DAN ARROW
and the
BLACK KNIGHT

By Edward S. Baker

A Black Opal Books Publication

Sent on a special assignment to learn if the New World Order will ultimately carry out its plans to eliminate most of human life, Dan Arrow travels into the future in a TR-42B triangle, only to discover that he has been murdered in the near future and his beloved Mona has married his murderer.

Shocked and angered, he moves from body to body and zips back and forth through time, trying to prevent his own murder while simultaneously attempting to foil the NWO's world domination plans. Diverted from his mission by the Black Knight satellite, he finds himself in the past with a woman who thinks she could be carrying his child. Then, on a future Earth that no longer resembles the planet he loves, he catches up with Mona and, together again, they face a nemesis with a name from the past: Nargas!

Can Dan save the Earth as we know it? Can Dan and Mona prevent Nargas from implementing the first commandment of the Georgia Guidestones? Will Dan and Mona ever be able to live a normal lifespan together?

**OTHER NOVELS
BY EDWARD S. BAKER
(in order of publication):**

Dan Arrow and the New World Order

Dan Arrow and the Hollow Moon

Dan Arrow and the Three-Headed Ophidian

DEDICATION:

This novel is dedicated to my wife Edna who has traveled through time with me.

It is also dedicated to those among us who believe in conspiracy theories in general and especially to those who believe that:

1. The TR squadron really exists, and those black triangles seen by civilians are ours.
2. The creation of the US Space Force occurred as a black-ops project almost fifty years ago.
3. The USA already has military bases on the Moon, Mars, Venus, and Jupiter.

ACKNOWLEDGMENTS:

A tip of the hat to the ladies of the Galway (NY) Writers Group who laughed aloud as they read Chapter One, and for their never-ending suggestions and encouragement to writers of all genres.

Special thanks, as well, to Susan at Black Opal Books for keeping this novel on track for publication during the COVID period. Her kind assistance and communications have been so appreciated by this author.

FOREWORD:

Private detective Dan Arrow met FBI Special Agent Mona Casola on a case that ended in non-disclosure agreements. It was during that case that they began dating. But, when Mona told Dan that she loved him, he dropped her like yesterday's meatloaf. Then, as the gods would have it, one of Dan's clients was murdered and Dan had to contact Mona because the FBI had classified the murder as a suicide. Thrown together again, their search for the killer took them into deep underground military bases where they found space aliens working with representatives of international governments to create a New World Order. Mona was captured and impregnated by the Reptilians' Commissar Nargas. But Dan freed her, and the duo foiled the NWO's plans and their supreme leader's migration from an old body into a new one. Hoping to abort the hybrid child, Mona discovered that the child had been plucked from her womb. She was angered both by the impregnation and by the theft of her child.

Returning to Washington, DC, Dan and Mona were met by their alien friend Waam, who asked for help in finding his nephew's killer. Their investigation took them inside the Hollow Moon, where the NWO was building an army to conquer the Earth, once a pandemic had been unleashed. Mona's identity was quickly discovered and, once again, she was collared by Commissar Nargas. Dan managed to rescue her and her hybrid child, but in the process, he nuked the interior of the Moon and cracked its outer shell. Returning to Mars, the duo was captured by Nargas, but Waam came to their rescue, sending the NWO leader and evil Commissar flying into the fires of the sun.

At home with their hybrid daughter Stella, Dan and Mona learned that the leader of the NWO was, in fact, still alive and selling opportunities for humans to be migrated into younger clones of themselves. Attempting to capture the NWO leader, Dan pursued three clones, any one of which could have been the NWO's leader. His investigation took him to Antarctica, where he nuked an underground fortress, and then to the NWO headquarters in Astana, Kazakhstan, where he was captured and beaten to near death. Telepathically, Stella let Mona see Dan's predicament. She flew to Astana where she was present when the NWO leader killed the reptilian queen and was, in return, killed by her guards. Mona then rescued Dan, returning his electrical essence to safety in a short-term storage device. With moments left to save him, she migrated Dan into the body of an alien grey. It's not the best of circumstances.

Chapter 1

Mona had been on the phone with her sister Wendy for almost fifteen minutes before Wendy asked, "So, what's really eating at you, Mona? You're talking around stuff, and something isn't right. Is Stella okay?"

Mona broke into tears. "It's Danny," she wept. "…Well, it's not Danny. He's trying. It's me. I can't take it. I don't think I'm going to make it, Wendy."

"What, as a mother?"

Mona pulled a tissue from the box on her nightstand and patted the tears from her eyes. "No, as a wife."

"I don't understand," Wendy replied. "You love him, don't you?"

"It's not that. You haven't seen him lately, Wendy. He's not Danny."

"What do you mean? Is he abusing you?"

"No, nothing like that." Mona sighed, paused a moment, and then said, "Let me try to paint you a picture."

"Oh, God," Wendy said, worried that things were really bad for Mona.

"Have you seen those new advertisements on the internet about moving you from your old body to a new one?"

"No, but I've heard about them from the girls that I drink with."

"Well, they're real."

"No shit?"

"Yeah, they're real. So, while you were babysitting Stella last month, I flew to Kazakhstan to rescue Danny from a prison cell in Astana."

"Prison? Danny was in prison?"

"Yeah, he was arrested while on a covert mission. It was a top-secret assignment."

"Okay, yeah. I guess I understand it now when you tell me that something is top secret. You can't tell me everything, and you really shouldn't be telling me anything. I understand that. Shit, I'm still reeling from when you told me all about the aliens and your trip to the moon. I still want to believe that you were putting me on."

"You haven't told anyone have you?"

"God, no. It was so bizarre that they'd wonder what I've been smoking."

"Do you remember seeing Danny when I got back from that mission?"

"No, it was just you and that small grey alien. Remember? I thought it was a kid in a costume, and I assumed that Danny was debriefing with the FBI or CIA. Why were you with that alien, anyway?

"That was Danny."

"Bullshit, Mona."

"No bullshit, Wendy. When I found Danny in Astana, he'd been tortured and was near death. The doctor who was with me used the same technology that they're advertising on the internet to remove Danny from his dying body and put him into a holding device. When we got him to safety, we had him moved to a new container because the storage device was running out of power."

"So, you moved him to another device?"

"No, think of your body as a container, Wendy."

"This is all too confusing, Mona."

Mona puffed a breath of frustration. "Look, it *is* possible to move a person from one body to another. It's alien technology that's been given to certain governments. Just stay with me, okay?"

"Okay," Wendy replied, but she couldn't make herself sound altogether convinced.

"So, the scientists who facilitate this movement call the body a 'container' and they call the movement process 'migration'. Are you still with me?"

"Yes, Mona. God save me, yes."

"So, when we found Danny in Astana, he was dying. We had no option but to migrate him into a storage container. Then, when we got him back to a friendly facility, we migrated him from the storage container into a living container, but the only container that was available was that little grey alien."

"So, your big, strapping Danny Arrow is now a little grey alien?"

"Well, yeah, except that it's only supposed to be temporary until they migrate him into a clone of himself in about eighteen months."

"This is too much, Mona."

"That's my point, Wendy. I can't take it. Danny isn't himself. He's small and frail. He doesn't eat meals with Stella and me, but he sits with us and talks to us in that high-pitched helium gas voice. When we get into bed at night, he smells like a mixture of raw hamburger and goat cheese, and he snores with a shrill wheezing whistle. I can't stand it."

"If he doesn't eat with you, what *does* he eat, Mona?"

"He doesn't eat like us, Wendy. Nutrients have to be absorbed through his skin. Our guest room bathtub is constantly full of ground meat and Gatorade that he has to sit in every few days. I can't go in there because it looks so gross and stinks so bad. And he's too weak to empty the tub out when it's time to change the slop. Instead of letting the liquid drain, we call the Villaggio septic cleaning company. They send a truck and a guy puts a long tube through the bathroom window and pumps the stuff out of the tub."

Wendy tried to bolster Mona's resolve. "This isn't like you, Mona. You've always been more masculine than feminine when it comes to gross stuff. You outperformed a bunch of guys at the FBI training camp, didn't you? What's changed you? Are you pregnant?"

Mona sighed. "Yes, maybe three months."

"Oh, I knew it! I'm so excited for you two. Have you told Mom yet?"

"Nobody knows but you and Danny. Promise me that you'll let *me* tell Mom."

"Okay, but it's going to be difficult not to say something about it."

"Listen, Wendy, my pregnancy just complicates the issues with Danny."

"No, Mona, the pregnancy explains how you feel. You're going through hormonal changes. Until you come to grips with the changes in your body, you're going to feel fat and ugly and undesirable. It's all hormonal imbalance."

"I don't know, Wendy. But I find that everything about Danny is…well, it's disgusting."

"It can't be that bad, Mona. You love him. Eighteen months isn't that long."

"It gets worse, Wendy."

"I don't know how…"

"Grey aliens are sexless, Wendy, but Danny thinks I need sexual relations, so he tries to do things for me to bring me pleasure, but when he tries to touch me with his three skinny fingers I want to vomit. Did you know that grey alien fingertips have little suction cups on them? I try to fake enjoyment, but I'm pretty sure that he knows it isn't working for me. Just having him in bed with me reminds me of when I was held captive on a leash by two draconian greys. I feel so guilty. It's a horrible situation and I don't know what to do."

"Are you coming to your little sister for advice?"

"If you have any. If not, just letting me vent helps."

"When Mom has trouble with Daddy, what does she do?"

"She gets out of the house for a while."

"Exactly. Why don't you get out more often? Go spend more time doing that thing that you're learning how to do."

"Do you mean remote viewing?"

"Yeah, that thing. If you go to more lessons and practice more in the classroom and less at home, you'll get better at it, and you'll also be spending a little more time away from Danny. You know, a little less time in the house is a little less time that he can gross you out and a little less time to feel revulsion. It could help the eighteen months go by faster."

Mona blew her nose into another tissue. "Yeah, maybe," she replied. "Maybe a little less time feeling sexually frustrated and, at the same time, a little less time feeling guilty about being completely repulsed by my husband."

Chapter 2

Mona was at her remote viewing training session when the landline telephone at home rang. Because my container's voice was squeaky, normally I wouldn't have answered the phone, but I figured that it was probably the septic guy trying to set up an appointment, so I picked up the receiver. I guess I wasn't thinking.

"Would Mr. Arrow be there?" a woman asked. She sounded like she was in her late fifties, and her accent was definitely British.

"This is Mr. Arrow," I replied.

"Oh, you sound so much different than I had anticipated."

"My voice is being electronically scrambled for security purposes," I lied. "How can I help you?"

"Mr. Arrow, my name is Loretta Gates. Marlene Powers gave me your number because she thought that you might be able to help me."

"What's your problem, Mrs. Gates?"

"It's about my son Max. He was found dead in his hotel room in Warsaw a couple of weeks ago."

"I'm sorry for your loss, Mrs. Gates. What were the circumstances?"

"The Polish authorities say that his death was from natural causes, but I have reason to believe that it was murder."

"Why's that?" I asked.

"About a month before his death, Max texted me and told me explicitly that if anything were to happen to him, I was to launch an investigation."

"Had he been threatened in any way?"

"That's hard to say, Mr. Arrow. He was almost forty, so he didn't share as much information with me as he would have if he had been twenty if you know what I mean."

"Yeah, I get that. Sure."

"Max was into conspiracy theories, Mr. Arrow. He was making the rounds of the international UFO conferences, giving presentations about various types of extraterrestrials that are watching the earth and interfering with mankind's genetics and politics. He told me that he was afraid that certain people didn't want this dark information to be shared with the general public. Eliminating him was one way to keep it all secret."

"Now I get the connection between your son Max and Billy Powers. They were both doing the same thing."

"Yes, Mr. Arrow, exactly. And, Billy Powers was strangled to death, but my son was poisoned. I'm convinced of that. Why else would a healthy young man just pass away for no reason? His girlfriend found him dead on the sofa after she came back from her daily jog. The poor dear was very upset. He was alive when she left and dead when she returned about an hour later."

"Has anyone done an autopsy?"

"I had his body shipped back to England for autopsy, but it's been over three months and I haven't received any type of report. When I call, I am supposedly transferred to the autopsy office, but the phone call is always cut off and all I'm left with is a dial tone. If nothing else, I'd like to have his body returned so I can have it cremated and give him a proper Anglican burial."

"So, how do you know Marlene Powers?" I asked.

"I've never met her. We've just spoken by phone and by Skype. She read about Max on the Anonymous website on the internet and called me. She thinks Max might really be alive. Do you think it's possible, Mr. Arrow? Do you think I'll ever see my little Maxie again?"

"Mrs. Gates, before I ever got involved in this extraterrestrial stuff, I'd have said 'No,' but the more I get involved in it, the more I realize that just about anything is possible. Just ask Marlene about it the next time that you speak with her."

"I really hope so, Mr. Arrow, and I will."

Mrs. Gates gave me contact information for Max's girlfriend and for the coroner's office in Kent, where Max's body supposedly was undergoing autopsy. I asked her for a small retainer to use for probable and unforeseen expenses. The next day, she wired $5000 to the Villaggio Branch of the First Virginia Bank, and I had half of it dumped into an account that was attached to my personal debit card. It felt good to be back in the detective business, but I didn't expect to find Max Gates alive. At least not in a container that his mother would recognize.

Chapter 3

At nine in the morning, I called Max Gates' girlfriend at the number in Cornwall that Mrs. Gates had given me. She didn't answer, so I left a message. She didn't return the call, so I tried again in the evening after Stella went to bed. This time a woman picked up the phone. "Gretta here," she said in a deep, groggy voice.

"Miss Faust, this is Dan Arrow," I began. "I left a voicemail this morning…"

She cut me off. "Do you know what time it is, you fucking twonk? It's bloody one in the morning."

"I apologize for calling you so late. Would early afternoon be better?"

"Yeah, bugger off until four tomorrow, kindly." She hung up.

Mona came down the stairs and into the living room. "That was a quick call," she said, sitting down in the stuffed chair across from me.

"I think I just met your British cousin," I told her.

"Was she Italian?"

"No, but she had the vocabulary of a Marine."

Mona smiled at my analogy. Until Stella came into our lives, every sentence that Mona uttered contained an expletive. But now as a mom, she was less likely to unleash a barrage of four-letter words because of Stella's keen hearing and her rapid learning aptitude.

"Come sit beside me," I said, patting the cushion of our sofa.

"I'm good here," Mona replied.

I tilted my head to the side and nodded. Mona had been stand-offish for the past few weeks. I mean she was polite and courteous and did what she always had done for me, but it seemed like those things were done more out of obligation than affection. But who could blame her? I was stuck in a skinny grayish-blue container, and I was incapable of the manly things that I used to be able to do. Even loosening a screw cap on a new jar of jelly was now beyond my physical capability. And she seemed to be spending more time away from home than in the past, especially at the remote viewing training center. If I were a jealous man, I'd be wondering if she was really there, or if she was somewhere else engaged in something unthinkable. But, then, only a short time ago her remote viewing ability had saved me from certain death in Astana, so I encouraged her to go every time that she asked if I minded her slipping out for a little while.

"Ms. Faust doesn't want to talk until tomorrow afternoon," I said.

"Would you like me to talk with her?" Mona asked. "Sometimes a woman can pull a secret from another woman."

"Yeah, that would be good, baby. I have to begin every phone call with the lie that my voice has been digitally scrambled for security purposes."

"What do you need from her?"

"Mostly information about her boyfriend's death. Apparently, she found the body when she came back from jogging. It's a case like Billy Powers'. Her boyfriend might have been migrated, but actually, it's more likely that he might have been murdered."

"And then, he simply might have died from natural causes," Mona reminded me.

"Yeah, but he had been giving presentations about alien intervention into human affairs at international UFO conspiracy conferences. He also texted his mom to say that if he was found dead, she should launch an investigation."

"Then it was definitely a murder, huh?"

"Probably."

"Have you contacted the coroner yet?"

"Not yet. They're five hours ahead of us in England, so he's at home sleeping right now."

"No wonder that girl doesn't want to talk to you until tomorrow afternoon."

Mona and I watched television for an hour and then went to bed. She slept with her back to me. In the middle of the night, Stella woke up complaining about a bad dream. Mona brought her into our bed and she slept between us until morning.

After I woke, I immersed to my neck in my bathtub full of ground meat and Gatorade for about half an hour, enjoying the feeling of newfound energy that such baths gave me. When I heard Stella's rapid footsteps on the carpet in the hallway, I knew that the day had begun, so I stood and turned on the shower. The warmth of the water felt good as it ran across my skin, carrying with it little pieces of red and brown meat that fell back into the life-giving slop in the tub. Following the usual protocol, I picked up one foot, rinsed it off, and then stepped out of the tub. As I did, I raised and rinsed the other foot. This made Mona happy because if I didn't wash them all off, the little pieces of meat would find their way onto the floor all over the house, which she found disgusting. Then, I opened the drain and let some of the liquid out of the tub so it wouldn't overflow the next time I bathed. I would have to wait for Mona to loosen the caps on ten Gatorade bottles before I could refill the tub. She'd help me later in the day, probably when it's Stella's nap time.

While the girls ate breakfast, I drafted a list of questions for Mona to ask the Kent Shire Coroner when we called. After breakfast, Mona set Stella up in the family room to watch educational television while she and I made the calls. We used the speaker function on her iPhone, and Mona threw away my questions before punching the number into her cell phone.

"Morgan Parrish's Office," the receptionist said when she answered the ring.

"Good afternoon," Mona said. "This is special agent Casola with the United States FBI. Would Mr. Parrish be available to answer a few questions about one of your cadavers?"

A few moments later, a man's voice came on the line. "This is Parrish. Did you say FBI?"

"Yes, this is Mona Casola, special agent with the FBI. I am wondering if you can answer a few questions that I have about one of your cadavers? The deceased's name was Maxwell Gates."

"This is the United Kingdom, Agent Casola. You have no authority here, but I'd be happy to answer any questions of a general nature."

"Thanks, Mr. Parrish. Our questions are related to suspicious circumstances surrounding Mr. Gates' death. If necessary, however, we can ask MI7 to interrogate you on our behalf."

"No need to bring in MI7. What is it that you want to know?"

"First, Mr. Gates' mother asked for the autopsy several months ago and she hasn't yet received a report. When can she anticipate one?"

"As soon as MI9 authorizes me to release it."

"Why would MI9 be involved in this matter?"

"You tell me. They're the office supposedly involved in covert operations, and they bloody contacted me to inquire about his death before his body even arrived. It was in terrible condition, you know, his body was. All black and looking quite peculiar for someone supposedly deceased just that morning."

"All black? What would cause that?"

"Paint would do it, make a minger out of a body, but it was poisonwood sap what did it to that bugger."

"Poisonwood?" Mona asked.

"That would be it. It's a relative of what you Yanks would call poison ivy, except this is a little more wicked. Turns the skin black in short order. Whoever this bloke pissed off did him in and then poured poisonwood sap all over his body."

"Was there any evidence of strangulation as the cause of death?"

"Internal there was, but the poisonwood sap removed all traces of external evidence."

"So he was definitely strangled?"

"That would be right, maybe by a piece of cord, but I don't know if that was the actual cause of death. There were lesions of the afferent nerves, which would lead me to believe that myocardial infarction got him before the strangulation was completed."

"So it's possible that somebody was in the act of strangling him, but didn't complete the strangulation because the victim had a heart attack during the process?

"That would be correct. The lesions would have interfered with the primary purpose of the afferent nerves, which is to conduct pain. Thus, Mr. Bates died painlessly…well, except for the strangulation, of course."

"Thank you, Dr. Parrish. May I call you again if I discover additional evidence that leads to more questions?"

"Oh, I forgot to mention something, Agent Casola. Mr. Gates suffered from diabetes. The lesions in his afferent nerves were a byproduct of diabetic neuropathy. Poor bloke probably didn't even know that he was diabetic, young like he was."

"Diabetic?"

"Right. His sugar was low, maybe low enough to be near the coma stage, but he wasn't there yet. He fought his attacker and took some skin under his nails."

"Did you do a DNA analysis of the skin and send it to Scotland Yard for possible perp ID?"

"Strange it was, the skin sample was probably contaminated by the poisonwood sap. It came back as non-human, possible source reptilian, unknown species. Odd, right?"

"Well, thank you, again, Dr. Parrish," Mona repeated. "You've been most helpful. At the risk of sounding like a broken record, may I call you again if I discover additional evidence that leads to more questions?"

"Certainly. Whatever. Just don't involve MI7."

"Of course not," Mona replied and hung up.

Mona looked at me. If I had been in my old container, my eyes would have been wide open and my eyebrows would have been raised. "Definitely termination by the reptilians," I told her.

"Possible migration, Danny…but I don't think so unless they botched it because they didn't know he had diabetic nerve problems."

☙❧

We waited until 11:00 am our time and then Mona dialed Max's girlfriend. The voice that greeted her said, "Better timing this time around, ain't it, ya blighter."

"This is Agent Casola of the American FBI," Mona said, rolling her eyes at me. "Is Ms. Gretta Faust there?"

"That's me, mum. I thought ya was the knobber what woke me at one this morning."

"Ms. Faust, I'm investigating the death of your boyfriend Max. Is this a good time to talk?"

"I wouldn't call him my boyfriend. He was a friend and he was male. My pet name for him was my 'mighty Man Friend,' but we wasn't shagging buddies. I'm no scrubber."

"But you were staying in the hotel room with Mr. Gates at the conference?"

"Yeah, we often did that to share expenses. Blimey, the blooming room had two beds."

"So, tell me about the morning that you found him dead," Mona asked.

"He was already up when I got up. He had been for a walk and brought tea and hard rolls back for breakfast. I drank my tea but left the hard roll for after my run. When I went out, he was going to review his notes for his presentation at ten o'clock. When I got back…"

"What time was that?" Mona asked.

"It was near nine when I got back. There he was, stretched out on the sofa like a mummy. I barely recognized him, what with his skin all black like that."

"So, what did you do?"

"I called the front desk and asked them to send up the house doc. The codger what come took one look at Maxie and called the Bobbies."

"Did anyone else come to see him…I mean other than the physician and the Bobbies?"

"One very tall bloke, but he didn't stay."

"Can you describe him?"

"There ain't much to describe. He was wearing sunglasses and looked like he needed to get out in the sun, being pale like that. It was his height what took me by surprise. He was maybe two and a half meters."

"What kinds of questions did he ask?"

"He didn't ask none. He walked in, looked at Maxie, and walked out. If it wasn't for his size, I wouldn't have given him a bloody look."

"What was he wearing?"

"Just a black trench coat and a black fedora. He might have been from Scotland Yard."

"I wouldn't bet on it," Mona replied.

Mona took Ms. Faust's address, asked her to call if she thought of anything else, and then said goodbye. There was no question that Gates had been terminated by extra-terrestrials. If he had been migrated, there would have been no reason for the Man in Black to come see if he was dead because they'd have his electrical essence in a portable container and they'd already know that his physical container was empty.

Chapter 4

A couple of days later, Mona had a late session at the remote viewing training center. She explained to me that the energy that carries the images that she receives is different in the evening, sort of the way that AM radio signals travel differently during the day than during the evening. She asked me to feed Stella but that she'd grab a burger in the training center's cafeteria during the break in the class.

For dinner, I fed Stella her favorite: chicken fingers, cooked carrots, and French fries. The chicken and the French fries went into the oven, and I heated the carrots in the microwave. There was no sense in burning my frail container by trying to cook on the surface of the stove.

After dinner, Stella read to me. Her favorite book at that moment was *Kylee and the Knock Man*, which she already had read aloud several times. But that was okay because I like the story. I put her into bed with her iPad at 8:00 pm, and then looked in on her at 9:00 pm to be sure she was asleep. She was, so I shut down her iPad and closed the door to her room.

At 10:15 pm Mona came home. Her eyes were red and teary and the skin on her neck was blotchy. It was obvious that she was upset.

"What's wrong, baby?" I asked.

"Nothing," she replied.

"I know better than that. Did you view something that was upsetting?"

"I don't want to talk about it," she snapped. She went into our bedroom and shut the door.

Mona doesn't like it when I pry into her life like an officer of the Inquisition, so I knew better than to press her any further. When she was ready, she'd let me know what was bothering her. So, I sat in the family room and watched several reruns of *Hawaii Five-O*. When I found myself nodding off, I tried the bedroom door, but it was locked. I went back to the family room and slept under a comforter on the sofa.

෪෨෪

"Can you talk?" Mona texted into her iPhone. Within thirty seconds her phone rang. "Wendy?" she asked.

"Yes, Mona. Is everything okay?"

Mona took a deep breath. "I fucked up, Wendy. I fucked up big time."

"Oh God," Wendy gasped. "What did you do?"

"I've been going to remote viewing training a lot lately like you suggested. Tonight, it got out of hand."

"Oh, Mona, quit beating around the bush and tell me what happened."

"I kissed my remote viewing instructor."

"Oh, shit, Mona. You didn't, did you?"

"It was after the training session. He and I were the last to leave class. We walked out together talking about what I've been viewing. He thinks I'm the best remote viewer he's ever seen, even better than he is. It was cold, so we got into my car to continue talking. It was all innocent, Wendy. But things drifted away from remote viewing and to family. I told him about Danny—you know, how Danny was migrated into an alien's body."

"Isn't that supposed to be above top secret?"

"Sarge has above top-secret clearance. He *is* an RV instructor, you know."

"It sounds like you're trying to rationalize what you did, Mona."

"Okay," Mona admitted, "maybe I shouldn't have told him, but I did."

"It's too late now, Mona."

"And I told him how I'm repulsed by Danny in his little grey sexless body. And I told him that I suspect that Danny knows how I truly feel. Sarge seemed really concerned about me. He and I have become very close over the past few months. Well, he stroked my face and wiped away my tears, and gave me a hug."

"Oh, shit, Mona."

"Well, it just happened. We just sort of kissed." Mona paused to collect her thoughts. "It was a small peck at first like you'd kiss your best friend, but then it became more passionate, you know, with tongue and heavy breathing."

"Mona, you're three months pregnant. Please tell me that you didn't have sex with him." Wendy demanded with dread in her voice.

"No, I didn't have sex with him."

"Thank God."

"But he touched my breast."

"Oh, nooo."

"It felt sooo good. Making out with him raised all sorts of primal urges in me, Wendy. I haven't been touched by a man in months, and I've missed it."

"Oh, Mona, you're in such trouble."

"I pushed him away, Wendy. He wanted more, but I pushed him away."

"Mona, you let him put his tongue in your mouth and touch your breast. You're only kidding yourself if you think that pushing him away this time will stop him from coming back for more the next time. You've created a buck in rut."

"I know, Wendy. I'm a cheater."

"You're not really a cheater, not yet anyway. You didn't have sex with him."

"But I wanted to. I let him touch me. That's as good as being unfaithful."

Wendy concurred. "I think you've called it for what it is, Mona."

Mona burst into tears.

Chapter 5

While Mona slept in, I turned on the television to see if the Redskins' quarterback was going to be able to play on Sunday. His shoulder had been badly bruised in last week's game, and the prognosis wasn't good for his return, maybe for the rest of the season. But the news wasn't what I expected. Instead, every channel was running a headline story about the accidental death of the popular movie star Nevada Ritter, whose horse had rolled over on him while shooting a film on location in the Mexican desert. Women around the nation were sobbing that the handsome action hero was never going to ride again, and, in Hollywood, animal rights activists were picketing the studios, claiming that the horse had been injured in some way during the filming. Go figure.

My cell phone rang about an hour later. It was Mona's boss, Mack, which usually meant that he needed me for something clandestine. He said that he had been busy since early morning on the phone with Hollywood producers who had millions of dollars invested in a film that was not yet completed. He had informed them that a perfect double for Nevada Ritter was alive and well if they cared to meet him. So, the purpose of Mack's call was to ask me for Billy Powers' phone number.

"Are you planning to be his agent?" I asked.

"Well, I thought I could help Powers negotiate a good deal and perhaps, at the same time, negotiate a small percentage of Nevada Ritter's last film for myself."

"You'd better get cash, Mack," I replied, "because Hollywood is famous for making million-dollar movies that earn no taxable profit. With no profit, you'll get no percentage."

"Thanks, Dan. I'll remember that," Mack replied.

I gave him Powers' phone number in Olney, Maryland, and we said goodbye. But, twenty minutes later he called again.

"Was Powers receptive to the opportunity?" I asked.

"I got a busy signal each time I called. His wife has probably taken their phone off the hook so she can have her way with him. You know how they are…I'll have to try again later. But, I had another thought, Dan."

"What's that?" I asked.

"Are you tired of living in that Grey container yet?"

"Oh, yeah," I replied, feeling a shot of self-pity. "Mona has to do everything for me, and she's already annoyed at the thought of another year of this lifestyle."

"Do you remember that Ritter had another clone in storage in Italy, Dan? Since he won't be needing it anymore, maybe we can talk the Ummites into loaning it to you until yours is ready."

"I'd forgotten about that, Mack. You're a genius. Can you see if you can set that up for me? I'd like to surprise Mona."

"Yeah. Let me call you back." He hung up for the second time.

Ten minutes later, Mona came down the stairs, Stella holding her hand and walking beside her. When they reached the bottom step, Stella broke away and ran to me. "Morning, Daddy," she cried, giving me a big hug.

"Don't hug Daddy too hard," Mona cautioned her.

"It's okay, baby, she knows I'm in a delicate container."

I gave Stella a gentle squeeze and patted her back. She kissed my cheek and then toddled over to the coffee table, picked up her iPad, and began playing some new video game.

"Did I hear your phone ring?" Mona asked.

"Yeah, it was somebody wanting me to switch our digital provider," I lied. "I thought we'd already put our phones on the 'do not call' list."

"You know how those companies are, Danny. They think that if they bother you enough, you'll finally cave in and buy their product. I hate them."

It was mid-morning when my cell phone rang again. Mona answered it and brought it to me in the guest bathroom, where I was bathing in the usual ground meat and Gatorade soup. She held her nose with one hand while sticking the phone out with the other. "It's Mack," she said, rolling her eyes because she knew that his calls always meant that I'd be dragged away on some sort of Bureau business.

"Can I call him back?" I asked. "I'm eating dessert right now."

"Take the damn phone and let me get out of here," she said.

I sat up in the tub and wiped my hands on a towel before taking the phone. When I did, Mona left the bathroom, closing the door firmly. She made no pretense about her disdain for the look and smell of the slop that nourished my grey container.

"Hi, Mack," I said into the receiver. "Do you have good news for me?"

"It's all set. Dr. Spann would be pleased to migrate you into Ritter's other clone. He needs the space, anyway, because he's received a request from the Vatican for a special cloning. He'd like to do the migration within the next couple of days. Can you be away for three or four days, Dan?"

"If you tell her that you need me, Mona will let me go. Hell, you're her boss, aren't you?"

"Yeah, but she can be tough to handle when one of my decisions is contrary to her opinion. But you know that— you're married to her."

"How about you tell her that you need me for a special Homeland Security briefing on the Antarctic meltdown, and that I'll be gone for four or five days. Can you send a chopper for me? I can't drive."

"Yeah, the Antarctic meltdown would be plausible, especially since it's causing such havoc with the weather. I can have the chopper there in about four hours. It'll take you to Andrews and then we can catch a hop from there to Italy."

"Sounds like a plan," I replied. Hell, I'd enjoy being out of the house for a few days, especially if it meant that I'd come back in the container of an adult male human being.

"Put her on the phone," Mack told me.

I stepped out of the bath and opened the door to the hallway. "Mona, Mack wants to talk to you." I shouted at the top of my squeaky voice.

Mona came to the bottom of the stairs. "Get back in the tub, Danny. You're dripping that shit all over the carpet."

"It's Mack. He wants to talk to you."

Mona snorted a puff of annoyance and then climbed the stairs to retrieve the cell phone. "Give me that and get back in the tub," she said when she took the cell phone from my hand. As I climbed back into the soup, I heard her ask, "So where are you sending him this time, Mack? And is it really all that important?"

❦

The sound of beating rotors let all of the Villaggio know that a helicopter was setting down in my backyard. Mona looked out the front window. "The neighbors know that something out of the ordinary is happening here this afternoon. What am I going to tell them? Why couldn't Mack have sent Waam to whisk you away silently?"

Waam is my Ummite friend who's wanted by the New World Order for conspiracy in the damage to the Moon and for the destruction of the secret facility hidden beneath the Antarctic Ice. "You know that Waam's in hiding," I replied. "Besides, this is just a federal inquiry and briefing. Waam's physical presence would send the senators into a frenzy and would blow the lid off the UFO denial conspiracy."

"I guess you're right," Mona said. "I can't wait until we're beyond all this secrecy as a country."

Stella gave me a hug and a kiss on the cheek and told me that she'd miss me while I was away. After Mona opened the back door for me, she gave me the quick kind of hug that you'd give an acquaintance and wished me a safe flight. I think she actually was glad to be rid of me for a few days. If nothing else, there would be less work for her to do while I was away.

I waited for its rotors to stop spinning before I climbed aboard the Blackhawk chopper that sat in my backyard. At only sixty pounds, my alien container would have been tossed like a feather in a cyclone if I'd walked outside while the rotors were still turning.

As I climbed in, I thought that the pilots would find my alien body startling, but they simply welcomed me aboard and told me that Agent Smith would be meeting me at

Andrews. Obviously, I was not the first grey they had seen and they must have assumed that I was of some importance or else I wouldn't be traveling somewhere with Mack Smith.

The flight took a little over ninety minutes, and I passed the time by looking out the window at the headlights of commuters whose cars were winding away from Washington toward homes in the Virginia suburbs. It wasn't that long ago that Mona and I had lived in Washington, and it wasn't until we had Stella that we even had considered moving away from the urban environment. In fact, the tales told by friends who commuted each day— the traffic jams, the accidents, the breakdowns, the road rage—had been enough to keep us settled in an apartment close to work. Now, however, we were safely snuggled into rural America, far from the crowds of the city and, because of our special arrangements with the FBI, we didn't have to commute to work. Well, except for missions to strange places around the world, all expenses paid for by Mack Smith.

As his chopper spun to touch down in a painted circle at Andrews, through the lights from a Hummer I could see Mack standing on the tarmac in a khaki trench coat, looking ever so much like an FBI agent. I waited for the rotors to stop spinning, and then climbed out of the Blackhawk.

"I had forgotten how small your container is," Mack told me as we shook hands.

"Thanks, Mack, you really know how to make a guy feel good about himself."

The Hummer took us to a distant runway where two F-35B Lightning Joint Strike Fighters were waiting to whisk us away to Italy. "Why don't you ride in the pink one and I'll ride in the blue," I suggested.

Mack laughed. "Our rides have been assigned already, yours with a booster chair on the co-pilot's seat so you can look out the window."

Nice, the way he verbally abused me, huh?

"The reason we're riding in these special fighters," Mack told me, "is that they can land and take-off vertically, like a Harrier, but they're twice as fast on a slow day."

That sounded good to me because I was anxious to see Dr. Spann, and I was sure that the vertical landing capability of our F-35B's was going to come in handy when we eventually touched down in the mountains of Italy.

My pilot was a female Navy Captain named Lohre. She had volunteered for this run because she had been suffering too much desk time and needed to get in her required 25 hours of flight time for this month or else she'd be grounded until she re-took certification examinations. She was taken back when she first saw me standing next to Mack. "Pardon my reaction, sir," she told me later, when we were over the Atlantic, "but when I first saw you, I thought you might have been a blowup doll that Agent Smith was bringing on the flight."

More abuse, and this time from a woman I didn't even know. So, perhaps Captain Lohre had a good poker face and perhaps she had never seen a grey alien before. "That's okay," I replied through my helmet's communication system. "I've been told worse. By the way, the name is Arrow."

"Are you really from outer space, Arrow? I've seen a couple of UFO's but I always thought they were probes, maybe sent here from several light years away, the way we send probes to Pluto and Venus."

"What you're looking at when you look at me is a reticulan grey alien," I said. "This species is from Zeta Reticuli."

"How long did it take you to travel here? Did you have to go into suspended animation on the trip?"

"Did I say that I came here from Zeta Reticuli?"

"I thought you did, sir."

"This species does, but I was born here on Earth."

"So, you could say that you're a first-generation Earthling?"

I didn't want to confuse her, and I didn't want to give her too much information, especially the stuff that was above top secret, but I was getting boxed in by her line of questioning. I changed the subject. "Haven't you heard the rumors about the existence of several races of extraterrestrials working with a shadow government here on Earth?"

"That's the stuff of science fiction movies and maybe the tabloids."

"You should go to the movies more often," I replied.

Our conversation was interrupted by the squadron leader who announced that we were being tailed by an unidentified aircraft. As it approached, I turned to look for it. Out of the darkness behind us, I could see a military tureen. I couldn't tell if it was NWO, Draconian, or Ummite.

"I think we should consider taking evasive action," I told Captain Lohre. She relayed the message to the squadron commander.

"Negatory," he responded. "Agent Smith called for an escort. That aircraft is coming along to protect us. It's a new one on me. I don't recognize its radar blip."

"Holy shit," Captain Lohre exclaimed as the aircraft pulled beside us but one hundred feet above. "It's a goddamn flying saucer."

"It's an Ummite military tureen, Captain," I said. "You should pay more attention to the tabloids. Maybe someday you'll take a ride in one of those babies. They can do light speed, and if you're inside when they do, you'll think you're standing still."

"You've been inside one of those?" she asked.

"Did you take a good look at me back at Andrews?"

"Point taken, Arrow."

Chapter 6

While our F-35B's sought a place to touch down at Montano Antilia, the Ummite tureen that had accompanied us entered the mountain as though its granite surface wasn't there. "Look at that," Captain Lohre exclaimed as the tureen simply disappeared into shimmering rock.

"Don't try to follow it, Captain," I warned. "Just find a level spot and touch down. Agent Smith and I'll walk from there."

Captain Lohre and the squadron leader discussed several possible vertical landing sites before settling on an outcropping of rock that appeared to be somewhat level and would hold both fighters. Then, they coordinated their positions and touched down together.

As we climbed down from the aircraft, we were greeted by three people who emerged from the cliff beside us in a vehicle that looked like an enclosed ski lift gondola, except that when it stopped, it hovered six inches above the ground. Our pilots were amazed at that, and they welcomed the opportunity to ride with us through the granite mountain into the facility that was hidden beneath.

"There's no sense having you wait for us up here while Mr. Arrow conducts his business," Mack told them, "when you can have a light meal and coffee on me in the cafeteria below. He should be no more than an hour."

When we exited the gondola in the hangar below, the pilots got their first close-up look at the Ummite tureen that had accompanied us on the journey to Italy. It was a typical military tureen, gray-green in color, sixty feet across, and only twenty feet high at its center.

"Any chance of going inside it?" Captain Lohre asked.

"Let me see what I can do," Mack replied, "but I can make no promises."

Two reticulan greys came toward me from the medical wing. Both were wearing faded green medical scrubs. "Are you Arrow?" one asked me.

"How did you know?" I replied.

"My name is Tryl and this is Baaz. Dr. Spann has been anxiously awaiting your arrival. We are to take you to see the status of your own clone, and then to see the clone that will be on loan to you for the next nine months. Your migration is set for thirty minutes from now. Are you prepared?"

"I'm beyond prepared. No offense to you guys, but I don't understand why you'd ever **want one of these grey containers.",**

"And we have no comprehension of why you would ever want to live in a primitive human container," Tryl replied.

"You ought to try one for a couple of days. The sex is great."

"Sex? Do you mean species reproduction?" Baaz asked.

"Yeah. Except that having sex isn't just for reproduction. It's for fun."

"I don't really understand," Baaz replied.

But, how could he understand? He was a sexless grey. "Why don't you wait until Dr. Spann has a slack period, and then ask him if you can try out a male human container for a week," I suggested. "Think of it as a vacation, maybe a little migration-facilitated R & R. You'll have more strength than you've ever imagined, and…well, as they say on Earth, 'A roll in the hay, and you'll never go grey.'"

"W-w-what?"

"He's making fun of us, Baaz," Tryl interjected. "Some humans are definitely more primitive than others." He turned to me and said, "Please follow us, Arrow. And give my friend Baaz a break from your juvenile humor."

Wow. This guy had known me for less than two minutes and he'd already figured me out. I wondered if he'd spoken with Mona.

I told Mack and the two pilots that I'd see them in an hour or two for our flight back to Andrews. Then I followed Tryl and Baaz through the cloning facility and into the growth chambers, where the lighting was dim and bodies of all ages and shapes hung suspended in slender transparent cylindrical units, like the ones I had seen below the Denver Airport when I was trying to rescue Mona last year.

We had passed half a dozen growth chambers when Tryl paused at a tall cylinder that was filled with translucent green fluid, similar to pastel lime syrup. Inside was a kid that I guessed would have been in elementary school if he weren't floating inside a glass cylinder in Italy, tubes coming from his nostrils and mouth, and wires attached to his forehead and chest. Next to the cylinder stood a pole onto which were mounted several electronic devices with screens that provided constant monitoring of the clone's condition, including its approximate age in Earth years. This kid's age read YRS: 05, MTH: 04, DYS: 16, HRS: 22, MIN: 46, SEC: 55.

"So, this kid is about five and a half years old. When does he come out of the tank?" I asked.

"This is your clone, Arrow. Don't you recognize yourself?" Tryl asked.

I guess I should have been paying more attention to what he had told me earlier, but the green fluid and tubes contorted my clone's lips, and his hair had not yet been cut, so it hung below the shoulders and he looked a bit like a wild boy. Hell, in every picture that I'd seen of myself at that age I'd had a haircut and was dressed for some type of family party. And my Dad never took any pictures of me buck naked. I had to admit that it was kind of neat to see myself as a kid.

I studied the clone for a few moments and then asked, "How old will this clone be in Earth years when I migrate into it?"

Baaz touched some buttons on the primary monitor and replied, "The growth chamber is set to release this container in eight of your months and sixteen of your days. At that time, this container will have developed to approximately 29 Earth years in human age."

"Thanks, Baaz. That's really good news."

I patted the glass side of the cylinder to wish my clone goodbye until nine months from now. The noise startled him, and he stirred briefly before returning to a state that resembled sleep. "It's like he's still in the womb," I said.

"He is," Tryl told me. "Come, Arrow, we have another clone to inspect."

I followed Tryl and Baaz out of the darker growth chamber facility and into a small room with white walls and bright fluorescent lights. I had to squint for a few moments until my eyes adjusted to the brightness.

Against one wall sat a surgical table where Nevada Ritter lay in state…well if it were really Nevada Ritter who, instead, was lying in state somewhere in Southern California, hopefully with a fresh coat of pancake, compliments of a good make-up artist. This container, however, was breathing unassisted, with pink flesh, a fresh haircut, and manicured nails. Wires connected its chest, head, and pointer finger to a mobile monitor that stood nearby. With all the new Bluetooth technology, you'd think they'd have had a wireless setup.

"Here it is, Arrow," Tryl told me. "Mr. Ritter was hoping to migrate into it later this season but, as you know, he met an unanticipated and unfortunate end. I liked his films."

"Yeah," I replied, "but the storyline was basically the same in movie after movie."

"That's Hollywood," Baaz added, like someone who knew the movie industry well.

"So, is there anything I should know about this clone?" I asked, standing on a stool to look down upon it.

"Its Earth age is approximately thirty-one years," Tryl told me. "We have been exercising its muscles via electrical impulses for the past month, so you should experience no weakness during normal daily functions. We think you'll be pleased with it. Try not to damage or injure it in any way because eventually, it will bring a handsome sum from some millionaire who wants a new container."

I knew it was only a loaner, and I didn't have any plans to get involved in heavy action, so I said, "I'll do my best."

"No tattoos," Baaz cautioned.

"No problem. I don't like needles." I turned to Tryl and asked, "So, why don't you use wireless technology instead of all these connected wires?"

Baaz answered me. "That question is best addressed to me, Arrow, because I am the technology expert. As to your question, wireless technology is open to interference from other electronic devices, as well as television and radio signals. We avoid a plethora of problems by utilizing old technology."

"That makes sense," I replied, although I still believed that wireless technology would be a smarter and less confusing way to achieve the same end.

"Are you ready to change containers, Arrow?" Tryl asked. "Dr. Spann should be prepared for you by now."

"Let's do it," I said.

We walked into an adjoining room, where a nurse waited to assist me into a surgical gown for migration. Tryl and Baaz wished me a speedy journey and said farewell. The nurse told me to undress and then she pitched my clothes into a trash barrel because I wasn't going to need them anymore. She took my vitals, and then she had me sit in a wheelchair, which she pushed into the migration room. When we emerged through the swinging door, Dr. Spann turned and greeted me. "It's nice to see you again, Agent Arrow."

"You too, Doc," I replied.

I turned when I heard a banging noise behind me. It was Ritter's clone, being pushed by a tall Ummite assistant. "Be careful, Nonnie," Dr. Spann cautioned. "We don't want any bruises."

"Yes, Doctor, I'm sorry."

The nurse moved me to a wooden table with stainless steel legs. Beneath its sheet, a thin foam cushion softened the hard surface of the oak against my back. Then, she attached electrodes to my skull and across my chest, similar to the set-up for an electrocardiogram. The wires all connected to a single metallic device that resembled a small flashlight with a cluster of pins instead of a lightbulb at the end. She inserted its end into the migration machine and twisted it to lock it in place. Then she gently pushed my table backward until I could see the fans of a rotor surrounding my head in a large arc. Turning to Dr. Spann she said, "All good here."

Nonnie the Ummite was performing a similar procedure on Ritter's clone. When he was finished, he told Dr. Spann, "The recipient has been prepared."

Dr. Spann turned to me. "Close your eyes, Agent Arrow, and when you wake up, you will be in the new container."

I closed my eyes, took a deep breath, and exhaled to rid myself of the nervousness that filled me. I could hear the rotors begin to turn and could feel the gentle breeze that their spinning created. Suddenly I felt the sensation of vertigo and drifted into sleep. I dreamed that I was riding on a roller coaster, climbing quickly up to the top of the first and highest drop, and then rocketing downward through a full twist and a straightaway before slamming to a screeching halt in a bale of hay at the bottom. Then all was blackness. I heard several voices speaking rapidly, but perhaps in a room far away because I couldn't decipher what was being discussed. I felt my body arch upwards uncontrollably and then fall back into a reclined position. The voices were becoming more distinct. Darkness gave way to light, bright light. I tried to shield my eyes, but my arms were strapped down.

"Agent Arrow, welcome back."

I recognized the voice. It was Dr. Spann. *Oh yeah*, I realized, *I'm in a new container.* As I struggled to sit up, I could feel fingers removing the straps that bound my wrists, and several hands pressing against my back to lift me into a vertical position. I inhaled deeply, and instantly felt the weight of this new container's chest muscles on its skeletal structure. I marveled that I felt tall, muscular, and masculine again. Was that testosterone I could sense in my loins? Joy of joys!

Chapter 7

Mack stood to greet me as I entered the family waiting room. I was dressed in a military jumpsuit with a flight jacket and jungle boots.

"Dan?" he asked with a smile. "Is that you or Nevada Ritter?"

I grinned back.

"So, how does it feel?"

"I'm seeing things from a better point of view, Mack. It's nice to be tall again, and this container has some beef compared to that grey carcass that I left behind. I can't wait to give this container a test ride!"

"Are you hungry?"

"Naw, just horny right now."

"Oh, I pity Mona," Mack snickered.

"Are our bus drivers still around? I'm anxious to get home."

"They should be back any minute. Let's go join them topside."

Mack and I found the gondola where we had left it, climbed in, and were escorted to the top of the mountain by one of Dr. Spann's staff who operated the vertical lift technology. As we climbed upward, I kept admiring my new container's reflection in the chrome framework that held the gondola's glass panels in place. I looked like Billy Powers, who, in turn, looked like Nevada Ritter. I liked the container's jawline and twinkling eyes and the breadth of its shoulders in contrast to its narrower hips. It was the container of a natural-born superstar. No wonder ladies swooned when Ritter smiled at them. I hoped that Mona would prefer this container to the grey alien that I had left behind somewhere in the migration facility.

We emerged through the rocky side of Montano Antilia within one hundred feet of the two F-35B's which had brought us to the mountain only two hours before. Our pilots were not there to greet us. Though the outside air was cool, it was not cold, so Mack and I sent the lift operator back down to spread the word that we were topside and waiting for our ride home, just in case the pilots had found their way back into the facility.

Fifteen minutes later, the rock wall beside us began shimmering, so we stepped back and watched the gondola emerge from the granite. As it set down, Captain Lohre and the squadron leader stepped out. "What a fantastic experience," Captain Lohre said to Mack. "Not only did we get a tour of the cockpit of the tureen, but a pilot took us on a trip around the planet. We were back here in less than half an hour. Isn't that amazing?"

"They never took it out of first gear," Mack told her. "Those babies can do better than light speed once they're out of the atmosphere."

"I'm so exhilarated," the Captain said. "I'll never be satisfied flying anything that *we* have."

"Ask your commander for a transfer to the TR squadron, Captain. If he knows about it, he might authorize your transfer. If he doesn't know about it, he'll start asking questions, and eventually you still might get there."

"What do they fly, the TR squadron?"

"I can't tell you because it's above top secret. I've told you too much, but your excursion today already has introduced you to more classified information than you're certified to know."

Captain Lohre looked around and then asked, "I assume that we'll be taking off as soon as Arrow gets here?"

"That little guy won't be taking the ride back home, Captain," I said. "You'll be taking me back, instead."

"Oh," she replied. "I'm pleased to meet you. My name is Lohre, but you can call me Nicki."

I reached out and shook her hand. "The name is Arrow."

Captain Lohre's face froze for a moment as she tried to comprehend how her previous passenger's name and mine were the same. Then she shook her head and told Mack, "I think I have a dozen questions to ask you, but I think I already know what you'll say."

"Probably," Mack replied.

❧❧❧

Our flight back to Andrews took an hour longer than our flight to Italy, probably due to the prevailing westerlies that slow all westbound flights. When we finally landed at Andrews, we were greeted by Mack's black Hummer that was waiting to return us to the helicopter pad, where I said goodbye to Mack and caught my flight back to Villaggio Ibrido. I arrived in my backyard absolutely exhausted, but it was evening, and I had been away for only twenty-five hours Eastern Standard Time.

The pulsating noise of the helicopter's rotors beating the hell out of the air brought Mona from the living room to the kitchen window. I climbed out of the Blackhawk and waved farewell to the pilot as he lifted off. Mona opened the back door as I approached. "May I help you?" she asked. Then a moment of fear overtook her as she recognized Billy Powers and she cried, "Don't tell me…something's happened to Danny. Is he dead?"

I took her in my arms and kissed her, deep tongue. She slapped me hard with a ferocious right cross, pressed the heels of her hands into my shoulders, and pushed away from my grip. Then she screamed. It was bloodcurdling. I was so caught by surprise that I immediately released her and stood watching as she hurried inside and slammed the door behind her. The lock clasp set with a loud "click."

I knocked on the door and cried, "Mona. Mona, baby, it's me. It's Danny."

"I'm calling the M.P.'s," Mona screamed at me through the locked door.

"No, baby, don't do that. It's me, Danny."

"Bullshit, Billy Powers."

"No, baby, please let me in. I just left you yesterday to meet with Mack, remember?"

I could hear her talking on the phone. "Sergeant, this is Mona Arrow. I have an intruder at my house. Yes, I will. Yes, I have a gun upstairs. Okay."

"Mona, no. It's me, your Danny. Don't have me arrested."

Within seconds I could hear the sirens wailing and knew that the M.P.'s would be here momentarily. I turned my back to the door and listened to a zipper pull on my flight suit scratch the paint on the door's steel surface as I slid to a sitting position on the ground. "Aw, fuck me." I was too tired for all this drama.

When the M.P.'s found me on the back stoop, they asked for identification. Of course, I didn't have any. On went the handcuffs. They lifted me to my feet and checked me for weapons. Then they checked my pupils and had me blow into a breathalyzer. I just kept telling them, "I'm

Agent Dan Arrow. I live here." That didn't seem to convince them.

They marched me around to the front of the house and rang the doorbell. Mona came to the door. "Is this the man who accosted you?" one of them asked.

"Yes, that's him," Mona said. "I've already rinsed my mouth with vodka. Do you think that'll kill any viruses that he's carrying?"

"Ma'am, you're going to have to come down to the Provost Marshall's Office to swear out a formal complaint."

"Can I meet you there? I have a daughter here at home with me."

"You can follow us down, but we won't be leaving without you."

Mona went back inside our home. A few minutes later, she reappeared with Stella beside her. Both were dressed in light jackets in case the late afternoon air became chilly. "I'll have to get my car," she said.

As she reached for Stella's hand, Stella broke away from Mona and ran to me with opened arms, crying, "Daddy. Daddy." She threw her arms around my thighs and hugged me. The M.P. who was holding my handcuffs released his grip, and I dropped to one knee and gave Stella a kiss on her cheek.

"How's Daddy's girl?" I asked with my hands still locked in the metal bracelets behind my back. "I've missed you."

"Who are these men, Daddy? Why are they hurting you?"

"They aren't hurting me, baby. There's just a little misunderstanding. Mommy and I will talk this out and everything will be fine. Maybe we'll go out for an ice cream cone later."

Stella turned to Mona and said, "Look, Mommy. Daddy's home."

Mona's mouth dropped open. "Where did we meet?" she asked me, raising an eyebrow.

"On a missing person's case I was investigating that involved the FBI. We started dating almost immediately. After six months, you told me that you loved me, so I quit asking you out. Last year I called you because I needed info on FBI records involving Billy Powers, who had been strangled. Your guys called it a suicide. We found Billy about a mile beneath Denver. You missed Wendy's wedding. You and I traveled to the Moon together, where we found Stella. You saw me freezing in Antarctica, and you recently saved me from certain death in Astana. You brought me home from Italy in an alien costume. Now I look like Billy Powers and that dead cowboy actor Nevada Ritter."

Mona's mouth was still hanging open.

"So, are you gonna let me come into my own home, or are we gonna continue standing out here making a scene for the neighbors?"

"Uh...?" she stammered.

"Your father doesn't like me. My ex-secretary Hal probably doesn't either." I couldn't think of anything else at the spur of the moment. "Come on, Mona. Tell them who I am and let me come home."

"Mommy?" Stella asked. "Are you mad at Daddy?"

"Little girl, is this your Daddy?" one of the MP's asked Stella.

"Uh-huh," Stella replied.

As the MP unlocked my handcuffs, he said, "It looks like we have some kind of domestic dispute here. It doesn't look like there's been any violence." He moved his hand back and forth at Mona and me. "Now, can you two work this out peacefully, or do we have to take both of you in and let you explain this to the Commander?"

"I promise that I'll be good," I replied. "How about you, baby?"

Mona nodded her head. "Yeah, he's a pain in my ass, but there's no reason for us to bother the Commander with this quarrel."

"So, you're not afraid to be in your home with him?" one of the MP's asked Mona.

"No," Mona replied. "If he gives me any shit, I'll kick his ass out again."

Stella asked, "Why would you kick Daddy's ass?"

Mona rolled her eyes. "Never mind, honey. It's just an expression that adults use. Little girls never say those words." She thanked the two MP's for coming to her rescue and apologized that it was an unnecessary call.

"Y'all have a nice evening now," the M.P. said, touching the brim of his hat with his forefinger.

When the MP's drove away, their emergency lights off and sirens silent, I saw the living room curtains close in the house across the street. I figured that we were going to be the topic of conversation for a few months into the future. I wanted to blame Mona for being so dramatic, but then I guess it was really my fault. I had wanted to surprise her, and I guess I had.

∽∾∽

After Stella went to sleep, I climbed into bed with Mona, who had wrapped herself between the sheet and the blanket. It had been her "don't touch me" safety place for years. We lay in the dark without speaking for a while and then Mona finally broke the silence.

"When were you going to tell me that you could migrate into a human container?" she asked.

"I knew that you disliked the grey container, so when I learned from Mack that Nevada Ritter's extra clone might be available, I hoped to surprise you. I thought you'd really like to be sleeping with a man again instead of with an alien."

"But don't you think you should have talked to me about it first? Maybe I'd have liked the chance to get used to the idea before you sprung it on me."

"I'm sorry, Mona. I guess I wasn't thinking straight."

"Danny, how could you possibly think that in your absence I'd let Billy Powers or Nevada Ritter kiss me? What kind of girl do you think I am?"

"Mona…"

"Shut up, you asshole."

I was really feeling low. "Okay."

"You'd still be in the lock-up if it weren't for Stella, Danny. She's the only one who can recognize you, I mean the real you. She can see your true essence and containers can't fool her."

I wanted to say something, but I knew better than to open my yap.

"You're right about one thing, and that's that I miss your touch and I miss feeling you inside me. As a wife and a woman, it's been really hard these past few months."

Mona reached over and took my hand. "You're the biggest lug I've ever known, Danny. You can be so loving and caring at one moment and then you can do something so stupid the next."

"Mona…" I said.

"Shut up, Danny. I don't want to hear you say anything." She threw the covers back, exposing her breasts. "Don't say anything. Just make love to me. I know that's what you want."

I wasn't sure what to do, so I just laid there. Touching her might have been a trap, where it might appear to Mona that I was only interested in gratifying myself. But if I didn't touch her, she might feel unwanted or undesirable. It was a quandary beyond my ability to resolve. But I think that Mona sensed my dilemma because she moved my hand to her breast, thank you. That was all I needed—a sense of direction.

We made love for over an hour, her body shuddering half a dozen times as I tried to make up for time lost while away from her and, especially, time lost in the container of a sexless grey alien. When I finally let go, Mona was on top. My new container arched as spasms overtook its nervous system. *Yes*, I thought, *this is what I was meant to be, a human volcano erupting on the southern coast of Italy.*

Mona collapsed beside me. As we lay silent, she began to weep.

"Was it good for you, baby?" I asked.

Mona didn't answer, but I could hear that she was still weeping, occasionally sobbing. There's nothing that tears me up as much as Mona weeping. Was she happy? Did I hurt her accidentally? What could possibly be wrong?

"What's wrong, baby?" I asked. "Are you alright?"

Mona shook her head. Something was wrong.

"Mona, tell me what it is, baby."

She reached for the box of tissues that was on her nightstand, blew her nose, and then curled into the fetal position, closing herself off to me. Not knowing what else to do, I curled up beside her and put my arm around her. After a few minutes, I tried again, "Mona, I love you."

"I know you do, Danny. I love Danny Arrow, too."

"What's the matter, baby?"

"This is all wrong, Danny. I want you back."

"I *am* back, baby."

"No, you aren't. You don't look like Danny Arrow, your voice doesn't sound like Danny Arrow, your body doesn't feel like Danny Arrow, and, worst of all, your skin…it doesn't smell like my Danny. I feel like a cheater, Danny, like I just cheated on you."

"Oh, come on Mona. I'm me, and the body and smell that you want will be back in less than nine months. And with a bigger schlong, if I remember what you ordered."

"We live in such a topsy turvy world, Danny. I never expected to see you again after our first break-up, but I did. I never expected to be impregnated by a lizard from Draco, but I was. I never expected to have my baby plucked from my belly before it was full term, but she was. I never expected to see my child again, but I did. I never expected that my daughter would have to be hidden away from regular society, but because of her eyes and her intelligence, she does. I never expected to be artificially impregnated again, this time by a praying mantis, if you're right about that…and I am *definitely* pregnant again. I never expected that you would be migrated into a grey alien's container, but I was there when you were. I never expected to be sleeping beside a grey alien, but I have been until this evening. I never expected to make love to another man, but I just did…and it was in our bed, Danny. Why can't my life be normal?"

Chapter 8

While she was busy giving Stella a bath, Mona's cell phone rang. She pulled it from her pants pocket and sat on the toilet so she could watch Stella play while she answered the call.

"Casola."

"Agent Casola? Gretta Faust here. We spoke a few weeks ago. It was about my friend Maxie's death. Remember?"

"Yes, Ms. Faust. How can I help you?"

"Well, it's like this. I was cleaning through Maxie's stuff and I found a key to a box at the train station. So, I went down to see if it would still fricking work. You know how the authorities will sometimes empty the boxes and change the locks if nobody pays the rental?"

"Yes, so what did you find?"

"He had a bloody notebook stuffed in there. It was all his notes about the bloody aliens that are here on Earth. Didn't know if you might want it or if I should pitch it in the rubbish."

"It might help me to solve his murder. Could you overnight it to me?"

"Will do, probably after midday. Can you spring for the postage?"

"Sure."

Two days later the package arrived from the U.K. Mona handed it to me. I opened it and began reading through Max Gates' notebook. After a few sections that read like Powers' notebook—you know, possible types of aliens and their assumed home planets and/or dimensions—he got into some interesting information about the alien agenda. It was all tied to the New World Order and its hopes to create a single government on Earth, a government that promoted no religion and bred dependent citizens.

As I read Gates' materials, suddenly a name that I knew very well popped up—Nargas. According to Gates, Nargas' hybrid son Anion had developed plans to take over the world and free the planet from Draconians, as well as humans. Similar to the original plans of the allied reptilians and NWO, he planned to follow the principles of the Georgia Guide Stones by exterminating 95% of the Earth's human population. He sounded like another genocidal maniac. However, unlike the NWO and the reptilians, his goal was to give the Earth to Human/Draconian hybrids, like himself, so that the Earth would soon be ready to take its place among the many planets and alien races that form the Galactic Federation.

I felt a small conundrum: Anion Nargas' plans sounded like good news for kids like Stella and her two hundred schoolmates at the Villaggio, because the Earth would be theirs to try to save from pollution, deforestation, and global warming. If anybody could reverse the trends that seem to be painting a negative future for Mother Earth, it would be those kids. They have all the skills and intelligence to save the day. However, Anion's plans wouldn't be so good for people like Mona and me because we'd be among the first to be exterminated. And you know how I felt about that as I read what Gates had to say about it.

There was no question about what I had to do. I had to find this asshole Anion, see what he was up to, and stop any activities that would enable him to achieve his goals.

I shared the contents of Gates' notebook with Mona, by playing with Stella while Mona read the pages that I had dog-eared.

"Why does the name Nargas always seem to find its way to megalomaniacs?" she asked. Then she told me, "You've got to share this info with Mack."

I agreed with her.

I called FBI headquarters and asked for Mack Smith. His secretary told me that he was out, but that she'd have him call me in the afternoon. I paced the floor for over an hour and finally my cell phone rang. It was Mack.

"So, what's the important news?" he asked.

When I told him about the information from Gates' notebook, I could hear Mack's wheels turning. As the FBI representative to the NWO, he was always privy to information that nobody else had. And his role as a double agent was always a length of razor wire that he had to negotiate. Let's face it. He had to provide American governmental support for many NWO functions while, at the same time, providing secret NWO information to those of us who were trying to subvert the NWO agenda. If he were caught, it was certain and instantaneous death. So, I wondered how this new information from Gates meshed with other things that Mack knew. In the end, he simply said, "I've got to check out some stuff that I've heard, stuff that I'm not able to share with you now. You'll have to put your trust in me Dan. I'll get back to you in a few days."

No sooner had I hung up with Mack than Mona came into the room, her eyes filled with tears. I wondered what

I had done. Instead of complaining to me, she gave me a hug, still weeping.

"What's wrong, baby?" I asked.

"It's my mom. Wendy just called. Ma is in the hospital and the doctors are suggesting that she be sent home and that Hospice be called in. She's been diagnosed with liver cancer and it's already spread to her brain."

I knew that if Hospice was recommended, it would be only a very short time before Mona's mom would be cashing in her chips. "Damn, baby, I'm sorry. I don't know what to say."

"Just hold me, Danny."

After a long minute, Mona released her grip, blew her nose into a tissue, and said, "I think I'm going to have to go Katonah to visit with her for a few days. I'll take Stella."

Katonah is just north of New York City, in an area that the locals call "Upstate New York," even though it's still in the southern half of the state, at least six hours by car from the northern border with Canada. "Would you like me to drive you there?" I asked.

"I think we should fly. Wendy lives only an hour away from Ma and she has a car. I'll get her to buy a car seat for Stella. She's going to need one anyway."

"Is she expecting?"

"No, but she and Darren are trying. If she's anything like me, she'll be pregnant before I get to her house tomorrow."

We packed two suitcases, and then I drove Mona and Stella to Roanoke, where they caught a mid-afternoon flight to White Plains, NY, about twenty minutes south of Mona's mom's home.

On the way back to the Villaggio, I thought about the synchronicity of my being offered a new container at the same time of Mona's mom's imminent death. If I still had been in the alien grey container, I wouldn't have been able to drive Mona to Roanoke. Sometimes things work out for the best.

∾

Mona, Stella, and Wendy arrived at Mona's mom's home after a short night's sleep at Wendy's. Inside, two middle-aged Hospice nurses were attending to Mona's mom.

"How is she?" Mona whispered to one of the nurses as she entered her mom's home.

"Mrs. Casola is resting now. She'll be happy to see you, though. She keeps asking for both of you."

"Good. Is she eating well?"

"She eats a little of everything that we offer her, but I would never say that she has a complete meal."

"I guess that's to be expected."

"Yes. Cancer does that to you, especially with all the medication that the doctors prescribe."

"How's Dad?" Wendy asked.

"He's meeting with the funeral home director, working out arrangements for care of the body, followed by the priest for choosing the songs at the mass and selecting the cemetery site. He should be home in a couple of hours."

Mona's eyes became teary again. She felt like a fountain.

Although Stella didn't know exactly what was causing Mona to cry, she knew that her mom was sad and so she hugged Mona's leg to try to comfort her.

When Mrs. Casola was ready to greet visitors, Wendy and Mona crept quietly into the bedroom and gave their mom a kiss on the cheek.

"There she is," Mrs. Casola said softly when she saw Stella. "How's my little girl?"

Stella pressed into Mona's body and swayed back and forth. "It's okay, Stella," Mona told her. "This is my mommy. She's your grandma and she hasn't seen you since you were a baby. She loves you."

Stella reached out and took Mrs. Casola's hand. When she did, she realized what was happening and said, "It's okay. Sick go away."

"Isn't she cute," Mrs. Casola said, looking into Stella's eyes. "You're really very pretty, aren't you?"

"How are you doing, Ma?" Mona asked. "Is there anything we can get you or do for you?"

"No, I'm fine. These nice ladies have been taking good care of me, and now that you're here, I have everything that I could possibly want."

The nurse opened two folding chairs so that Mona and Wendy could sit down. Stella climbed onto Mona's lap.

"I'm glad that you're both here at the same time," Mrs. Casola told her daughters. "I have something very important to share with you. It's something that happened a very long time ago and I've never told anyone, but I think it's time that I do."

"What is it, Ma?" Wendy asked.

"It's about the gnomes."

"The gnomes?"

"Yes. When I was a young wife, your father and I wanted to have children in the worst way, but we had no luck in conceiving. The harder we tried, the more depressed we both became." She paused for several seconds and then said, "You know, we were married for over five years before I became pregnant with you, Mona."

"Yeah, Ma," Mona replied. "A lot of people have that problem until they have their first child, and then the babies come one after the other."

"Yes, it's true," Mrs. Casola laughed. Then she continued, "Your father blamed himself, thinking that he was infertile due to an injury from playing football, what you call 'soccer.' But I was convinced that it was my fault, that I wasn't pure enough to have a child."

"That's not true, Ma," Mona said. "You're the purest person that I know."

"You know how we all are, Mona, blaming ourselves as the worst critics we could ever face. So, I blamed myself, and I went to confession every day, and I prayed to the Blessed Mother that she bless our marriage with a child. But nothing happened."

"Then Zia Nettie, my aunt, told me about Saint Gerard Majella, the Patron Saint of Motherhood. He was Italian, you know, from the town of Muro, not far from Potenza, where your father's family lived. She said that if I prayed to Saint Gerard, I would have many children. So, I began praying to him. Every day I drove to the church in Somers, where they have a shrine to St. Gerard inside the church. I lit a candle every day and prayed that he would find me worthy to become fertile and bear children who would grow up in the faith."

"So, what about the gnomes, Ma?" Wendy asked.

"Well, not long after I began making the daily trip to Somers, I was visited by the gnomes. They came into our bedroom one night while your father and I were sleeping. I felt their hands touching me and I woke to see six of them standing beside me and at the foot of the bed."

"I'm surprised that Daddy didn't shoot them," Wendy said.

"Oh, I imagine that he might have tried if he had awakened to see them there, but he had had a hard day at work and he never heard them or saw them. He just kept sleeping, the way that men do."

"Go on, Ma, tell us more," Mona prompted.

"The gnomes told me that I wouldn't be hurt, but that I had been chosen as a special woman to receive the gift of a child. They lifted me up and carried me right out the window of our house."

"Were they gnomes or angels?" Wendy asked.

"They didn't have wings, so they weren't angels, not like the ones they paint in the church booklets. They had small bodies with large heads and big eyes. But they floated through the air as though they had wings on their ankles. And they took me right out my window as though it were open and carried me into a giant egg that was sitting at the top of the big spruce tree that was in our back yard."

"This was one wild dream, Ma," Wendy said.

"This was no dream, sweetheart. That's why I am telling you, so you'll know how you came to be."

Wendy was going to say something, but Mona touched her arm. "Go on, Ma, tell us what happened."

Inside the egg is where the angel waited for me. She was very tall and wore flowing robes. She wore a hood that covered her head, but I could see her eyes. They were big like a bug's."

"Like a praying mantis?" Mona asked suspiciously.

"Yes, exactly."

"What did she do, Ma?" Wendy asked.

"She told me that I would have several children and that she would watch over my children. That she would see me again because this was not my last visit with her. Then the gnomes inserted a needle into my tummy. I cried out that it hurt. When I did, the angel touched my forehead and all the pain went away. I must have fallen asleep because when I awoke in the morning, I was in my bed, lying right beside your father."

"It had to be a dream, Ma," Wendy said.

"I told you that it was no dream, sweetheart. When I went into the bathroom that morning, there was a small mark on my tummy where the needle went in, and a small drop of blood on the inside of my nightgown."

"What did Daddy say?" Wendy asked.

"I never told him. I never told anybody about the angel or the gnomes. When we discovered that I was pregnant, I just told everybody the truth—that I had prayed to Saint Gerard and that he had sent his blessing down upon me and your father."

"Did you ever see the angel again?" Mona asked.

"Oh, yes," Mrs. Casola replied, taking each girl by the hand. "On her first visit, she brought you, Mona. On her second, she brought your sister Mary. And on her third visit, she brought you, Wendy. I was blessed three times by Saint Gerard because the gnomes carried me into the egg to see the angel three times."

"Ma…," Wendy started to say. But her mom interrupted her.

"All three of my children are very special. You are gifts from the angels and the angels will watch over you for the rest of your lives."

"We've been blessed to have you as our mom," Wendy said.

"Yeah, Ma. And thank you for telling us about the gnomes," Mona replied. But she was already putting two and two together. It would be hard for anyone to convince her that her mom hadn't been abducted by aliens about thirty-four years ago and that she, Mary, and Wendy weren't the products of some sort of experiment in intergalactic breeding.

Chapter 9

Mack came to the Villaggio for an unexpected visit while Mona was still in Katonah with Wendy and their dying mom.

"How's the new container working out?" he asked.

"I really like it. It's nice being a human again. I think that being a grey alien has to be just about the worst situation that any living being faces."

"Why's that?"

"They're frail and vulnerable, and they're subservient to just about every other galactic species. On top of that, they don't have sex."

"Do you mean that they have no gender?" Mack asked. "I think that in many work and social situations not having gender could be a good thing."

"No, I mean that they don't enjoy sex. They don't have a clue what it is. When I was trapped inside that grey container, I was like a neutered dog. If I hadn't known how nice sexual relations can be, I wouldn't have had a clue as to why people and animals hook up."

Mack shook his head and chuckled. "Sometimes you're a weird one, Dan,"

"Yeah, that's what Mona says." I took a mug from the cabinet and poured myself half a cup of Death Wish Coffee, then filled the rest of the mug with hot water. "Can I get you a cup of coffee?" I asked.

"Sure," Mack replied, "and then we can get down to business."

I had suspected that he wasn't here on a social call.

I handed Mack a mug of undiluted coffee and then he began, "The Black Knight has moved into a lower orbit, one that's less focused upon the North Polar Region. Something is up, and we need to know what it is."

"What's the Black Knight? Isn't that a Batman movie?"

"Not even close, Dan. It's a satellite in orbit around the Earth. According to some, Nikola Tesla was the first to discover radio signals from the Black Knight satellite back in the late 1890s, but he didn't know the source of the signals. Others, mostly astronomers, began monitoring its radio signals back as early as the 30s and '40s, and they were able to pinpoint its approximate location."

"Any school kid knows that there were no satellites circling the earth until the 1960s," I said.

"That's the point, Dan. It isn't ours. The first photo of it was taken in the 1950s when Grumman Aircraft Corporation plotted its orbit and calculated its weight."

"So what is it?"

"Some say it's space junk, probably Russian, but it's been sending radio signals to the Epsilon Bootes star system for as long as scientists have been monitoring it. Its polar orbit is what interests most scientists because a polar orbit gives you the opportunity to map land masses and oceans and to monitor activities on a planet."

"So, you think that somebody has been monitoring Earth from this satellite?" I asked.

"Yes, and sending data back to Epsilon Bootes for almost 13,000 years."

"So, why don't we shoot it down and take it apart to see what it's doing?"

"Each time we've tried, it's moved away from the vehicle that we've sent, or else it's shut down all systems in that vehicle. The same thing has happened to the Russians and SpaceX. The problem that we're facing now is that the Black Knight has made a radical adjustment in its orbit, now circling at the 38th Parallel, and no known governments have bothered it to cause it to move. We need to find out what's up."

"Isn't that the demarcation between North and South Korea?" I asked.

"Yes, and whoever is monitoring us may be concerned about North Korea's recent upsurge in nuclear missile testing. But the 38th Parallel also crosses the USA, Europe, Asia, and Russia. Something like this could make our enemies nervous and set off World War III."

"So what are you suggesting that we do?"

"We need to check out future events."

"And how do you plan to do that, hire a psychic?"

"No, something more precise. I want you to go there and report back what you've found."

"You've got to be kidding me."

"No, I'm dead serious, Dan. We've recently finished perfecting the technology to help you do just that. You'll fly to the future in one of our three new black ops triangles, a TR-42C. 'TR' stands for 'Time Runner.' It looks like the black triangles that you've seen before and it's already been tested. In fact, we have done some experimental travel into the past. I think that when you saw that triangle several years ago, you actually might have seen a TR-42C from the future."

"You really *are* serious, aren't you? Why don't you send somebody else?"

Mack didn't seem to hear my question about sending someone else. Instead, he just kept rambling on about the mission that he'd planned for me. "We have a shortlist of important stuff for you to find out: First, you have to try to determine the purpose of the Black Knight satellite and its ramifications upon life on Earth. Why has it changed its orbit? Is it hostile? Is it only monitoring Earth life? What cataclysmic damage might it cause to Earth? Second, when you get to the future, you have to see if Anion Nargas has been successful in implementing his pandemic. If so, how many people have survived? How are they governed? What has been the impact on the environment and upon our national electronic infrastructure? And, if he has been successful, you must learn what he did and when, so we can try to stop him and change the future that you've seen."

"That's a shitload of stuff to figure out, Mack. Why not send a crew of your FBI operatives?"

"There's too big a chance that our operatives, as you call them, could run into themselves in the future. That wouldn't be good. You, on the other hand, are in Nevada Ritter's body, and if you run into yourself in the future, the 'future you' will be in your own clone and you'll know why Ritter is there. Make sense?"

"Not really, but I wouldn't mind seeing the future, at least a little of it."

"There's more, though, Dan. The third thing I need you to do is to report back on the draconians. Have they finally come out of their deep underground military bunkers on Earth? Who, if anyone, is utilizing the Moon and how is it impacting those on Earth?"

"Jesus, Mack, I could be gone for a year before I have the answers to all your questions."

"Yeah, but the nice thing is that to those of us who are in this timeline, you won't have been gone for more than a day or two."

"How do I accomplish that?"

"When we set your return vectors, we'll set them for today at noon. See how simple it is? The only person who'll feel as though he's been gone for a year will be you."

"Time travel will probably cause some sort of impact to my container. Won't it be a year older? What happens if I lose a leg or get a new scar…how will I explain that?"

"We haven't figured that one out yet. Maybe we'll just use plausible deniability."

"You mean we'll simply deny that anything is different?"

"Yeah."

"What aren't you telling me, Mack?"

"Most important, I guess, is that I need to get you out to Nellis Air Base as soon as possible. Maybe tomorrow. Will Mona be okay with that?"

"I'll call her and tell her what you're up to. I'm not sure when she'll be coming home. If we can overlap her absence and mine, then neither one of us will be home alone for long."

⧉

I Facetimed Mona to fill her in on the new mission that Mack had planned for me. She wasn't happy that I was going on another mission, so I didn't tell her that I'd be traveling into the future. Instead, I told her that I'd be going to Nellis Air Base for a few days, and she reminded me that she wouldn't be home for a few days, either. So, we agreed to Facetime every evening just to apprise each other of what we were doing. Then Mona told me what her mom had revealed to her and Wendy.

"Are you thinking that you might be a hybrid?" I asked. Knowing Mona, her brain had made that connection before her mom had delivered all of the information.

"The thought has crossed my mind."

"Maybe Dr. Spann can suggest a way to determine that, baby. The Ummites are good with that sort of thing."

"When do you think you'll see him again?" Mona asked.

"I'm not sure, but I'm going to be with Mack for a day or two, so maybe I can get him to contact Dr. Spann so I can talk to him."

"Thanks, Danny. I love you."

"I'm only thinking of you. I love you, too."

ⅇⅉⅇⅉ

That afternoon, Mona used Wendy's home computer to do an internet search for DNA analysis companies. She found more than a dozen that would evaluate a person's DNA and identify biological heritage by percentage. She called three before she found one that would overnight the DNA sampling kit to Wendy's house for a small extra fee. She ordered two kits by phone, and they arrived the next afternoon. Mona and Wendy both collected the required samples of their saliva and skin cells, and then Wendy mailed the samples to the laboratory that same afternoon, while Mona took a short nap with Stella.

Chapter 10

I flew by chopper to Andrews Air Base again and then caught a standard hop to Nellis Air Base with Mack. The flight to Nevada took five hours, and Mack used most of that time to brief me more fully on the TR-42C experimental time travel program.

According to Mack, the U.S. government has operated a small fleet of black triangular craft for almost forty years. With propulsion systems that were retro-engineered from alien technology by our scientists, these vehicles can exceed light speed and, thus, far surpass anything operated by NASA. The Apollo lunar program that the world watched on television was simply a diversion, intended to keep the public in the dark about our real space exploration program, one that was funded by the government's black ops budget and one offering no public launches.

This special black-ops space exploration initiative was intended to give us a technological leg up on all our enemies. Through the program, U.S. astronauts have explored the ruins on the dark side of the Moon and actually have driven alien mining operations off our planet's nighttime orb. But, of course, we haven't colonized the Moon because of the presence of the reptilians, who have been living in the Moon's hollow interior for a thousand years. Now, because I nuked the interior of the hollow Moon, the reptilians are the only species capable of living there since they are immune to the high radiation levels. It's the same thing our scientists discovered when they studied the impact of radiation on plant and animal life in the desert where we conducted our first atomic bomb tests in the 1940s—reptiles are the only species of any kind that is not subject to mutations due to radiation. Back to the present, though. Although we haven't colonized the Moon, we have, however, colonized two bases on Mars, one on Venus, and another on Pluto, where water and a minimal atmosphere actually are present.

More recently, however, has been the upgrading of the TR squadron to include three TR-42C's. While the TR on the older models stands for "triangle," on the newer models, it stands for "time runner," because that's a new capability made possible by the fact that they can travel up to twice the speed of light. According to Mack, once the TR's exceed light speed, time and space as we know them cease to exist. Instead, onboard computers can lock onto any point in our timeline, and when the TR slows down, you're there. It's the same location but in a totally different day and time.

The kicker came when Mack told me, "We've gone up to ten years backward in time and then have returned to the starting date, Dan. It's been very successful. However, I haven't been completely upfront with you. We've never gone forward in time unless going backward first. Your trip into the future will be our first attempt to go forward and then return to the present. You know, forward and then backward."

No wonder he didn't want to send any of his own operatives. This was an experiment, and I was expendable. "Can we do it?" I asked.

"Theoretically, we should be able to do it, and your pilot is convinced that it should be a piece of cake, but there is always the risk that the two of you might find yourselves stuck in the future, unable to return."

"Thanks, Mack. I knew that you were only thinking of me and my safety when assigning me to this mission."

⁂

When we landed at Nellis, Mack took me to the medical center for a pre-flight physical. It was standard practice, the same as what our astronauts are put through before they're strapped to a giant roman candle and shot into space. The center was in a nondescript faded green steel building, and only the black caduceus which had been stenciled onto the entry door's window glass let you know that it was a medical facility.

We were greeted by a sentry who asked our business. Behind him, I could see that the floors were polished concrete and the lighting was fluorescent. Certainly, it was no upscale facility, and it couldn't hold a candle to the Ummite migration facility in Italy.

"Pre-flight physical, TR Squadron," Mack told the sentry.

"Take a right at the first hallway, third door on your left," he told us.

I saluted him as I walked by. The sentry gave me a dirty look, his eyes following me as we passed.

When we got to the examination center, they were expecting us. Mack stayed in the waiting room while the nurse led me to an examination room where she instructed me, "Strip everything, including your skivvies."

"Even my socks?"

"Yes, everything."

It was then that I noticed her five o'clock shadow and her protruding Adam's apple. She was a he. But I guess that was no big deal, especially in today's armed services. Hell, if I was one gender and wanted to be the other, the armed services would be the perfect place to be, because they'd cover all the costs of my gender-change operations and concomitant counseling sessions. Maybe I'd do a three-year stint, but I'd save a bundle on medical expenses.

So, I did as the nurse asked—I stripped. Maybe I was in Nevada, but it was cold inside that room with no clothes on and if the examination didn't start soon, I was going to freeze my balls off.

After a couple of minutes, the nurse returned, accompanied by Dr. Renquist, a guy in his mid-forties with a receding hairline and slight graying at the temples.

"I presume that you're new to the squadron, Agent Arrow," he said.

"Yup," I replied. "Is it that obvious?"

"You're my first patient who carries no military rank, although I see that you're a Special Agent with the FBI."

He took my temperature and blood pressure, checked my reflexes, and had me pee into a plastic cup, I assumed for analysis of possible drug use as well as diabetes. Then he listened to my lungs and my heart.

"Interesting thrill in your heart," he muttered.

"Thrill?"

"Yes. It's backwash, usually due to a valve not closing properly. I'm going to want to do an ultrasound as well as an EKG."

Dr. Renquist told me to get dressed and he left the examination room.

Mack came in while I was tying my shoes. "The doc's a little concerned about your heart," he said.

"What could be wrong with it?" I asked. "It's brand new and Dr. Spann didn't see any anomalies when he checked me out in Italy."

Ten minutes later I had an IV in my arm and was running on a treadmill while Dr. Renquist was watching my heart on a monitor. When I was running three-quarter speed, he told the nurse to inject dye into my bloodstream. As she did, I could feel its tingling spreading through my veins, taking about twenty seconds to fill my entire body with warmth.

The treadmill suddenly stopped, and I was directed to lie on my side on a table, while Dr. Renquist smeared some gel on my chest and moved an ultrasound wand across my left pectoral muscle. On the monitor, I could see my heart doing double time as it worked to recover from the exercise that it had just been through. The doctor pointed to a section of my heart on the monitor and then ran his finger around the heart's outer wall. "Looks like the beginning of rejection," he muttered.

"Rejection?" I asked.

"Possibly, Agent Arrow. It's not altogether rare, but migrants are sometimes subject to host rejection."

At first I thought that he thought I was a migrant laborer, but then I realized that he was referring to the fact that I had been migrated into this container in Italy. Obviously, he was aware of the migration process.

Dr. Renquist turned to his nurse. "Please go find Agent Smith and bring him to the cardio room. We'll meet you there."

I got up, wiped the gel off of my chest with a small towel, and followed the doctor down the corridor, buttoning my shirt as I walked.

We reached the cardio room at the same time as Mack and the nurse arrived. Dr. Renquist excused the nurse and sat at a conference table with Mack and me.

"We have a problem," Dr. Renquist told us. "Agent Arrow, I'm fairly certain that your container is rejecting your electrical essence."

"What makes you believe that?" Mack asked.

"Already one heart valve has begun to function erratically, and the outer layer of the heart is dying from lack of oxygen. In addition, the EKG shows signs of brain wave denial."

"Denial?" I asked.

"Yes, Mr. Arrow. The brain sends a signal to the heart and the heart does not respond, as if denying that the signal exists."

"What does this mean?" Mack asked.

"Do you want the meat without any trimmings?"

"Yeah, doc, get to the point," I said.

"I give you no more than two days to live, Agent Arrow."

"What are our options?" Mack asked.

"Is your old container still viable?" the doctor asked.

"It's in Italy and probably has been disposed of by now," Mack told him.

"Maybe you should call your insurance agent and double up your policy," the doctor said to me. "It would certainly benefit your wife." Maybe he was trying to be funny, but I didn't laugh.

"Agent Arrow is supposed to leave on an important mission tomorrow morning," Mack said. "It's a matter of national importance."

"National security?" Dr. Renquist asked, looking at Mack for confirmation.

"Yes," Mack replied.

Dr. Renquist drummed his pointer finger on the table a couple of times and then said, "I have a container here at Nellis that I could loan you, but I would have to have it back within two weeks. That would give you time to find a suitable replacement for Agent Arrow."

"What kind of container, Doc?" I asked. "I've been in a small Grey, and I'm not going back into one of those."

"Are you familiar with the Jonathan Silverman situation?"

I looked at Mack and shrugged my shoulders.

"He's a Navy Seal," Mack said, "one of the guys on the team that got Bin Laden. He was kidnapped while on vacation with his wife in Israel. His wife was found beaten to death, most likely stoned, near the Palestinian border. Silverman was later featured in a video that was posted by ISIS, apparently being held captive somewhere in Syria."

"Yes," Dr. Renquist said, "and a team of Seals is currently here at Nellis, training to extricate him. They'll leave on their mission within ten days. If they're successful, he'll most likely need to migrate into his clone. But I can loan it to you until he returns to Nellis."

"Seals have clones?" I asked.

"It should come as no surprise to you, Agent Arrow. We've had the migration technology for almost two years now, and we've grown clones of every Navy Seal and Marine Recon member who's stationed here, just in case there's a training mishap. The Silverman clone has been ready for migration for the past month."

"You've had the migration technology longer than the NWO," I said in surprise.

"The NSA stole it from the reptilians and the CIA perfected it before the NWO did," Dr. Renquist continued. "Our guys obtained it from the CIA. I understand that some of the newer facilities that are being opened around the globe offer pain-free migration. We aren't there yet, but our Seals and Marines don't mind. They live for a little pain."

"Can I see the Silverman clone?" I asked.

"Sure. Follow me to the container storage room."

Mack and I followed Dr. Renquist through the building to a room that looked like it could have been a basketball court sometime in the past. The floor was crawling with wires and tubes that twisted and turned like snakes as they wound across the concrete and connected to more than thirty growth tubes. It reminded me of the re-birth facility in Astana and the alien facility beneath the Denver airport.

Dr. Renquist found specimen number 23. He flipped the number tag around and double-checked the identity information on its backside, reading it aloud, "Yes, this is Silverman. Age: 31. Ethncity: Hebrew. Blood type: A+. Height: 73 inches. Weight: 195 lbs. No known allergies."

I took a hard look at the container, although if I had less than 48 hours to live, I really didn't have a choice. It looked somewhat Middle Eastern, with jet black hair, and large pores on its cheeks. Overall, though, I thought that Mona might find it attractive and I said that aloud.

Mack chuckled. "Dan," he said, "you remind me of Rock Hudson in that movie with Doris Day, where he thinks that he's going to die, so he starts trying to find his wife her next husband."

"Gimme a break, Mack. You didn't see how she reacted to me when I came home in this container." I pinched the skin on my neck to drive the point home. "What's she gonna do when I show up as somebody else for the second time this week?"

Mack turned to Dr. Renquist. "When can we migrate Dan into Silverman's clone?"

"I'll need half an hour to warm up the machine and to prep my staff. The two of you can wait in the lounge. Coffee is free." Then he turned to me. "Except for you,

Agent Arrow. You shouldn't eat or drink anything until after the procedure."

So, we found our way to the lounge, where assorted snacks and sandwiches were available in vending machines. The coffee was in one of those machines with the funny name, the one that fills a single cup at a time by dribbling hot water over coffee grinds that come in a small plastic cup. I was just as glad that I wasn't supposed to drink because I never liked the plastic back taste of the coffee that comes from those machines. No wonder the most popular options are the flavored coffees—you know, hazelnut, chocolate mint, and butterscotch—basically coffees for people who don't like the taste of coffee…or plastic.

When Nurse Klinger appeared, I knew it was time to ride the roller coaster again. She escorted Mack and me into the Nellis version of a migration facility. It was a well-lit space, about the size of my living room back home. The walls were painted light green and Fresnel's hung from cables that disappeared into the darkness above. The migration machine stood in the middle of the room looking like something that had been put together by high school boys in a tech class.

"Basic," Mack said when he saw the technology that Dr. Renquist planned to use.

"It's the same unit that Dr. Laskey was going to use to migrate Hitler into his clone back in Livermore," I replied. "This is going to be like getting a tooth filled by a dentist with an old-fashioned foot-pump drill. He wasn't shitting us about Seals living for pain."

"Hitler, Nelson, and Powers all survived the experience, Dan. So will you."

Dr. Renquist interrupted our conversation. "Agent Arrow, if you would please strip to your skivvies, we can begin the process."

"What about this container, Doc?" I asked. "It's on loan from Italy, and I really need to get it shipped back there."

"We'll try to save it, but the decay of the heart tissues has already begun, so the container will be weakened, at best, and may be altogether dysfunctional for its next recipient."

I didn't like the sound of that, and I knew that Dr. Spann wouldn't be happy that I'd ruined his prized container. But, I'd let Mack handle those details. Maybe he'd give Spann a couple of hundred thousand from his black ops budget to replace the lost revenue that Spann hoped to squeeze from a Hollywood-type who wanted to live in Nevada Ritter's clone.

I dropped my trousers and removed my shirt and shoes. The nurse escorted me to a wooden table with no pad to soften its oaken surface. She stuck electrodes onto my chest and head and after I laid down, she moved the usual rotating paddles into a position around my head. Then she did the same to Silverman's clone, except that he didn't get the paddles. When all was set, she turned to Dr. Renquist and told him, "All set here."

Dr. Renquist nodded and then told me, "This procedure will have some bumps and twists that you didn't experience in Italy, but you'll be fine."

I nodded and gave him the "thumbs up" sign.

"Close your eyes, Agent Arrow," the nurse told me. "It'll be easier on you."

A friend once told me never to trust a woman with a five o'clock shadow, but I did as the nurse suggested. When I felt the gentle breeze from the rotating paddles, I knew that the ride was about to begin. Vertigo rose in my head, I felt that my eyes had crossed, and then things went black, as though I had passed out. Then the dream began, I was climbing up to the top of the roller coaster again. As I crested the top of the first and steepest rise, I suddenly experienced the sensation of freefalling, as though I had jumped out of an airplane without a parachute and was hurtling toward the ground at a hundred and fifty miles per hour. Suddenly, however, I felt a burning sensation on my back, as though I had entered a bone-dry water slide and friction was doing its thing. The slide turned left and then right and then quickly dropped until I felt a ripping sensation at my side, as though two sections of tubing had been poorly welded together, leaving a sharp edge that tore my flesh as I passed. "Goddam juncture in the electric cable," I told myself. As the ripping sensation subsided, I felt the tube drop again and another jagged juncture tore at my hip. I was about to swear when suddenly the tube lurched upwards, slamming me against its side as it spiraled to the right, and then I felt myself crashing into the bale of hay that signified that the ride was over.

It was dark and I heard voices in the distance, just like I had experienced at the end of the migration in Italy. I lay motionless for what seemed like an eternity, but suddenly I felt my body arch. Then it arched again. I heard alarmed voices but couldn't understand what they were saying. I heard a buzzing sound and my body arched a third time. The voices seemed less anxious. Soon, light began to appear, at first hazy and then brighter, as I came to physical consciousness.

"Lay still, Agent Arrow." It was the nurse. "Lay still until you become adjusted to your new container."

A few minutes later Dr. Renquist asked, "So, how does your new suit feel, Agent Arrow?"

"Actually, pretty good. The ride was ugly, though, Doc. You've got to get some upgraded equipment."

"You gave us a few moments of anxiety, Agent Arrow. We weren't sure that we were going to be able to restart your heart. But the third shock seemed to do the trick."

"Thanks for not giving up on me, Doc. It's nice to be back."

"I'd like to keep you here overnight for observation. It's just a precautionary thing. Nothing to worry about."

I didn't believe that Dr. Renquist was giving me the whole story, but I thought it best to do as he suggested. This was his clinic and he knew its capabilities, so I was in no place to argue.

Mack came to see me about ten minutes later. "So, what's bothering the doc?" I asked him.

"They had trouble getting the clone's heart to start, but it seems to be pumping just fine right now. I think he wants to monitor it overnight. So, you'll get a good night's sleep tonight and we'll meet your pilot and see the TR-42C in the morning."

Mack gave me my cell phone before he left to find a berth in the BOQ, the Bachelor Officers Quarters that are found on all military bases. After a standard mess hall dinner of mystery meat and gravy with a side of mashed potatoes and canned peas, I gave Mona a call.

"Danny, is that you?" she asked. "You sound funny over this connection. Where are you anyway? And why didn't you Facetime me?"

I explained that the Nevada Ritter container was rejecting me and that if they hadn't migrated me into a new container, she'd have been a widow in a couple of days.

"Don't do that, Danny. Don't go dying on me. I can't do this without you."

We agreed to FaceTime after she acknowledged that she wouldn't recognize the guy on the other end as being me, not even being me as Nevada Ritter.

After we hung up, I called Mona's cell phone again, this time using Facetime. "Let me look at you, Danny," she said before I could even say, "Hello."

I held the phone away from me while standing near a lamp so its light would let her see more of me than just a close-up of my face. Then, following her instructions, I slowly moved the phone to the right and then to the left side of my face.

"I guess you'll do," she told me. "But I'm not sure I'll be able to kiss you when I see you again. It's going to take some getting used to, like when you came home the last time."

"Thanks, Mona. This one is a surprise on me. I'm glad that you understand."

"This is just a continuation of what I told you before. I never expected any of this when I first met you, and this ride that we call a relationship just keeps taking so many unexpected twists and turns. How can I kiss you or make love to you when you aren't the Danny Arrow that I love?"

"It is me, and I am your Danny Arrow," I reminded her, "unless it's just my container that you love."

"But you don't look like you or smell like you, Danny. We've gone over all of this before. I feel like a cheater. It would be better if you came home as a blowup doll. At least then I'd feel like a weirdo, but not like a cheater."

"I know, hon. I'm sorry. But I'll be back as your Danny Arrow very soon, I promise."

♥♥♥

Mack woke me at three in the morning. "Come on," he said, "we're getting you out of here. Your TR has been fueled and the pilot is conducting pre-flight checks. We need to get you into a flight suit and out to the runway as soon as possible."

"Why this time of the morning?" I asked.

"America is asleep, Dan. We always fly at night when the chances of being seen are next to nil."

"And what about the doctor? He'll be coming to check me out in a few hours."

"He'll get over it."

Chapter 11

She was standing on the side of a well-worn cattle path when the farmer found her. Her clothes were new, perhaps freshly washed and her dark hair was clean and brushed, but she was barefoot. In his native Spanish language, he asked, "Are you lost, little girl? Where are your parents?"

The child did not speak, so the farmer continued his business of distributing honey-glazed oats to his Altiplano cattle in the adjacent field. When two hours had passed, the farmer began to walk home for his midday meal. The little girl who had watched him work was still standing in the same location. He proffered his hand and she took it. They walked to his home together.

"What have you brought me, Mateo?" his wife asked when she saw the little girl accompanying her husband.

"I don't know, Milagros. She has said nothing. She watched me work the cattle for two hours. I think she may be lost."

"We cannot keep her. Her parents must be frantic with worry."

Milagros offered the girl a basket of cuñapé. The girl reached into the basket and quickly ate two of the corn and cheese balls. Milagros turned to Mateo and said, "Pour her a glass of milk. She's hungry."

Mateo found a cup and filled it with milk from the quart-sized bottle in the couple's small refrigerator. He handed it Milagros, who handed it to the girl. She seized the cup with both hands and drank its contents in large gulps. As she did, a thin line of milk dribbled from the edge of her mouth and dotted the front of her dress.

"Go to the village, Mateo, and bring the Prefect. He'll know what to do."

Mateo did as instructed. An hour later he returned with Senor Ricaldi, the sound of the Prefect's car telling Milagros that help had arrived.

"Ola, Senora Soleta," the Prefect said as he entered the small home.

"Ola, Senor Ricaldi. This is the girl."

The little girl stood resolute beside Milagros.

"Where is your mama, little girl?" Senor Ricaldi asked.

She did not respond.

"Do you understand what I am asking you?"

She did not respond.

"Perhaps she's deaf?" he asked.

Milagros smacked a wooden spoon on the table behind the girl. She jumped in surprise.

"That should answer your question, Senor."

"Then perhaps she is from Paraguay and does not speak our dialect."

"We cannot keep her, Prefect. You must help us find her parents."

"There have been no reports of missing children, Senora. Perhaps we should take her to Sucre. The authorities there shall know what to do with her."

"I will accompany you, Senor," Milagros said. "See how your gruff manner frightens the child?"

"You're probably right, Senora Soleta."

Milagros gathered some cookies and a jar of milk for the hour-long journey to Sucre, the judicial capital of Bolivia. The road was narrow and wound around tight curves that followed the fences of farms that existed before the introduction of automobiles into the backcountry of Bolivia. Soon, however, buildings replaced cattle and sheep along the roadside, and as the Prefect's Mercedes SUV entered the city limits of Sucre, the quiet of the jungle and grasslands gave way to the noise of urban commerce.

The girl seemed interested in the city, sitting up and looking eagerly at the buildings as the SUV passed them. When the Prefect guided his vehicle onto a side street, the girl pointed at the marquis of the Hotel Independencia and exclaimed in English, "There. The International UFO Conference."

"What did she say?" Milagros asked the Prefect.

"I think she pointed to the Hotel Independencia. Perhaps she stayed there with her parents."

The Prefect did not stop but continued to the headquarters of the Cuerpo de Policia Nacional. The little girl rose to her knees and slapped on the Prefect's shoulders from the back seat. "Go back. Go back. The International UFO Conference."

"Is she American?" Milagros asked.

Three blocks later, the Prefect pulled to a stop in front of the National Police Corps headquarters. He opened the back door so that Senora Soleta and the little girl could get out. Once out of the car, the little girl started running back toward the hotel.

"Stop her! Stop Her!" the Prefect shouted to people on the street.

A young man with a basket of mangoes dropped them and grabbed the little girl as she ran by, lifting her into the air and holding on tightly as she struggled to free herself.

When the Prefect reached the young man, he gave him a reward of one hundred Bolivianos, took the young girl in his arms, and marched her up the street and into the Police Corps headquarters. Senora Soleta followed.

"This little girl," the Prefect began, "was found wandering alone outside of my village of Padilla this morning. If she has parents, they have not reported her missing. She is foreign, American we think."

"The desk sergeant asked, "And what should we do with her?"

"Help me find her parents. If you cannot find them, put her into the State orphanage. My village has no such facility to care for so little a child."

"And where should we begin to look for them?"

"Perhaps the Hotel Independencia. She seemed excited when we passed by it."

The Prefect filled out the necessary paperwork, reporting the child as abandoned by her parents. Then he and the senora drove back to Padilla, their mission accomplished.

ഗഗ

At seven in the evening, two officers of the National Police Corps walked into the Hotel Independencia accompanied by the little girl. "Come," she told them, pulling one officer's arm as she urged him onward. "The International UFO Conference."

The officers stopped at the front desk and spoke briefly with the manager, who pointed them down the hallway to the conference center where hundreds of people from around the world had gathered to learn about the latest UFO sightings, alien intervention and interactions, and governmental cover-ups around the globe.

As they entered the room, the group's moderator was preparing to announce the after-dinner speaker, an

Egyptologist with irrefutable evidence of alien assistance in the construction of the Sphinx more than 20,000 years ago. The Police interrupted the moderator before he began his introductory remarks. "This little girl has lost her family," one officer said. "She does not speak Spanish and we do not speak English, but we believe that her parents may be attending your conference or perhaps someone here knows who they are."

The moderator bent down and whispered to the little girl in English, "Do your speak English? Are your parents here?"

"I'm Maxwell Gates, Charlie. I was abducted, but I'm back. I need to speak to the conference attendees."

"Good God. Didn't you commit suicide in Warsaw?"

"It was a set-up. Tall Nordics did it, helped by the greys of the Watchers. I was migrated into this little girl's container. But it's me, in the flesh."

The moderator walked briskly to the podium. "Friends, I have a surprise guest who would like to speak with us this evening. This may be of vital interest to our UFOlogist community. After his address, we will resume with the regularly scheduled presentation."

He turned and motioned for the little girl to come to the podium. She looked no older than five, still in her milk-stained dress and still barefoot. She took her position on the stage beside the podium, as though she had done it a hundred times before. The moderator removed the microphone from its stand and handed it to the child.

"It's so nice to see so many of you here today," the little girl said into the microphone. The audience of 300 paying members and guests seemed as puzzled by her remark as they were by her evident ease in front of so very many adult strangers.

"Let me begin." She paused for a moment. "My name is Maxwell Gates." Several gasps erupted from the audience. "I was abducted by aliens several months ago while preparing to make a presentation to a major UFO conference in Warsaw, Poland. They migrated me into a small, hand-held device, the size of a pack of cigarettes that they pressed to my solar plexus. I don't know what they did to my body, but it must have looked like a murder or a suicide. I awoke in this new container less than a day ago."

The audience erupted into conversation. The moderator shouted to the crowd, "Let him speak. Please, friends, let him speak." The audience slowly quieted.

"Hello, Jonathan," the little girl said to a man seated at a third-row table. "I haven't seen you since the conference in Edinburg where you moderated my presentation on the New Alien Agenda." Jonathan put his hand to his lips in disbelief.

"And hello, Martha," she said to a woman at a front-row table. "I haven't spoken with you since we shared lunch of foie de gras and wine on the banks of the Seine in Paris."

Martha gasped, "It IS Maxie Gates." A loud murmur arose from the audience.

"Thank you, Martha. I'll give you and your journal exclusive rights to my story. Please see me after this event."

The little girl cleared her throat. "If I may continue, ladies and gentlemen…Before being dropped off in the ranch country of Bolivia, the aliens left me with a warning for all of mankind. They told me to tell you that we are mishandling our planet and destroying its ecosystems, much the same way as the technologically advanced human civilizations before ours did. And because they cannot let us continue this destructive path for the sake of our living planet, they will destroy our civilization as they have done in the past to three other civilizations, returning the Earth once again to a more primordial condition. We have only a short time, a few years, to change the error of our ways, to end the violence, to reverse the pollution, and to end deforestation of the rainforests. If we do not do so, the next generation to remain on our planet will live once again in caves."

The conference again erupted into conversation at each table. Then hands flew into the air as conference attendees had myriad questions to ask Max Gates who stood before them in the container of a five-year-old human female.

Standing beside the police on the side of the stage, the moderator turned and in Spanish told them with a smile, "Gentlemen, I believe that you've found this little girl's family. Thank you for bringing her home."

Chapter 12

Mack and I exited the jeep and walked into the hangar where a large triangular-shaped craft was waiting. Its outer shell was made of a strange metal composite with a mirror-smooth matte black finish. It had no visible engines. Under its three edges were rows of clear lights, three on each side. It stood silently on three thin legs, one at each point of the triangle and each with a rectangular foot, about 24 inches by 18 inches in size.

"Here she is, Dan," Mack said as we neared the Time Runner.

I reached out and touched the smooth skin of the TR-42C. Two sides appeared to be almost sixty feet long, but one was less, maybe thirty-five or forty, and at its center the craft was approximately twenty feet thick.

"No, not the Time Runner, Dan. Here's your pilot, Commander Nicole Nardini. She's been with the unit for four years and has combat experience in the TR-38's. The TR-42's haven't seen combat, but they're fully equipped if the need ever arises."

Commander Nardini stepped out from under the wing. She was dressed in a blue flight suit, helmet under her left arm. Her red hair was short, but not close-cropped. Her face bore the freckles that you would expect on a redhead, and she was attractive, if not beautiful. But I guess that her physical attractiveness depended on your taste, and you know that my experience with redheads has been lukewarm at best. As a group, they're freaking crazy.

"Agent Arrow?" she asked, extending her hand.

I shook her hand politely, trying to be firm, but not overbearing. "Glad to meet you Commander."

"Please call me 'Nicki,'" she told me.

"Then, call me 'Dan,'" I offered.

"How's the ship?" Mack asked.

"Totally ready to go, Agent Smith. I talked to her a few minutes ago and she told me that she's excited about seeing the future."

This lady was really gung ho. "So, what do I need to do to prep for the trip?" I asked.

Nicki pointed to a tent that had been set up in the corner of the hangar. "Your flight suit and foot gear are in there, waiting for you to put them on. We checked your sizes with Dr. Renquist. Once you're dressed, you can kiss Agent Smith goodbye and we'll see him yesterday."

"Huh?" I asked.

"I asked Commander Nardini to set the return coordinates for yesterday at noon," Mack told me, "so when you contact Mona, you'll have already returned."

"Too late, Mack. I called her last night. It would be less confusing to all of us if we returned at noon today."

Mack nodded.

"Okay by me," Nicki replied. "I'll reset the coordinates before we launch, so we'll return about ten minutes after we launch."

"One last stupid question, Mack. What do we do for spending money in the future?" I asked.

"Commander Nardini has a small strongbox with one hundred ounces of gold, mostly American Eagles, but a few Krugerrands have been thrown in. You should be able to trade them for modern currency at any bank."

That sounded reasonable, as long as the gold standard was still in place when we arrived at the future. But I knew that we'd be shit out of luck if in the future the monetary standard had changed to silver, or platinum, or maybe clean water.

Nicki urged me again to go change into my flight suit, so I did. I suppose that beating the sunrise and launching before the general populace wakes to start the workday is a smart thing. When I came out of the dressing tent, I held my arms out like a runway model and twirled in a circle. "Nice, huh?" I asked. "It's a perfect fit."

Mack got down to business. "Be sure to keep your TR cloaked in the future, and when you land, do it only when whatever place you choose isn't busy."

"Got it," Nicki said. "Just like when we landed at the Denver airport back in 2010. We avoided the busy runways, and nobody knew we were even there."

"I thought you said that the TR-42's are new additions to the fleet," I said to Mack.

"She means that she landed at the Denver airport in 2010, but she didn't go there until last week."

"You'll get used to it, Dan," Nicki said. "Time means nothing. We're here in this time because this is where we're playing out our lives. But, we could really be at any place at any time doing the same thing. I mean, you and I could launch today and in less than an hour land in Denver five years ago but, instead, we're hopefully going to launch and in less than an hour find some place to land fifteen years in the future. Got it?"

I nodded, but I have to admit that it was hard getting my head around the concept. I'm no linguist, but I could see that language doesn't seem to provide the words necessary to easily understand time when it isn't chronological. Does that make sense? I mean, how could I be here at 9:00 am today, and then at 10:00 am be here yesterday, and then at 11:00 am be here next week, but all in the same day? My head was spinning with this new perspective.

It was time to board, so I shook Mack's hand and told him that I'd see him at noon today, barring anything unusual occurring over the next fifteen years. He handed me my helmet, smiled, and wished me a safe flight. "Stay out of trouble, young man," he told me as I climbed a mobile aluminum staircase and stood on the wing of the TR-42. I saluted him and then followed Nicki to the hatch. She entered first and I followed her. Once I was inside, she brushed beside me as she closed and locked the hatch. The aroma of her perfume was new and interesting to me, and I could feel arousal in my new container, but I pushed that physical reaction aside because I've been a one-woman man ever since I married Mona. When Nicki turned to go to the pilot's seat, I quickly relocated my eyes from her body to the cabin's walls.

The interior of the TR-42 was more spacious than I had expected. It wasn't as large as one of the Ummite military tureens, but there was enough room for a crew of five or six to be comfortably seated—two seats for the pilot and co-pilot, one for a navigator, one for a gunner, one for a systems technician, and one for a passenger or possibly a medic.

The interior walls were molded plastic or a metal composite in the standard dull military green of most government-owned vehicles. The crew's seats were padded with camouflage upholstery, and a white plastic door on one wall was labeled "HEAD," so I knew where to go if I had to barf on our voyage. In front of the pilot's seats were enough dials, gauges, and switches to make a 747 look like a child's toy. Above them at eye level, five screens were brightly lit up, giving the pilot a 360-degree visual of the vehicle's surroundings, plus one for above and one for below.

"It looks intimidating, Dan, but it's really not much different from flying a basic jet fighter. Once you input the desired coordinates, the computer does the rest. Elon Musk has adapted much of this baby's GPS-based self-guided software for use in his driverless cars. After we lift-off, you can sit in the pilot's seat if you'd like."

"I'll sit in the co-pilot's seat if that's okay. Where are the other crew members?"

"It's just the two of us on this flight. If things go as planned, then we might get an additional crew member next time. The squadron command is all about safety, you know. And, since this flight is really an experiment in time travel, command didn't want to put too many people in jeopardy."

I expected the TR-42 to be pulled out of the hangar by a tow motor, the way passenger planes are moved onto the runways at commercial airports. However, alien technology was at play in this craft. Once Nicki started the propulsion system, she retracted the three landing struts and the TR simply hovered silently above the concrete floor of the hangar.

I checked the five screens above the control panel and could see that Mack and two technicians had moved to the sidewall of the hangar. When Nicki asked if I was ready, I gave her the thumbs-up sign, and we quietly drifted out of the hangar and into the darkness of the early morning sky. As we slowly moved toward the runway, Nicki flipped a switch and pointed upwards. I looked up and saw that the ceiling of the craft had become clear, and I could enjoy a full view of the stars and galaxies overhead. I wished that Mona could have been with me because as much as I like seeing a cloudless night sky, she romanticizes such opportunities.

Nicki tapped a couple of buttons and we rose straight up to 25,000 feet. Then she tapped a couple of computer keys, touched a small digital screen, and hit 'enter.' The TR launched forward, I couldn't guess how fast, but a mild queasiness in my stomach told me that we were accelerating.

"What are we doing?" I asked.

"I've used the computer to set the coordinates for a trajectory between here and Jupiter that has no known debris or space junk to interfere with our flight. We're now accelerating and will be doing so for about twelve minutes. When we reach the speed of 186,000 miles per second, our screens will flash. From there, we'll accelerate to 245,000 miles per second. At that point, our computer will engage the year 2033. We'll then begin the deceleration process. If everything goes according to theory, we'll find ourselves hovering twenty-two miles above Nellis. That's when things get dicey."

"What do you mean 'dicey?'"

"Well, we don't know if Nellis will still be here and if it will be friendly territory. If the reptilians own it, we may get shot down. We also don't know if the future military will have developed newer technology, like something that enables them to see us through our cloaking. If they have and they perceive us to be a threat, we don't know what kinds of weaponry they may have developed that could shorten our trip."

"Don't you mean 'blow us out of the sky?'"

"You've got the picture," Nicki replied.

"One other thing, Nicki. If we've been traveling away from earth at light speed for over ten minutes, how will we end our journey hovering above Nellis, which should be a gazillion miles behind us?"

"It's unreal, isn't it?" she said with a smile. "All laws of space and time as we know them seem to unravel once we pass light speed. All matter becomes energy. All we have to do is reconfigure the energy to be where and when we want to be and, as the energy slows down, it becomes matter again. It's like there is no past, present, or future. Once you hit light speed, they all exist at the same time and place. It's like there is only one place and one time. You just plug into where you want to be and when you want to be, and you're there. It's alien technology at its finest, and though we've harnessed it, we're just in the infancy stage when it comes to understanding how to utilize it to its fullest capability."

"I guess I just don't understand."

"You don't have to understand. Just know that it works. Alien technology enables us to bend the laws of space and time. Our first glimpse of it was when we were given teleportation technology."

I nodded at her, unsure of what she thought that I already knew.

"The first time that I teleported to the Martian facility," Nicki said, "I couldn't understand how they could unscramble all the atoms and electrons in my body, send them across space, and then reassemble them in the underground facility."

"The one on Mars?" I asked, leading her to give me more information.

"Yeah. But I didn't have to understand it. I just sat back and enjoyed the ride because the technology works. It's the same thing with time travel. I don't fully understand how it works. I leave that to the physicists. I just pilot the craft and go from today to yesterday and then back to today. I love it."

So, now I knew that we have teleportation technology as well as time travel technology, but John Q. Public is totally unaware of it. Why is the public being kept in the dark? There could only be one reason. It had to be for purposes of military advantage. As I turned this new information over in my mind, I felt that our government, well, at least the black ops portion of the government, was intentionally keeping us in the dark. We, the general public, are like the Stone Age tribes deep in the jungles of the Philippines and Borneo who have no access to simple technologies that would make their lives easier and healthier. Shame on those who hold the secret technology for not bringing the public into the knowledge loop. Well, maybe…I'd have to think about that.

Two quick flashes of red light followed by a burst of white from the monitors above the console let me know that we had reached light speed. "That didn't take long," I said.

"And the next 59,000 miles per second will take less than a minute," Nicki replied.

I watched the monitors, but there was nothing to see, except Jupiter in the front camera's monitor and Earth in the rear's monitor. Jupiter seemed to be growing in size and, as expected, Earth was shrinking. The side camera monitors were blurry, with an occasional white line quickly passing across one screen or the other.

Suddenly, I felt the mild sensation of motion in my stomach again. I looked at Nicki for confirmation. "We're decelerating," she said. "You'll get used to it."

"I've felt similar sensations in Ummite tureens," I told her.

"And if we didn't have internal gravity technology, inertia would have slammed both of us flat against the interior walls. It's good stuff, huh?"

I remembered Commissar Nargas slamming me around the interior of his personal tureen when we were returning from the dark side of the Moon to its hollow interior. It was an unforgettable object lesson in the value of internal gravity technology, and an experience that rendered me unconscious.

Motion on the right-side camera monitor caught my eye. It was our Moon. And the front monitor projected an image of our Earth, unquestionably above the west coast of the United States. Definitely we were hovering above Nellis, possibly in the stratosphere. Rays of light were sweeping across the middle of our country's landmass, meaning that morning was arriving. I could see where we were, but I remained baffled about how we had arrived here when we had been heading away from Earth toward Jupiter at better than light speed.

"Are we cloaked?" I asked.

"Thanks for reminding me." Nicki hit a switch with her left pointer finger. "We are now."

I felt a lot more comfortable knowing that we were cloaked. Waam's Ummite tureen had cloaking capabilities, and cloaking had saved us from being detected by passing NWO tureens after we had taken out the Hive technology that was being used to make UFO abductees commit atrocities. I wondered if the Ummites had passed this technology along to us, or if we had somehow hacked its secrets from their computers. I made a mental note to find out when we got back to the present. Or was it now the past?

"I'll drop us down to the runway and set us down near the end of the taxi strip," Nicki said.

"No, don't do that," I told her. "I want to begin my investigation at Little Devil's Stairs, Virginia."

"You're the boss, Dan. What's there?"

"Villaggio Ibrido."

"Never heard of it. Do they sell Italian food?"

"It's a small community, a black-ops special project. We'll have to approach carefully and find a good place to land near the housing area. It looks like suburbia, but it's not. Well, not exactly."

Nicki took control of the TR-42 and guided it east until we were over Atlanta. From there, she turned north and followed the Appalachian Mountains until indicators on the control panel told her that she was approaching Little Devil's Stairs. I searched the monitors, analyzing the pattern of the buildings and streets beneath us until I could see my house. The Villaggio looked about the same, maybe a few more homes and stores, but still appearing from the sky to be a sleepy hamlet in the mountains.

"There," I said, pointing to a small field a few hundred yards from my house. "Can you set us down there?"

Nicki checked a few gauges and replied, "Yeah, I think so. The field is mostly wildflowers and weeds in hard packed soil. It should hold the weight of the TR."

She set us down and opened the hatch.

"Stay cloaked," I reminded her. I borrowed a clipboard and a gel pen and headed out the hatch. "I should be back in less than an hour."

"Roger," she replied.

I crossed the field, hopped a split rail fence, and followed the asphalt street into my neighborhood. The trees and bushes were definitely larger than I remembered, but I was now fifteen years in the future and they had enjoyed that much growing time. As I passed the first home, I saw two cars in the driveway, neither of which I recognized, so they had to have been late models. I didn't even recognize the emblems on their grills. New companies, I supposed.

At my house, I walked up the driveway. As I did, a dog barked loudly inside. Before I could knock, Mona answered the door. She was older and a little heavier in the hips. Her eyes looked tired and her chestnut brown hair was peppered with streaks of gray. "Can I help you?" she asked. She didn't recognize me from our brief Facebook call fifteen years ago.

"I hope so, ma'am," I replied. "Would you be Mrs. Arrow?"

"I used to be. The name is now Molandowski. My husband is Sergeant Major William Molandowski, head of the RV Training Unit."

You could have knocked me over with less than a feather. Mona had married someone else. What happened to me? To us?

"Thanks, Mrs. Molandowski," I replied, doing my best to hide my surprise. "Then I guess that I'm trying to gather information about your former husband. Wasn't he the one who cracked the Moon?"

"I don't know who you are or why you're here. Do you have any identification?"

Mona was still on the ball, not giving out any personal information to a stranger. "Yes, ma'am." I showed her my new I.D. "My name is Jonathan Silverman. I'm attached to a TR squadron in the West. I can't tell you where, exactly, because it's classified. I'm actually trying to locate your ex-husband. It's related to a top-secret mission that went down a few years back."

"Top secret, huh? Well, you've run out of luck, pal. My ex isn't here. You'll find him buried at Quantico National

Cemetery. He died on one of your fucking top-secret missions almost fifteen years ago."

My jaw dropped open. I couldn't believe what she was telling me. "Are we talking about the same man, Special Agent Daniel Arrow?"

"That would be the poor bastard," Mona replied.

"How did it happen, ma'am?" I asked, truly concerned for my own immediate well-being.

Mona sat down on the front steps. "Do you have a cigarette?"

"No, ma'am. I don't smoke." I wanted to say, "You don't smoke either," but I didn't know if that was still true about my bride in this strange future.

"Sit down."

I did as she requested.

"Your name is familiar to me, but I'm not sure where I've heard it."

"I'm sure we've never met, ma'am. This is my first trip to the East."

"Where's your car?"

"I flew in, ma'am, and walked here. I'll be picked up later."

"So, what do you need to know?"

"About your late husband, ma'am, Agent Arrow."

"Look, at the time of his death, I was in New York, visiting my mother. She had been diagnosed with cancer and was under hospice care."

"Yes, ma'am."

"My husband was on some special top-secret mission in the West. When he got home, he was immediately contacted by his supervisor, who sent him on an overnight mission to assist with securing some nukes that had fallen into the hands of terrorists. All I know is what I've been told. It was a raid on the warehouse where the nukes were housed. Danny was shot in the back of the head three times at point blank range, .45 caliber, I believe. The bullets exited through his face, so I never got to look at him again. The funeral arrangements were made by the FBI, and it was closed casket because of the damage to his face."

"I'm sorry, ma'am."

"I left my mother's home in New York the moment that I got the news and I went directly to Quantico to attend the funeral. He was the love of my life and I never saw him again. I would have given just about anything to have had another weekend with him, but I got cheated out of that."

"Cheated, ma'am?"

"Yeah. I thought my mother was going to die in a day or two, but her cancer went into remission. Instead of attending her funeral, I attended his."

"Remission, huh? That was fortunate and a rare thing."

"Yeah. She's still with us, except that she's incontinent and in a nursing home in New York. And my Danny has been gone for almost fifteen years. I should have been with him and not her. If I had, maybe he'd still be here."

"Did you two have any children, ma'am?"

"Danny and I had two children, a daughter and a son. He never even saw his son, Daniel. The kids are on their own now, one working as a spook and one finishing college."

Good. I had hoped that Stella wasn't home because she'd see right through this new container and know exactly who I was.

"It must have been tough raising two kids on your own," I said.

"It was for about four years, and then I remarried." Mona sighed, removed her slipper, and scratched the ball of her foot. The blood red polish on her toenails was chipping off. "You got anybody special?" she asked.

"Naw. Like I said, ma'am, I'm working in a top-secret place, so we don't get out much."

"Well, soldier, when you find that special person, you'll learn that it's nice having someone around to help with the little day-to-day things, especially if that person is your soul mate. If anything happens to them, you'll miss sharing the day-to-day things. Eventually, you may find someone to help fill the void. At least that's what I did. It isn't the same as your first true love, but you learn to love them in a different sort of way."

"So, you still love Agent Arrow?"

"Yeah, I hate to admit it, but I do. I still miss the lug. Oh, he could be a pain in the ass, but we had a thing. I hope that someday you'll find somebody who means that much to you. Not everybody does."

"Ma'am, has anyone ever said that they've seen your husband somewhere, or somebody who looks like him? I mean, is it possible that he isn't dead but was maybe injured and forgot who he was or something like that?"

"You watch too much television, Silverman. Do you honestly think that he's out there somewhere and will wake up one day, remember who he is, and come home to me? Ha!"

"Well, ma'am, my Ma told me that just about anything *is* possible."

"I used to believe that, too, but I guess I've become a pessimist." Mona put her slipper back on her foot. "So, where does your mom live?"

"She died about a year ago, ma'am."

"She wasn't in line for a new container?"

"She didn't believe in it. She felt like when it was her time, it was her time, and buying more time in an unnatural manner wasn't what God wanted us to do."

"As tired as I feel, I may have to agree with her. There's a container in Richmond with my name on it, but I'm not sure that I won't give it away to some poor slob who has leukemia or something."

"So, you'd give up the new container and go looking for Agent Arrow...on the other side, so to speak?"

"Yeah, I probably would."

Chapter 13

Her mother called him "Will," but Stella called her stepfather "Sarge," as did most of his Army and Air Force co-workers. Although as her stepfather he was now a member of her family, there was something about Sgt. William Molandowski that just didn't sit right with her. And, in spite of her psychic capabilities, Stella hadn't figured it out yet. Sarge seemed too interested in her and went overboard in trying to be close friends with her, making Stella uncomfortable with his proximity.

After graduating with a doctoral degree from the University of Virginia at the age of 12, Stella was hired by the CIA where she divided her time between its Global Missions' Offices of Space Reconnaissance and Advanced Analytics. She had just flown home from New Mexico for a week to celebrate her sixteenth birthday. When she arrived home, her mom was not there. Instead, she found a note which explained that Mona was at the Remote Viewing Center for an afternoon's session focusing upon an unknown target on another planet, but that she would be home by four to greet Stella and to make dinner. Stella was alone in her room when Sarge knocked on her door and brought her interesting news.

"I have someone who'd like to meet you," her stepfather told her.

"And who might that be, Sarge?"

"Does the name 'Commissar Apkallu Nargas' mean anything to you?"

"No. Should it?"

"Hasn't your mother told you about your father?"

"Yes, my dad was Dan Arrow. I have memories about him from when I was a little girl."

"Yes, he was your dad, but he wasn't your father, at least not to the full extent."

"Explain what you mean, Sarge. I hate innuendo."

"You're special, sweetheart. You know, part of a new wave of genetically enriched human beings. Star children."

"Yeah, so I'm a hybrid. Some people call us 'freaks.'"

"You're a genetic combination of human male, human female, and extraterrestrial DNA. People would kill to have your I.Q. and psychic abilities."

"Sometimes I'd kill just to be a normal human…but what about this Commissar Nargas?"

"The Commissar was a very powerful military officer in the Draconian Empire. In fact, he was the architect of the Draconian initiative within the New World Order."

"Yeah, and it fizzled."

"Not completely. Let's just say that it went back underground. But that's not important right now. While he was alive and on assignment in our solar system, Commissar Nargas worked with reticulan, draconian, and human scientists to perfect the next generation of human beings. In two cases, he donated his own DNA for use in the experimentation. You are one of the two offspring of that experimentation."

"And what happened to the other?"

"That's who wants to meet you. He's your true half-brother, sharing DNA from your biological father, the Commissar."

"And what about from my dad?"

"Your brother's human male DNA came from another donor, a different man who was known to the NWO as 'His Excellency' and who had been chosen to be its supreme leader. While you are descended from one royal line, your brother has royal blood from two lines, human and draconian."

"What is his name?"

"Anion Nargas."

"And why does he want to meet me?"

"Isn't it natural for siblings to want to know each other? What harm can come from it?"

"I'll ask my mother about this," Stella replied. "I think this is something that she should know."

"I'm her husband, sweetheart. Let me talk with her for you. I think she'll be delighted that you have another sibling here on Earth. In the meantime, if it's okay with you, I'll bring you downstairs to meet Anion."

"Is he here? You brought him to our home without asking Mom?"

"He's waiting downstairs in the living room. And don't worry about your mom. I'll tell her about this meeting. I'm sure she won't be upset with you, especially since Anion is family."

Stella passed a brush through her dark brown hair, adjusted her jeans and flannel shirt in the mirror, and put a mint in her mouth. Then she and Sarge descended into the living room.

As they reached the foyer, a young man perhaps a few years older than Stella rose to his feet from the sofa. Stella studied him carefully. He was wearing a royal blue golf shirt, tan khakis, and baby blue sneakers. His eyes were almond shaped, like hers, and his hair very dark brown, almost black.

Sarge excused himself to make a phone call. At least that was the excuse he gave for stepping outside of the house.

"Hi. I'm Anion, son of Commissar Apkallu Nargas," the young man said, extending his hand.

"Stella," she replied, taking his hand.

As their hands touched, Stella perceived that, born two years sooner than she, Anion's early years had been much different from hers. Raised in an underground fortress by reptilian nurses, he hadn't enjoyed family life on the Earth's surface. His meals had been basic and his only form of entertainment had been formal study. Because of that, his knowledge of science, mathematics, and military tactics was beyond that of most humans. He saw little value in literature, music, and art, and he felt that human beings spent altogether too much time in pursuit of leisure time activities. Stella felt deep-rooted anger within him, but she couldn't detect its cause.

Similarly, when their hands touched, Anion perceived that Stella had enjoyed a comfortable, perhaps soft, childhood, filled with laughter and travel. Her psychic abilities were stronger than his own. She was an expert in all school subjects, including the literature and music that he disdained, but she knew little of military tactics. Because she had been raised on the surface, she was well-schooled in the social graces of human interaction. Overall, where his skills were weak, hers were strong. Thus, she would make an excellent partner to help him achieve his plans.

"We have learned much about each other, but there is so much more to learn," Anion said. "Perhaps we should begin with the fact that your life has been easier and more comfortable than mine."

"I guess that I had a good childhood," Stella said, "with the exception that my dad died when I was very young. I have a few memories of him, but I never really got to know him. I was raised by a single mom for almost five years, and then Sarge came into my life. Now that I'm on my own, I continue to have a good life, too. How about you?"

"My childhood sucked. My mother committed suicide on the day that I was born. She was an unwilling participant in our father's hybridization experiment and refused to raise a child like me. Instead of a mother and family like you had, I was raised by reptilians in a facility beneath Dulce, New Mexico. They met my basic physical needs, but they didn't really understand how to raise a human hybrid." He paused for a moment and then asked, "Do you have a social life?"

"Yes, a relatively active one for a sixteen-year-old professional. I don't have anyone special in my personal life because most of my co-workers are in their late twenties, but I do date. I've never mated if that's what you're asking."

"I already knew that," Anion said. "You know, from when we touched."

"I didn't explore that aspect of your life," Stella replied, feeling that her personal life perhaps had been violated.

"I don't date. The reptilians find me ugly, and the humans find me repulsive as well."

"Why? You look normal to me."

Anion lifted his shirt to his neck and turned around. On his back, from the middle of his rib cage to his beltline, his flesh gave way to green and yellow scales. "I was the first of our generation of hybrids. When they saw the outcome, our doctors eliminated the S27 genome before creating you. You're the lucky one, the one with no scales. No human female is interested in a man who is part lizard, and no reptilian female is interested in a lizard who is mostly human."

"Oh," Stella said, now understanding the source of his anger. "Surely you'll find someone among the Star Children who shares features similar to your own."

Anion pressed the toe of his left foot against the heel of his right and pried the sneaker off of his foot. Then, he pulled off his sock, revealing a scaly three-toed foot. "As you can imagine, I'm wildly popular around the pool in the summer," he growled.

"There's someone for everyone, Anion. You're good looking…but even the ugliest people find love," Stella told him. "For you, especially with your lineage and position, it should be easy."

"You're naïve, little sister."

"I'm deadly serious, Anion. I truly believe that among the hybrids you'll find a mate who shares elements of your anatomy and who'll love you for who you are, not the flesh of your container."

Anion sat down on the sofa and put his sock and sneaker back on.

"Have you thought about migration into a more suitable container?" Stella asked.

"Yes, but I'm afraid that I might lose my hybrid identity and psychic capabilities."

"But you seem angry about being in a hybrid container."

"Yes, for now, but once my plans come to fruition, I believe that my ultimate destiny—*our* ultimate destiny— will pave the way to a new and better world."

"Plans?"

"Yes, our father worked with the New World Order to create a warmer globe, a more perfect habitat on Earth to be shared by both Reptilians and Humans. Draconian scientists determined that neither race was perfectly suited for this environment; however, they suggested that a new hybrid race, one that included the best aspects of both races, could help the planet by evolving the human species into a more fitting custodian of this orb."

"That would be hybrids, like you and me."

"Yes, and all the hybrids in your little neighborhood and all the other hybrids in all the other special places around the globe."

"How many of us are there?"

"Close to 850,000 and growing every day."

"So, we'll share the Earth with humans and reptilians. As hybrids we can bring the best of both races to the forefront and we can help each to understand the other."

"No. The Earth should be ours. Humans should be exterminated, and reptilians should be driven off the Earth forever."

Before Stella could continue her line of questioning, the front door opened, and her stepfather walked in. "Enjoying getting to know each other?" Sarge asked.

"Yes, it's been interesting," Stella replied.

"Then you'll join me in bringing my plans to fruition?" Anion asked.

"I understand why you feel the way you do and how you've come to this plan. I won't say 'no,' but I want to consider its implications," Stella told him. "I probably need more information, like your intended timeline and how you plan to accomplish its major components…and what you see as my role."

"We'll have to meet again so I can share those details," Anion replied. "Maybe lunch in your little village?"

"Sure. Maybe in a few days. I'll be home for a week, and then it's back to work. Are you staying local?"

"Yes," Sarge answered for Anion. "He's bunking at the Remote Viewing Center for the rest of the week."

Anion gave Stella a brief hug and then left with Sarge, immediate destination undisclosed. Stella returned to her room, head spinning with new information about her reptilian heritage and the fact that she had a newly discovered half-brother.

Discovering Anion's existence would have been a different experience if he hadn't been so negative about humanity and about his hybrid container. If his plans to exterminate humans were successful, the Earth would certainly experience less ecological damage. And its abundant flora and fauna would face less violence at man's hand, if only from the dramatic loss in the number of beings who would dine on their bodies. At the same time, eliminating human beings would also mean condemning her mom to death, something that Stella could not condone.

Chapter 14

Nicki asked me where I wanted to go next, and I told her that I needed to find Mack Smith.

"Back to Nellis at noon?" she asked.

"No, wherever he is in this time," I replied.

"How are we going to find him?"

"He could be anywhere. Maybe he's in Washington, D.C., but I doubt it because he was nearing retirement when we left to come on this mission. Possibly he could be in Astana, Kazakhstan, or maybe in some retirement community in Florida or Arizona."

"Is there somebody you could call?"

"I should have asked Mona, but it didn't cross my mind until now. Maybe I should call the FBI."

Nicki flew us to a small shopping center near I-81, where the empty parking lot of a closed big box store gave us plenty of room to land undetected. This time she joined me when I took a walk in the future, and she brought along a couple of solid gold American Eagles to cash in for modern currency.

Our first stop was at a small branch bank, where the teller called the branch manager over to assist her when we tried to have an American Eagle broken down into spendable cash.

"This is the first time we've been asked to convert gold into dollars," the young manager told us. "We're generally skeptical of such requests because of concerns that the coin is stolen or counterfeit. You may have better luck at the jewelry store, three doors down." Nicki had hoped to buy a pre-paid credit card from a teller in case we needed it, but without cash, we were out of luck on that front, too.

As we left to find the jewelry store, I saw the branch manager pick up her telephone and begin speaking to somebody. I hoped it wasn't the local law.

The jewelry store held great promise because in its window was a sign that read, "Cash for Gold." Not much had changed in fifteen years.

After introductions, the jeweler took our coin into the back of his shop to check it for weight and purity, a simple chemical test that has been used by jewelers for the last century. When he came back to the front, he told us that the coin checked out, but that he didn't have enough cash on hand to give us more than fifty cents on the dollar. He told us that instead of wanting cash he hoped we would trade the coin for jewelry of equal value, but Nicki stressed that we were in a bind and needed the cash. So, he went into the back, probably to his safe, and brought us $3,200 in cash. I looked at Nicki as the guy counted out the bills. She mouthed the word, "Wow." It was clear that inflation had hit the value of the dollar, sending the gold to $6,400 per ounce. I wondered what a gallon of gas would cost, or better yet, what I'd have to pay for a burger at a fast-food joint. It was also clear that this guy was taking advantage of a couple in need by putting a cool $3,200 in his own pocket. What a crook. If I hadn't needed the cash and I weren't afraid of getting arrested in a world where I don't exist, I'd have rearranged his face. Instead of giving in to my normal anger, Nicki and I thanked the jeweler, divided the money equally, and stuffed it into our flight suit pockets.

Further down the sidewalk was a drugstore, where I knew I could get a couple of magazines, the newspaper, and, with any luck, a pre-paid cell phone. I paid the cashier $45 for the three magazines, $5 for the paper, and $75 for the cell phone. It came with twenty minutes of user time and instructions on how to purchase more if needed. Nicki found a rack with assorted pre-paid credit cards. I watched her fingers pass over cards with names that meant nothing fifteen years ago, New World Bank, Ivanka Funds, and Hollywood National Bank before she settled on two of the lowest VISA cards at $175 each.

Before cashing out, I put a Snickers bar on the counter and shuddered when I saw the clerk ring it up for $2.75. At 15%, sales tax was also an unexpected and sorry surprise. When I commented on the tax rate, the clerk told me, "I wouldn't charge any tax if I could, but it's that damn health care law. They were supposed to fix it, but you know how that goes." She pointed to a button on her collar that displayed a picture of a pill bottle with the standard red "No Smoking" circle imprinted on top of it. I assumed that the cost of prescription medicine was the primary driver of the high tax rate, but I'd have to check that out.

When we got back outside, I opened the cell phone package and discovered that it had no number pad. Instead, other than the on/off switch, a single button sat in the middle. When I pushed it, a robotic voice asked, "Where do you wish to call?" I asked for the phone number of the FBI in Washington, D.C. and, instead of being given a number, I was connected immediately to the general switchboard of the FBI. I asked for personnel. A couple of static clicks later a robotic voice answered, asking my business.

"I need a phone number for Agent Mack Smith," I said.

"I'm sorry, but Agent Smith has retired and is no longer available through the FBI system. Can I be of another service?"

"Can you connect me to Agent Smith's former secretary?"

Again, I heard a couple of static clicks as the phone was transferred to an unknown number. "This is Meredith," a woman's voice answered.

"Meredith, this is Dan Arrow. I need to contact Mack Smith. I know that he's retired, but I need to speak with him."

"Agent Arrow, aren't you dead?" she asked.

"I'm supposed to be, but it didn't work out that way."

"You know that I can't give out Agent Smith's private number. He's retired to upstate New York, in the Adirondacks."

"Yes, but years ago when I was in trouble, you called Mack for Agent Casola. Can you do that for me?"

"Agent Smith told me that I might hear from you someday. This is so odd, isn't it? I'm actually talking to a dead man. Give me a number where he can reach you."

I looked at the cell phone and read the number printed on its face in raised white letters. As I did, I noticed that area codes had been changed to one alpha and three numeric digits. "Yes, this is so odd, Meredith," I whispered to myself.

She hung up abruptly. Nice talking to you, too, I thought. Years ago, Mona had called her a "stupid bitch" for doing the same thing, but I didn't even think about it. I needed to talk to Mack.

Mack called after Nicki and I had climbed up the rungs which were implanted into the fuselage of the TR-42. "Dan, is it really you?" he asked.

"Of course it is," I replied. "You sent me on this mission just this morning. Well, fifteen years ago your time. Nicki and I made it safely to the future. Can we meet?"

"I knew you made it safely to the future because you made it back as planned at noon on the day that you left. Crazy, this time travel stuff, huh?"

"Where are you, anyway?" I asked. "Meredith said something about the Adirondacks."

"I was surprised when she called me. She's supposed to retire soon so she can spend time with her third husband. He's got stomach cancer, I think, but he doesn't qualify for a new container." Mack coughed and then said, "Fly to Lake Placid, New York. You'll see an old grass airstrip there, about two miles northeast of the ski jumps. It's abandoned now. Land there and I'll come get you. I'll be driving a Tesla Jedi 4X4, jade green."

"See you in less than half an hour," I replied. I'd never heard of a Tesla Jedi, but the source of its name was a no brainer.

⌘

Mack looked thirty years older, like he was ninety instead of seventy-five, but I didn't rub it in. I had no idea what sorts of things he had experienced since I saw him fifteen years ago this morning. I just knew that his job was a stewpot full of stress, and stress can age a man faster than a nagging wife.

After reacquainting himself with Commander Nicki Nardini, Mack drove us from the abandoned airstrip to a local mom and pop where we ordered a late lunch and chatted while we ate.

Wiping fried chicken grease from his lips with the back of his hand, Mack asked me, "What have you learned thus far?"

"I'm dead," I replied.

"Yeah, I wish I hadn't sent you on that mission to secure the nukes."

"Did I go quickly, or did I suffer?"

"I don't really know, but I assume it was quick. You took three shots to the head at close range, like it was an execution. The lizards don't do that."

"You mean execute? Sure they do."

"No, I mean use .45 caliber bullets. Dan, you were killed by one of ours, not one of theirs."

Mack was right about that. So, I had two alternatives when I got back to our timeline, either refuse to go on the mission or be sure I'm not in front of anybody with a .45 handgun. I wouldn't know which option to choose until the mission is announced.

"What else have you learned?" Mack asked.

"Mona's remarried…to her Remote Viewing Instructor. I never trusted that bastard, but I guess he's been good to her. Hell, she hasn't kicked him out yet."

"You need to be careful of him, Dan. I don't trust him. I suspect that he's covert, from the next iteration of the New World Order. He may be more than that. I've heard from some of the active service guys that there's a new movement among the hybrids to take over the Earth for themselves."

"Really? Do you mean Stella?"

"Possibly. She *is* one of them—no offense intended to you and Mona, Dan."

"What about this guy who's married to Mona? If he's involved in this new movement, could he be a hybrid?"

"I doubt it because he's an Air Force non-com, but you never know. Have you met him?"

"I'm not sure I could handle meeting the man who's been sleeping with my wife."

"I believe that he's here on a special mission, one where his goal is to turn Stella against her family and the resistance. She has special skills, you know, skills that could be put to good use by the draconians and the NWO in their quest to take over the world."

"Maybe I can put a stop to that," I replied.

"It already may be too late to turn Stella away from supporting the NWO's agenda, Dan. Rumor has it that she's been promised a high position by her half-brother."

"Half-brother? Stella has a half-brother? Mona didn't tell me that she had a child with her new husband."

"She hasn't had any children other than Stella and Daniel. We've kept information about the half-brother from her, Dan. Our guys haven't told Mona that she's not the only one who Commissar Nargas used for breeding purposes. Nargas fathered another child with a human female, one who killed herself when she saw the child. He's mostly lizard, and he's a rising star among the reptilians and the NWO."

"What's his name?"

"Same as his father—Nargas. Anion Nargas. He's maybe two years older than Stella."

Then it struck me. In his notebook, Max Gates had written that Commissar Nargas had a hybrid son named Anion who planned to annihilate human life and turn control of the Earth over to draconian/human hybrids. Gates hadn't mentioned how Nargas planned to do that, but he'd mentioned that Nargas planned to follow the ten principles of the Georgia Guidestones. I wished that I had brought Gates' notebook along with me so I could re-read that entry, but it was back in my top dresser drawer in the Villaggio, where I hid it fifteen years ago.

Nicki interrupted my thoughts. "I'm sorry for butting in, but maybe you should go back and ask your wife some more questions, Dan."

"I don't think so," I replied. "I'm afraid that with too much contact, I'll give myself away. She saw me once via Facetime fifteen years ago, and more contact just might spur a recollection."

"Maybe Nicki should speak with her," Mack suggested.

"And what's Nicki going to ask her?" I replied.

"I can see if she knows anything about this Anion Nargas guy and if she thinks that Stella might be involved with this new movement," Nicki replied. She looked at Mack and asked, "Does this new movement have a name?"

"Yes, 'mondo Ibrido'. It means…"

"World of Hybrids," Nicki said, finishing Mack's thought.

So, it looked like we were going to fly back south to the Villaggio and I was going to stay with the TR-42 this time while Nicki interviewed Mona.

Mack paid for our meal and drove us back to the abandoned airstrip where the TR-42 was waiting for us. But before we departed, I needed to ask Mack one more thing.

"Mack, is there anything that you want me to tell you when we get back to Nellis fifteen years ago? You know, something that might make your life back then easier?"

Mack thought about it and said, "There's a bunch of stuff that you could tell me that would speed up our weaponization and time travel programs, but I'm afraid of causing a paradox. Maybe just tell me that I'm still alive, retired, and the NWO has not yet successfully taken over the world."

"Will do, buddy," I said. "You don't look too bad for an old man. Keep 'em hanging."

Chapter 15

Nicki and I flew back south and landed again in the field near my home in Villaggio Ibrido. As planned, Nicki left the cloaked TR and I remained behind, with the hatch to the wing open to allow the air inside the cockpit to transfer with the fresh air outside.

Sometime while I waited, I drifted off to sleep. I mean, I was awake and looking at the paper that I had purchased in the drug store and the next thing I knew, I felt vibration on the wing that let me know that Nicki was already back. Without looking up, I folded the paper and said, "That was brief. I guess Mona wasn't home."

Suddenly, a piece of surgical tubing whipped in front of my eyes and wrapped around my neck! The pressure against the artery on the left side of my throat was intense, but the tubing had caught momentarily on the right corner of the co-pilot's seat, leaving enough room for me to thrust my fingers and palm between the tubing and the right side of my throat. I pushed my arm upwards and stood, turning to look my attacker in the eye. I'd never seen him before, but he looked like a blond-haired, blue-eyed fifteen-year-old kid in an NWO uniform. Obviously, he wasn't well-schooled in the killing arts or I'd already have been dead.

Still holding both ends of the tubing, he pulled me forward, over the co-pilot's chair, and onto the floor of the cockpit. I fell awkwardly, but as I did, I was freed from the grip of the thin, tan-colored tubing. He pounced on me, clutching my throat and squeezing with all of his might. I lifted my right leg toward the ceiling, pulled it between us, and pried him off of me. As he fell backwards, I stood and watched his right hand searching his side for a weapon. A small pistol was seated firmly in a holster on his belt, held in place by a snap-release strap. As he stood, fumbling with the strap, I grabbed his wrist with both hands and pushed him against the white door of the TR's head. When we hit it, I thought I heard the door crack, but this was no time to think about damage to the TR's interior because this guy wanted to kill me. I made a mental note to tell Nicki to have the door inspected by the maintenance crew when we got back to Nellis.

Junior kicked at my crotch three times, missing the vitals, but hurting my inner thighs with each blow. The pistol slipped out of its holster, firmly in his grasp. Still holding his right wrist with both hands, I spun him around and we both fell outside of the hatch and onto the wing. I slammed his wrist against the wing's radar-resistant metal surface, but he didn't release the pistol. Instead, he punched me in the face twice with his left hand. I swung an elbow at him but missed, and we rolled off the wing to the ground. He landed first, and I fell on top of him, accidentally jamming the pistol into his chest as I hit. The pistol fired, and I could feel the strength leave his arm.

Holding his wrist with my right hand, I used my left to pry the weapon from his hand. I'd never seen a pistol like this one before. It was green plastic and stamped on the slide was the phrase "Kaz 9mm." I learned later that it was a special weapon used by NWO troops for close combat. "Kaz" stood for Kazakhstan, where it was manufactured, and "9mm" was obvious. I slid the pistol into the front right pocket of my flight suit.

My assailant was still alive, but the blood loss from the side of his chest let me know that he was using hollow points or, perhaps, dumdum bullets. Unless he got immediate help, he was a goner. Without a phone, I was helpless to call for an ambulance, and, besides, I had no identification that would land me anywhere except in the brig if the authorities came to the rescue. So, I asked questions.

"Listen, kid," I said, "why did you try to kill me?"

He shook his head as if to say "no."

"You're going to die unless you get to a hospital, and I'm not calling for help until you talk to me."

He shook his head again, but I could see fear in his eyes as he realized that he might die.

I repeated my question, "Who sent you to kill me?"

A tremor passed through his body, and I could see fear change to panic in his eyes.

"Tell me who sent you, and I'll call for the ambulance," I repeated.

"Com…Commander…Nargas," he sputtered.

"Do you mean Commissar Nargas?" I asked.

"No," he said, coughing blood, "his son, Commander Anion Nargas."

"Why did he send you to kill me?" I asked.

"Because…" he said, pausing as he drifted into semi-consciousness.

I patted his cheek to bring his attention back to me.

"Why did Nargas send you?" I shouted at him.

"Because you saw him," he whispered.

"What? Where?" I asked. "What do you mean?"

He looked at me with terror-filled eyes, and then his stare went blank.

I shook him and patted his face again, but my efforts were fruitless because he was now a cadaver waiting for a mortician, or maybe a vulture.

I fell onto my butt, breathing heavily, and wiped my hands clean on the short weeds beside me. *I'm getting too old for this shit*, I thought. Across the valley, in front of me, the Appalachian range stood purple against tufts of white clouds and a deep blue late afternoon sky. It's never a good day to die, but if you had to go, today was a beauty.

Motion caught my eye, and I looked in its direction. Nicki was returning to the TR, her head bobbing as she walked uphill toward the field where the TR sat cloaked behind me.

"I heard a shot, Dan," she said as she weaved through the weeds toward me. Then she stopped short. "Oh," she uttered when she saw the body in the weeds. "…What the fuck?"

"I got some information from him before he died," I told her.

"What happened?" she asked.

"He came into the TR and tried to strangle me."

"Really?" Nicki asked in disbelief.

"Yeah. He came up behind me when I was reading the paper. I thought it was you."

"I wonder how he knew that you were here. The TR is invisible."

"Good question, except that he was sent by Anion Nargas. It was something about the fact that I saw Nargas somewhere. That's what he told me before he died."

"Did you have to shoot him?"

"We were wrestling. The pistol was his and he was trying to shoot me. When we fell off the wing, the gun went off and he caught the round. I'm considering myself pretty lucky to be alive."

"What are we going to do with the body?" Nicki asked.

"Leave it here and let Nargas come looking for him. We've got stuff to do."

"If you can lift him onto the wing, we can drop him into the Shenandoah River, or maybe on top of one of these mountains."

"Yeah, you're probably right. I guess it wouldn't be too cool to leave him here where some kid could find him, especially if that kid is a hybrid who can figure out who killed him."

Nicki helped me lift the corpse onto my shoulder and then she climbed onto the wing to help me up as I climbed the fuselage rungs with an extra 180 pounds of weight. It was a struggle and a bit awkward, especially when I couldn't lift his body onto the wing without her holding its head and an arm, but eventually, we managed to plop the carcass onto the middle of the triangular wing.

After we rested for a few minutes, Nicki started up the engines. We quietly lifted into the air and silently drifted toward the purple mountains at no more than fifty miles per hour. When we reached the highest peak, she climbed a hundred yards above its summit and tilted the wing to let the corpse fall to rest somewhere below, where Nargas would never find it unless a homing beacon had been inserted under my attacker's skin.

❧❧❧

Nicki flew us into the stratosphere and let the TR drift above the Earth while we considered our next move. The attack on me had been entirely unexpected, especially if ordered by someone I didn't know and had never seen. The fact that I had survived was a plus, at least from my point of view, but seeing and having dealt with my attacker's bloody body was something that Nicki hadn't expected, and it left her unsettled. More than anything, she wondered how I had been found, especially when I was fifteen years ahead of where I was supposed to be, and I was sitting inside a cloaked military vehicle which had made an unscheduled landing in a field we had only seen from the air that morning.

"Did you see Mona?" I asked her, trying to move her thoughts onto a different topic.

"Yes, I did. Nice lady, but troubled about something," Nicki replied.

"How did you approach her, you know…ask her questions?"

"I was pretty straightforward. I showed her my credentials and told her that I was seeking information to assist in an inquiry. She told me that another serviceman had stopped in for the same reason earlier in the day. She was worried that that serviceman and I might be working at crossed purposes, or that perhaps we were enemies or that one of us was counterintelligence."

"How did you respond to that?"

"I gave her your pseudonym, told her that you and I are on the same team, that you failed to ask her a couple of important questions, and that the CO had sent me to follow-up while you are on KP duty. She laughed at that."

"So, what did you learn?"

"She's been out of direct service with the FBI for two years now, so she hasn't kept up to speed with what she called 'the New World Conspiracy.' However, she told me that Stella is working for the CIA and has shared a few bits of information that have caused her some concern. Mrs. Molandowski has heard rumors about the rise of a rebellion within the NWO, led by a hybrid who wants to alter the organization's agenda to eliminate both humans and draconians. Stella has confirmed that but hasn't told her mother that she knows this man or that he is her half-brother."

Nicki had referred to Mona as 'Mrs. Molandowski,' which sent a spasm of jealousy through my gut. "Does Mona know that Stella has a half-brother?" I asked.

"Yes, and she is very angry at her husband for bringing a Nargas into their home. She told me in confidence that she hasn't slept with her husband since he did that."

"Good," I responded. "I hope it stays that way."

"You've gotta stay focused, Hondo, and forget this stupid male territorial stuff," Nicki told me. "Remember that it's now fifteen years in the future and you've been dead for most of that time. What would you expect a healthy young woman to do, especially one with a career and a daughter to raise? If I were in her shoes, I'd have grabbed onto the first guy who looked my way and dragged him to the altar before he had the chance to change his mind."

I let out a puff of frustration. "Yeah, you're right," I had to acknowledge. Then I moved on to an important question. "Is Stella involved with the rebellion inside the NWO?"

"Mrs. Molandowski didn't give me any indication that she is. She may not know."

So, I was left to figure out where I might have seen Anion Nargas and why he wanted to kill me. This was a real puzzle. Hell, I hadn't remembered that Gates had written a note about him until Mack mentioned Nargas' name earlier in the day.

When we left Nellis this morning, Mack had wanted me to find out if the NWO had ever come into power and if Anion Nargas was ever successful in achieving his plans to eliminate both humans and Reptilians from the Earth so that hybrids could become the planet's dominant intelligent species. The only way to learn the answer was to go further into the future, maybe another thirty-five years, to a place where Nicki and I would be a total of fifty years out ahead of ourselves. So, Nicki and I decided to fly back toward Pluto at the speed of light until we were able to return to Earth thirty-five years later.

"Before we do that," I asked, "do you think we could check into a motel and get some sleep. I could really use a shower."

"Yeah, it's been a long day," Nicki replied.

Chapter 16

To find a motel, Nicki and I descended from the stratosphere to a lonely stretch of highway outside of Paintsville, Kentucky. We didn't pick that location for any specific reason. It was just where we found ourselves when the TR had descended along the 38th parallel to one thousand feet in elevation.

At an exit along a divided highway, we saw an economy motel with an empty field beside it, close to a wing where several eighteen-wheelers were parked, so we set down in the field and walked into the motel. The lady who checked us in seemed nice, though she kept looking at our small duffel bags as though she thought we should have more luggage. We pre-paid with cash rather than running credit cards through her machine, especially since we weren't sure that they would pass muster by the computer system.

The night clerk directed us to an all-night diner which snugged beside a gas station across the street from the motel, so we walked over and caught a quick meal before bed. Nicki had a chef salad with club soda, but I had a burger with onion rings and a couple of beers.

Back in my room, I took a shower, set the clock radio for 7:30 am, and hit the bed like a ton of bricks.

Sometime after midnight I awoke with a start, threw back the covers on my bed, and turned on the table lamp. "Bedbugs!" I screamed as three of them ran toward the bottom of the mattress.

My sleep had been fretful and somehow in the middle of a semi-conscious state, I realized that something had been gnawing on my ankles. "I can't believe that I've been dinner's main course for a colony of fucking bedbugs," I screamed at nobody.

I called the front desk, and some strange guy answered the phone. I hoped he was the owner, but with my luck, he was probably a third shift part-timer with no power to solve my problem.

"My mattress is infested with bedbugs," I told him. "My feet are covered with bite marks."

"It is no problem, my friend," he replied in a high octave falsetto. "I'll be right there."

A couple of minutes later there was a knock on my door. I opened it and let him in. He was thin, dark-skinned, and had short jet-black hair. In his right hand, he was carrying a can of Purdy's Bedbug & Flea Killer.

"Where is this bug that you want eliminated?" he asked.

"It's not one bug. My mattress is infested with bedbugs, millions of them."

I tore the sheets off the bed. Along the piping at the foot of the mattress, a dozen or more bugs scurried away from the light, some finding their way into the mattress through large holes in the fabric.

The night attendant sprayed the bottom seam of the mattress until it was saturated with Purdy's and the room reeked of the strong, recognizable chemical concoction that previously had filled the spray can.

"That should do it, my friend," he told me. "Now you can have a good night's sleep."

He left the room, slamming the door behind him. Somebody pounded on the wall from the room to my right. I guess I had been making too much noise.

In the morning I caught up with Nicki at the breakfast bar that was included with our $280 per room overnight's stay. She was drinking coffee and eating a gluten-free bagel with cream cheese.

"Sleep well?" she asked.

I suspected that she must have heard about my bed bug incident from the front desk clerk.

I pulled up the leg of my flight suit and showed her my bare ankle, covered with raised red bite marks. "Nice, huh? Did you get any of these?"

"Do you need to borrow some socks?" she asked.

"No, I've got a fresh pair in my room. I didn't wear any this morning, so I could complain to the manager when I see him. They had to bug bomb my room last night to kill a swarm of bed bugs."

"Bed bugs don't swarm."

"They do if they're hungry and somebody puts a load of fresh meat at their doorstep. My mattress was infested."

Later, when I complained to the manager, she arranged a ten percent reduction in my total bill. It was just enough to cover lunch, maybe.

After checking out, Nicki and I walked across the parking lot and into the field where the TR was waiting in the warm morning sun, cloaked of course. A lone black man with a heavy beer belly and salt and pepper hair stared at us, probably wondering where we were going. His staring didn't stop as we climbed the invisible fuselage of the TR, stood on the wing, and then entered the hatch, shutting it behind us.

Nicki started the nuclear engines and once they were warm, we ascended quickly to the thin atmosphere of the stratosphere. "Are you ready for hyper-speed?" she asked.

"No," I replied. "In my dreams last night, I remembered that Mack had mentioned the Black Knight. He told me that it had moved from an arctic orbit to the 38th parallel. That's where we were yesterday afternoon, but we didn't see it. I didn't even think to look for it. Do you think we can find it today?"

"Okay, can do. First, we'll fly to the North Pole and then I'll be able to set our scanners to pick up everything that's visible in the northern hemisphere."

Half an hour later, we were in position at absolute north and Nicki began the scan. Below and around us on the dark side of the Earth, the aurora borealis light show was going on. Nicki told me that electrically charged particles from the sun were colliding with oxygen and nitrogen in the Earth's atmosphere. It was nice to have an informed tour guide.

"Here you go, Dan," Nicki said, looking at a computer screen on her dashboard. "We've got over two hundred objects in orbit around the Earth in the northern hemisphere. Most are weather and communication satellites, some are military and others are commercial. Most are foreign—German, Russian, Kazi, Iranian, Chinese, and the list goes on. Several objects look like meteorites that are in orbit rather than burning up in our atmosphere as they fall to Earth."

"How about the Black Knight?"

"Maybe it's this one," she said, pointing to a set of coordinates labeled as "U2O," or "unknown orbiting object."

"Explain this to me," I asked, pointing to the coordinates.

She pointed to the first three sets of numbers. "These give longitude and latitude locations and altitude. The second sets of numbers give circumference, mass, and density."

"So, what do they tell us?"

"It weighs approximately sixty tons. It's a metallic alloy, hollow, with several interior spaces."

"So…?"

"If I were a betting person, I'd lay odds on this being a manufactured artifact, especially since it seems to be emanating a gravity wave signal of some sort."

"Then this is probably the Black Knight?"

"That would be my guess unless it's an abandoned space station."

"So, where is it located?"

Nicki hit a few keys on the inlaid keyboard, and then the screen lit up with an image of the object. Positioned with the Moon to its back, the Black Knight was dull black and bent in the middle like a beer can that some jock had crushed in his hand. A thin antenna protruded approximately ten feet from its base. No discernable lights or markings were visible. "It's back in an artic orbit, not too far from here," Nicki said.

"Let's go check it out."

Nicki double-checked the coordinates and drifted our TR-42 toward the Black Knight, utilizing hand controls rather than automatic pilot. A few minutes later, as we approached within half a mile, the Black Knight shifted several hundred yards to our left. Nicki adjusted our trajectory to approach closer. The Black Knight rose in altitude, so it would not interfere with our flight path. Nicki adjusted our trajectory a second time.

As if it knew that we were stalking it, the Black Knight belly-rolled and returned to its original position. Nicki adjusted the TR's trajectory for the third time. When she did, the TR's engines shut down and the interior suddenly became dark, with the exception of several dayglow strips which had been mounted on our interior paneling to make the position of certain controls more easily identifiable if we ever suffered an electrical outage. Like now.

"What the fuck?" I asked.

"We've lost all functions," Nicki shouted, her hands quickly testing a multitude of buttons and levers. "Even the primary computer bank is down. And our backup generator is non-functional."

"What's the protocol for a situation like this?" I asked.

"I just performed it. Nothing happened."

"Do it again. Maybe the second time is the charm."

Nicki began moving her hands more deliberately. She tried holding a small flashlight in her mouth, but even it wouldn't come on. "It's like we're experiencing a total drain of all electrical power."

"Mack told me that this has happened to others who approached the Black Knight, you know, the Russians, the Chinese, SpaceX, and even the Kazis. He told me that when they drifted far enough away, all power was restored."

"I hope it's the same for us," Nicki blurted. As commander of this craft, she was obviously concerned for her ship and for the well-being of her single passenger. "But we aren't drifting away, Dan. We're actually drifting closer to it, like it's pulling us in."

I could feel the motion of our TR in my belly, and we definitely were moving toward the Black Knight. But suddenly we stopped, and the TR's interior became deathly silent. Without warning, a bright sphere appeared, its intensity blinding us as it hovered four feet above the floor inside our cabin. I wanted to shield my eyes and to reach for my model 1911, but I couldn't move my arms. In fact, I was frozen in place. I'd been in similar situations, once in the facility below Denver and again when the praying mantis impregnated Mona. I looked at Nicki. She was obviously frozen as well, a look of total fear in her eyes. I wanted to tell her not to panic but I couldn't speak. I hoped that our captors weren't lizards because I knew that they'd already had enough of me.

Little guys with big heads and dressed like monks appeared from the shadows on all sides of us like they had entered through secret passageways. I knew it was some type of advanced technology and that they could appear from anywhere anytime they wanted. But this time, we had violated what they considered their space, and I hoped that they weren't going to terminate us.

Three of them touched Nicki and lifted her effortlessly into the air. The air around her began to vibrate like a desert mirage, and they all disappeared. I was next, and the same thing happened. Somewhere between being touched and waking up in a clean, white medical facility, I blacked out.

When I came to, I was sitting in a plastic or composite chair, still unable to move my arms and legs, but I could move my head and my mouth. Nicki was lying naked on a surgical table about ten feet away. Bright light emanated from the walls around us, and half a dozen little guys in maroon monk's habits were busying themselves around her.

I coughed. Two of the little guys turned and came toward me. Without saying anything to me, they let me know that their master wished me no harm and that I was to watch the surgery.

"What the fuck are you going to do to her?" I thought. "You didn't milk my sperm, did you?"

If you could say that one appeared older or wiser than the other, it would have been that one who waved his hand in front of my face. I noticed that he had a thumb like humans do, but only two fingers with blue-toned nails.

"Master Enki is happy to see you again," he said telepathically, "but he has no need of your fluids. He wants you to witness the surgery so that you will understand." He let me know that I was now able to speak.

"Understand what?" I asked, but the little guy just turned without responding, and he and his buddy went back to join the others around Nicki.

I fought against the invisible bonds that held me, but it was no use to struggle. Even if I had been able to break free, I had no ability to get back to the TR. So, I was forced to sit and watch as an observer to whatever horrors they were going to inflict on Nicki.

When a doorway of sorts opened at the far end of the room, I mean like when the light sort of divided itself and a tall thin figure appeared, the little guys separated into two lines and let him pass. I had seen him before, the same praying mantis-like creature who had milked my sperm and impregnated Mona with it. Was he "Master Enki?"

The mantis looked down at Nicki. I saw frenzy in her eyes and tautness in her neck muscles. The mantis placed his insectoid fingers on her temples and she appeared to fall into a deep sleep. Well, it looked like that because her eyes closed and her neck muscles relaxed.

The mantis then began directing his staff of little guys. One held a thin instrument with a glowing tip. That one cut a fine line around the base of Nicki's left breast. When he was finished, another guy flopped the beast upward onto her collarbone.

"What the fuck are you doing to her?" I shouted at them.

The mantis looked at me and squinted his eyes. Suddenly, I could no longer speak. He returned his gaze to Nicki, who was totally unconscious on the table before him. He nodded to one of the little guys, who used a tweezer-like instrument to remove small pieces of tissue from Nicki's breast. "What are you doing to her? Stop it," I thought forcefully.

One of the little guys walked over to me and telepathically told me, "As Master Enki wishes, we are removing diseased tissues from the female. If we do not, the disease will spread throughout her container and she will die before she has finished her assignment."

"Breast cancer? She has breast cancer?"

"Early stages, but when Master Enki has finished, she will be free from the disease. It is important that she live a longer period of time to fulfill her mission."

"Her mission?"

"As with your female," he replied. Then, he walked back to the table, where Nicki's breast was being re-attached and heat-sutured by some instrument that glowed with a warm purple light.

Mona? Like Mona? I grasped at possible meanings to what he had told me. What is Mona's mission or assignment? She's been impregnated twice. Is Nicki going to suffer a similar fate? Was this her mission? Maybe like Mona, had she been selected to raise a hybrid child in a human environment? Was she maybe going to be a living growth chamber for hybrid experimentation? Who donated the sperm anyway? I hoped that it wasn't mine. How could I explain the presence of my DNA in a child that I had not fathered by natural means, especially if I had spent significant time alone with Nicki in another place in time? It was all too much to think about.

I looked at the table again. They had sliced open a small portion of Nicki's abdomen, below her navel. Two little guys were holding the slice open, while a third was inserting a fleshy object, something like a raw oyster, into Nicki's abdomen.

"What are you doing? Don't hurt her," I thought.

The same little guy who had talked to me before waddled over to me. He told me, "As with your female, she is receiving a child, but with this female, we are accelerating the growth cycle by implanting a fetus that is already at the tenth week in your time."

What? Why? I thought.

He replied, "We are better able to manage the proper DNA sequence to ensure no abnormalities. Emotional responses are the most difficult elements to adjust, especially the anger response, which permeates your human species. Human-based hybrids appear less able to cope with anger."

I nodded.

He raised one eyebrow, "Witness the anger in Commissar Nargas' issue. It is almost uncontrollable."

"Stella? Do you mean my Stella?"

"No, the other one."

It was clear that he meant Anion Nargas. But why would he give me this information? What was I supposed to do with it?

Nicki's voice at the table turned my attention. The little guy hurried back to the others. As he did, he nodded to the mantis, who returned the nod. Then he joined the others in lifting Nicki to a sitting position.

Nicki seemed to be conscious of her nakedness, crossing her arms and holding her hands across her breasts. The mantis touched her temples with his fingers, and she dropped her arms to her sides. He then inspected the breast that had been subject to surgery, lifting it and pushing it from side to side with his hand, if you could call his claw a hand. There was no sign of surgery, no scar, no redness, no blood. Incredible. He looked into Nicki's eyes and she nodded, as though she understood what had just happened to her, and then she was helped down onto her back again by the little guys.

The mantis approached me. Telepathically, I heard him ask, "Do you understand what we have accomplished here?"

I was able to speak again, so I told him point-blank, "Yeah, you just impregnated an unmarried woman who has spent significant time alone with me. She's going to wonder how she got pregnant, and I'll be the target of her accusations."

"You were not the male donor, but it makes little difference because your doctors will clear you from blame. She will raise this issue and he will be a great leader among your species, finally uniting the myriad races."

"How do you know?"

The sides of his mouth actually formed a smile. "You already know that our species does not know time as you know it."

I nodded.

"Do you now understand the importance of what you must do?"

"The anger thing?" I asked.

His face turned serious. As he reached out to touch my temples, I heard him say, "Your role in this timeline is to stop Anion Nargas."

હગહ

My head hurt like I had had a bad dream after an all-night binge on cheap whiskey. I rubbed my eyes and then opened them. I was sitting in the TR's co-pilot's seat, and Nicki was beside me in the pilot's seat, breathing with a light snore. She was asleep, and she was dressed.

The cockpit appeared to be fully functional. All lights were on and the ceiling was projecting an image of the Earth, which shone brightly above us, reflecting the evening sun. I could see that we were hovering upside down a few hundred miles west of the California coast, but we were high enough in space that gravity didn't make any difference in terms of what was up and what was down if you know what I mean. When I stood, the TR corrected its position, rolling upright. I went to the head and relieved myself, using both elbows to hold myself erect. As I finished my business, pounding on the door let me know that Nicki was awake.

"Damn it, Dan, hurry up. I'm gonna puke."

I opened the door and before I could step out, I was pressed against the wall as she barged in and heaved into the john.

"Good morning to you, too," I said.

She heaved again.

I pushed her hips to the side and squeezed out of the head to give her some privacy. Then I went to the cooler and brought her a small bottle of water. "Rinse with this," I told her, the same way that Mona offered me water whenever I puked. Nicki took the bottle and waved me out of the head.

⁊ᴓᴕ

Nicki came out of the head wiping fluid from her lips with the back of her hand. She shook her head, as though emptying it of cobwebs, and then sat in the pilot's seat. She turned to me and asked, "What happened, Dan? We've lost ten hours. Where's the Black Knight?"

"I can't answer all your questions, Nicki. I woke up just a minute or two before you did. My first impulse was to pee."

"And mine was to barf. What happened?"

"The last thing I remember was our cockpit being invaded by an orb and a bunch of little guys who were dressed like monks. They used some kind of technology to freeze my muscles so I couldn't fight them. If I could have, I'd have killed a couple of them."

"I don't remember any of that. In fact, I don't remember anything after setting the TR in motion toward the Black Knight."

"You don't remember losing all power and the cockpit's being pitch black inside?"

"Really? That happened?"

"Yeah, it did."

"Jesus H. Christ! And we've lost ten hours. Do you think we were abducted?"

"It's a possibility. Maybe we ought to check ourselves for strange markings."

Nicki went into the head and stripped. Using a hand-held mirror and a wall-mounted mirror, she searched her body. Then she dressed and stepped back into the cockpit. "Nothing on my body. In fact, now that I've puked, I feel really good, like maybe the best I've ever felt in my life."

"That, in itself, is probably a sign of abduction," I told her. "They leave you post-hypnotic suggestions to kill your memory of the event and to make you feel really good." I was telling her the truth, but I wasn't planning to tell her anything that I had witnessed because I didn't want to upset her, at least not yet. Hell, it wasn't going to be too long before she realized that she was pregnant and, if she was anything like Mona, she was going to be pissed.

"Your turn," she told me, handing me her pocket mirror.

I got up and entered the head. What the hell, it was probably smart to check myself for small marks. I wasn't conscious the entire time, and the procedure that I witnessed didn't take any ten hours. The inside of the head didn't give me much maneuvering space, but I did my best. A small red spot behind my right ear gave me pause to feel the area with my fingertip. Something rectangular was under my skin. I dressed and returned to the cockpit. "I think they tagged me," I said, pointing to the red spot.

Nicki pushed my hair back and looked closely. Then she ran her fingertip across my skin. "Maybe they inserted a small computer chip there. Want me to cut it out?"

"No, not yet," I replied, "Unless an expert removes it, the chip will probably move on its own accord to another location. At least now I know where it is."

"Do they really move?" she asked.

"Yeah, like they have a brain of their own. Mona had two of them removed, and it does take an expert to pluck them out before they squiggle away."

Nicki returned to her console and punched some keys on the inset computer keyboard. "We're a few clicks west of the California coast and Nellis. Do you want to drop in and see what's going on?"

"No, Mack isn't there and most of the staff who were there when we took off are probably retired or at other duty stations. How do you think we'd be welcomed?"

"I'm not sure. Maybe we should continue with our plans to go thirty-five more years out."

"Yeah, that's what I'm thinking, but I could use a shower and a good meal. I could also use some time to clear the cobwebs out of my head. Any chance of landing and finding a motel before we launch into the future? One without bedbugs?"

Chapter 17

Nicki let the TR drop out of the stratosphere and settled it gently at 1000 feet. At that altitude, nighttime darkness had already driven the last fingers of sun's rays toward Hawaii and the other side of the Earth. As the TR settled, Nicki told me that something in the controls didn't feel right, but she couldn't put her finger on just what it was. Rather than hurry to the California coastline, she thought it best that we let the computer run a system diagnostic, a process that would take about an hour. I agreed with her. She told me that while the diagnostic was running, we wouldn't be able to run the TR's engines. So, we hovered quietly about a hundred miles west of Los Angeles. While we waited, I folded my arms and took a nap in the co-pilot's seat, but Nicki used that time to review her TR-42 Operator's Manual hoping to identify possible cloaking issues that could be remedied via field repairs.

When Nicki woke me, it was almost eleven at night. "We're into some shit," she told me.

"What did the diagnostic tell us?" I asked.

"The computer hasn't completed the process yet. It should have been finished an hour ago. It's like we have a virus."

"Oh."

"But that isn't the shit that I'm talking about. While we've been hovering, the westerlies have blown us close to the coast of California, like we're a hot air balloon."

"So, what's the problem?"

"We've been spotted by somebody on the ground, and they've got a searchlight on us. I think our cloaking device isn't working."

I got up and looked out the transparent shell of the TR. "More than one searchlight," I said. "I count five."

"Fuck," Nicki blurted, her word choice reminding me briefly of Mona.

Alarms went off inside the cabin. Nicki shouted, "Incoming!" I cinched my seat belt harness just as an explosion rocked the TR. "It blew up about two hundred feet below us!" Nicki exclaimed.

"That was no surface-to-air missile," I said.

"No! They're using old technology, maybe something from World War Two."

Another explosion rocked us. "That one was off our aft," Nicki cried. Whoever they are, they're really lousy shots."

"Where are we?" I asked.

"It's fucking Los Angeles," Nicki replied. "There are no modern military facilities near Los Angeles, at least nothing that would send crappy stuff like this in our direction. They haven't even scrambled any jets."

"When are we?" I asked.

"What do you mean?"

"When are we? Are we near 2030, or 1930?"

Nicki looked at the TR's gauges and said, "Holy shit, if this info is correct, we're in February 1942."

"So, the Black Knight relocated us," I told her, quickly counting on my fingers. "Not just ten hours later but seventy-five years in the past!"

"How? This seems impossible!"

Another explosion rocked our TR, maybe coming from high above us.

"I think your gauges are right," I said. "I mean, when did our military last use searchlights? I'll tell you, it was shortly after World War Two. So, if this is really 1942, the searchlights are an anti-aircraft protocol and the shit they're throwing at us is coming from anti-aircraft artillery bunkers in Santa Monica and the hills surrounding Los Angeles. They don't know our altitude, so they'll throw all sorts of stuff at us until they accidentally hit us. At that point they'll know what to use, and we'll be brought down like a sitting duck. Even if we wave the American flag at them, they'll keep shooting at us because they think we're a Japanese blimp or something."

"I've got the shields up, but I don't know what good they'll be against old-fashioned artillery. They work great against electromagnetic impulses and laser weapons. But nobody in design and engineering figured that we'd run into this stuff."

Two explosions occurred almost simultaneously, rocking the TR and changing our direction to the northwest so that we were drifting with the wind toward Pasadena.

"What about the cloaking system?" I asked. "Do you think you can repair it?"

Nicki opened her Operators Manual and began exploring the material on cloaking. "It's fifteen pages long and lists a dozen or more possible problems. I'll have to try each protocol. In the meantime, we're probably gonna keep getting artillery slung at us."

After a moment Nicki said, "You've gotta help me, Dan. On the panel beside the manual controls are six buttons, marked with A1, A2, A3, and B1, B2, and B3. There's also a red button marked "reset." We have to punch the reset button and then enter specific code sequences to try to restore cloaking. I'll read the sequences and you punch them in. If a sequence doesn't work, hit reset and we'll try the next. Okay?"

We were rocked by a round of three explosions, each seeming to be closer than the one before it.

"Yeah, Commander. Read me the first code." I hit reset and waited for Nicki to read the first sequence.

"Transformer relay blockage: A1, A1, B3, A3, B1, B1."

I hit the buttons as she read them. We heard a brief whine from the control panel, but the cloaking system didn't engage. I hit the reset button.

"Non-specific protocol misalignment: B3, B3, A2, A3, B1, B2." Nothing happened again. I hit the reset button, but it stuck in the down position. I beat on it several times with my finger and it popped back into the ready position.

"Pseudonym recognition error: B1, A1, A2, B2, B2, B3." Again, a whine in the control panel, but no cloaking. I hit the reset button again.

A series of three explosions erupted beneath us, sending sparks from a cabinet near the head. Nicki squealed, as though the pressure was too much for her to bear. It was clear that the anti-aircraft guns were getting too close for comfort.

"What's the next sequence?" I shouted at her, while I hit the reset button a series of times.

"Magnetron reboot: B3, B2, B1, A3, A2, A1."

I punched the numbers in. Immediately, a screen on Nicki's console computer began running ASCII code, scrolling line after line at breakneck speed.

A single explosion next to the TR sent it spinning slowly counterclockwise. And more sparks leaped from the cabinet beside the head. Nicki squealed again and put her hands over her ears.

"Come on, damn it," I shouted at the monitor. "Quit fucking around."

I hit the dash with my fist as though it were a hammer. Almost immediately, the monitor flashed, "Cloaking Engaged."

While we continued spinning in a counterclockwise rotation, the searchlights below us began moving erratically, searching the skies for us. We had been visible for more than an hour, but now from the perspective of the technology of the 1940s, we had simply disappeared. Thank God.

"What about the system diagnostic? Has it finished running yet?" I asked.

"Nothing to report yet, Dan. I'm worried that it may not be functioning correctly, and we might end up drifting with the wind for the rest of our lives."

I hit the dash near the main computer console. The monitor squiggled, as though it had been interrupted, but the message still read, "Diagnostic in Process."

"What did you do that for?" Nicki shouted at me.

"Hell, it worked for the cloaking system, so I thought I'd give it a try."

"You men are so predictable, Dan. If you can't fuck it, you try to beat it into submission."

Whoa. Her comment really took me back. She had exposed something about her past, something altogether unsettling, like a dark thunderhead deep within her psyche that let me know that her experiences with love and relationships with the opposite sex had been less than happy ones.

"Uhhh…," I said, unsure of how to respond to her.

Nicki realized what she had said and saw its impact on my face. "I'm sorry, Dan," she said sheepishly. "You're not to blame. You're a good man, married and faithful. You are, aren't you…faithful, I mean?"

"If you're asking me if I've slept with another woman since getting married, the answer is 'no.' The temptation is always there, but I've never acted on it. I don't want to hurt Mona or to destroy her trust in me."

"Well, I've never slept with another person, male or female."

"I don't need to know anything about your private life, Nicki."

"I want you to know, especially after what I said."

I just looked at her.

"When I was in college," she said, "I took the pledge to remain a virgin until I met and married Mr. Perfect. I met a lot of possible Mr. Perfect's, but one after the other all they wanted to do was to screw me. When they found out that I wouldn't sleep around, most of them dropped me like I was a leper. Two actually physically abused me. One even told me that if I didn't fuck him, he'd fuck up my face. He hit me several times, and when he pulled out a razor knife, I shot him in the gut with a .32 derringer. He lived, but I was arrested for assault. Fortunately, the charges were dropped or my career would have been over before it ever started. That's why I feel like I do…if men can't fuck you, then they try to beat you into submission."

"Well," I told her, "maybe you've been going out with the wrong kind of guys. I wouldn't throw all of us under the bus just because of a handful of assholes whose mindsets are still in the Middle Ages. Even some of the assholes might come around if they knew how you truly felt."

"I've sworn off looking for Mr. Right, Dan. I'm married to my career, now."

I felt sorry for Nicki because nobody should do to a woman the kinds of things that some men had done to her. But I knew that she wasn't alone. Hell, in the Middle East, many women are treated worse than dogs. They can't drive, they can't go anywhere alone, and when their husbands want to get rid of them, they can accuse them of just about anything and then stone them to death. If a woman is raped, she must find three male witnesses who will testify against the rapist. We all know how that works out. And in some parts of Africa, they still perform female castrations so women can't enjoy sex. Outside of the west and a few eastern countries, a woman's life isn't something I'd wish on a cat.

Then I thought about Nicki's situation, the one that she wasn't aware of yet. Since Nicki had pledged to remain a virgin and since she'd sworn off men, she was probably going to have one hell of a rough time accepting her condition when she found out that she was pregnant. When that time comes, maybe I'll suggest that she fly back to the Villaggio, so she can commiserate with Mona. There's no better guide through an ugly situation than someone who has already been there and done that.

A high-pitched computer beep interrupted my thoughts. The system diagnostic process had finished, and the monitor displayed the answer to our controls problem: System Override caused by extremely high magnetic field. The computer offered two remedies, manual repair or system reboot. Nicki touched the screen and selected system reboot. Everything inside the cockpit went dark for about five seconds, and then a single symbol appeared on the screen. It was a simple line drawing of a grey alien's head. Go figure. As the reboot continued, lights began flashing around the cabin, one here and then one there, as individual components came back to life.

Suddenly we were rocked by another explosion outside, and then a second. "When I hit reboot, it must have shut off our cloaking," Nicki exclaimed.

"Will it come back on by itself?" I asked.

"I hope so."

Another three explosions rocked us, one causing sparks to cascade from the ceiling.

As the sparks fell around us, the computer screen flashed the words "All Systems Go." Nicki reached for the cloaking button and switched it to the "on" position. Another explosion went off, but it was beneath us, and then another, further away. Then the barrage stopped. We were invisible again and the anti-aircraft guns had no idea where to aim.

Nicki took manual control of the TR and guided us away from the searchlights, flying slowly east from Los Angeles as we searched for a motel near a deserted space where we could land. When we flew over a small California town called Mecca, we saw a shopping center at the edge of a large field. "That'll do," I said.

Nicki guided us to a gentle landing, two hundred yards from the back of the shopping center, where a neon sign boldly announced "Plaza Garibaldi." Across the street was what I wanted most, a small mom-and-pop motel with three cars in its parking lot.

We secured the TR, leaving it cloaked but locked, and walked to La Coachella Motel, where we registered for two rooms at $12 each. From my perspective, 1942 was looking really good price-wise, but when the guy asked us for the money upfront and I handed him a $50 bill, he gave it back to me and told me that it was counterfeit.

"Why do you think that?" I asked.

"Look at the date, Mack. It says 2026," the desk clerk said. "And when have you seen Grant's picture so large?

And look at the funny colored lines in the paper. This is absolutely fake money. You got anything better?"

Nicki handed him a gold American Eagle. He turned it over in his stubby hand. His fingernails were edged in black, as though he worked as a laborer during the day and this was a night job.

"You too?" he asked. "Look at the date, lady. It says 2012. Where did you guys get this funny stuff?"

"At a bank in Virginia," I told him. "Listen, if you check that coin out, you'll find that it's 24 karat gold, regardless of the date."

"It's been nice, but you two can't stay here unless you have something worth $24."

"What would you like?" I asked.

"You got a gold watch?"

"No, I use my cell phone."

"Your what?" he asked.

"How about a pistol?" Nicki suggested.

"Whatcha got?"

"Give him your pistol, Dan. The green one."

I had forgotten about the Kaz 9mm that I had slipped into my flight suit pocket. I removed it, popped the clip, and cleared the chamber.

"Never seen one like this," the man said.

"It's made in Kazakhstan and uses 9mm parabellum rounds," I told him.

"It looks like a toy, made of plastic like that," the man said. "It's pretty light."

"Believe me," Nicki said, "it's no toy. And that plastic is the newest technology, stronger and lighter than steel. It'll never rust."

The man looked unsure. "What was that word 'bella-something' for the ammo?" he asked.

"Parabellum rounds," I replied. "'Parabellum' roughly means that if you want peace, you should prepare for war." I was proud of the fact that I knew some stuff about guns and ammo.

"Shoot it for me," he replied.

"Sure, where?"

He took us out the door and around the back of the motel, where several tin cans were sitting on a log. Behind them was a dirt berm. He hit a switch and a single light bulb came to life overhead on a pole. It looked like we had been escorted to his personal 20-yard shooting range.

I emptied the clip into my hand. I counted five rounds. I put one into the clip, slammed the clip home, pulled back the slide, aimed, and squeezed the trigger, sending an empty can hopping into the berm.

"Pretty good," the man said. "My turn."

I gave him a single round. He loaded the Kazi like he had owned one all his life. Then, he aimed and fired. Another can popped into the air and hopped away.

"Will this thing take 9mm Lugars?" he asked.

"Yeah, it'll shoot anything that's 9mm," I said, hoping that I was right about that. I really didn't know the answer.

"Okay, give me the other rounds and you can stay the night. No extra towels."

I handed him the three remaining rounds and then we walked back inside the office to get our room keys.

Nicki was two doors down from me. I walked with her while she checked her room. It was basic, but clean, with a Mexican motif. "I feel like I've walked into a room from the 1950s," she told me.

"Actually, it's not that modern. This is 1942."

She snickered, "Yeah, I guess you're right. See you in the morning, Dan."

After we decided to meet at 9:00 am, I walked back to my room. The motif inside was exactly the same as Nicki's room. I took a hot shower and climbed into bed, exhausted. Hell, it was already 1:30 am.

∽∾∽

I awoke at 3:00 am to pounding on my door: Bam! Bam! Bam! "Dan, open up. We've got trouble." It sounded like Nicki.

"What the fuck?" I muttered in a stupor from being jerked out of REM. I staggered to the door in my skivvies. "Nicki, is that you?" I asked before I unlocked the door.

"Yes, you blockhead. Now, open the door."

She was beginning to sound more and more like Mona. Maybe I have that effect on women. I freed the chain lock and then opened the deadbolt. Nicki stumbled in, being pushed by a large Hispanic man and two fat goons. The large guy's knuckles were tattooed with letters, probably by a ballpoint pen, and he was missing the top of his left ear. The fat goons were wearing black tee shirts, grey sweatpants and high top Keds. I guessed that this wasn't a social call.

"Sorry, Dan," Nicki said, regaining her balance and standing beside me. "They threatened to kill me."

"That would've been the easy way out," I replied.

"Carlos says you got Gold Eagles," the large guy said. His breath reeked of chilies and whiskey.

"Carlos?" I asked.

"You sold him some kind of toy gun a couple of hours ago. Where'd you get it?"

So, it was a sure thing that the night clerk liked to blabber. These guys were probably Mexican Mafia. In a few years, MS-13 would make them a thing of the past, but they didn't know that yet.

"We had an Eagle, but Carlos said it was counterfeit, so we dropped it in the grass out back. Maybe you'll find it when you're mowing his yard."

"What kind of smart ass are you, guero?" he asked.

"Give him the damn Eagle," Nicki said.

"I dropped it out back…honest."

The two goons each grabbed one of my arms and held me like a piñata. I knew what was coming, so as the big guy stepped forward to punch me, I launched a front kick that sent my big toe into his Adam's Apple. He fell backward, clutching his throat and gasping for air. I hoped that I had crushed his larynx, but I was barefoot and how much damage can a big toe do?

The goon on my right arm turned in my direction and swung his right elbow into my nose. Suddenly I was seeing stars and tasting blood. He hit me again and I blacked out.

When I came to, Nicki was wiping my face with a washcloth saturated with cold water. I looked around. We were alone.

"They're gone," she told me. "If you had just given him the Gold Eagle, none of this would have happened."

"That's what you think. They were gonna punch my lights out, anyway."

"It's because you had to wise off to them, Dan. Your testosterone was showing itself again. How's your groin?"

"It aches a bit. Why?"

"The guy with the trimmed ear kicked you there a couple of times after he recovered from your kick."

"That 'splains a lot, Lucy," I replied, trying to be funny. I was glad to have been out cold when he tried to smash my package.

Nicki helped me to my feet, and then I staggered to the mirror that was hanging on the wall above the vanity. My eyes were going to be black and blue for a few days, but my teeth weren't broken. Then, in the reflection of the mirror, I noticed that my wallet was lying open on the bed, no doubt empty, and my flight suit was on the floor with its pockets pulled inside out like elephant's ears.

"Did they get the Eagle?" I asked.

"Yeah, and all your paper dollars and coins from ninety years in the future. I think we'd better get going before anyone else decides to come meet us and see where we're from."

I agreed with Nicki's assumption. We needed to get back to the safety of the TR and plan our next steps. For me, the first step was sleep, even if it was on the TR's floor. My nose was hurting big time and I hoped that it wasn't broken.

We gathered our things, in my case a pair of underwear and my shaving kit, and quickly walked across the two-lane road that separated the motel from the small shopping center. Then we crossed the empty field, found the TR, and climbed onto its left wing. Before going through the hatch, I looked back toward the motel and saw seven men moving between our rooms. I touched Nicki's shoulder and pointed to the activity where we had been sleeping.

"I was right, wasn't I?" she said.

"I never argue with a woman," I replied, "especially when she's spot on. It was a good call, commander."

Nicki slid into the pilot's seat, turned on the TR's motors, raised us to 100 feet in the air, and then she set the controls so we'd hover in place while we napped. Of course, we were cloaked. She slept in her seat, but I found a spot on the floor where I stretched out until Nicki woke me at 10:00 am. It came quickly.

"I'm pretty sure you could sleep all day, Dan," she said, shaking me, "but I think we should get going. How are you feeling this morning?"

I rolled over and smiled at her but didn't say anything.

"Not too bad," she continued. "You've got some bruising on your face, but I expected the black and blue to be more pronounced. How's your groin?"

The best thing about being unconscious when you're being pummeled is that it just doesn't seem to hurt as much afterward as it does when you remember the pain that is being inflicted on you. It must be a mental thing. I mean, when you have surgery, you seem to recover faster if you aren't awake when the doctor carves into your flesh with his scalpel. At least your attitude is more positive. Right? Well, it's something that somebody might research sometime, as long as I'm not the subject of the experiment.

"I walked over here okay last night," I told her, "so I'm probably okay. I'm a little tight, probably some swelling. You're not asking to look, are you?"

Nicki stood and threw me a perturbed look. "I think you're more than okay, Hondo, especially with a crack like that."

I got to my feet and went into the head. The air carried the slight aroma of puke, so I figured that Nicki had been in before she woke me, and she was continuing to experience morning sickness. She hadn't said anything to me, so I assumed that she hadn't put two and two together, yet. I relieved myself. There was no blood in my urine, so I knew I was going to be okay in a day or so.

When I finished, Nicki set the TR on the ground, put an American Eagle into her pocket, and we walked to the front of the shopping center. There was no jewelry store and no bank, so we were out of luck in terms of trading in our gold for some cash and getting breakfast. However, outside of a small grocery store, we saw a newspaper vending box with the front page clearly on display behind a plastic cover.

"Check it out," Nicki exclaimed.

I bent down and looked at the cover story. The banner said, "Battle of Los Angeles," and the story described anti-aircraft artillery firing hundreds of rounds while searchlights panned the sky for a mysterious craft, thought to be Japanese, attacking our coastline.

"We were it," Nicki exclaimed. "Holy shit, we caused the Battle of Los Angeles."

"Let's get out of here," I said. "We don't need any more trouble."

Chapter 18

Stella's cell phone beeped, letting her know that a text message had arrived. She looked at the screen. It was from Anion, her half-brother. He was supposed to have met with her while she was at home visiting with her mom and step-dad, but he had failed to contact her after their brief initial meeting. She read his message:

Am in Dulce for a day. Hoping we can get together after work. R U available? A—

She keyed in a reply, I'm not in Dulce.

Anion challenged her: U R nearby. Can U come to Dulce after work?

Stella wondered how Anion knew that her black project assignment was located in a secret facility just outside of Dulce, New Mexico. She keyed again: You stood me up the last time we were supposed to meet. Are you planning to do that again?

Anion's reply came quickly: Sorry, little sister. Was called away. Didn't your father tell U?

Stella replied: Stepfather. No.

Anion's keyed: Let's do dinner at the El Ranchero. I'll be there at 6. A—

Stella recognized the El Ranchero as a Mexican restaurant located midway between Dulce and the small town of Lumberton. She replied: Okay. You're buying.

The conversation ended.

After work, Stella checked out of the secret facility, passing through several scanning devices and a hand inspection of her briefcase by security. It was standard daily protocol, but she tapped her foot impatiently as the security guard thumbed through the few papers that she was taking home. Then she boarded a gray school bus with blackened windows that shuttled her and thirty other employees to a fenced federal parking lot located at the edge of the town of Dulce. There, she climbed into the searing heat inside her emerald green electric Merica, a new marque manufactured in Dallas, turned on the air conditioning, and drove silently to her small apartment in Dulce. She had owned the car since turning sixteen, the age when she could legally drive in New Mexico. After checking her mail and taking a cool shower, she dressed in jeans and a loose-fitting cotton top and then drove to the El Ranchero, wearing mirrored sunglasses, as she always did when out in public.

Anion was already inside when Stella arrived at the restaurant. When she entered, he rose and waved her to the booth that he had selected, against the far wall and across the main seating area from the door.

Stella gave Anion a polite hug as she reached the booth and then settled in across from him. The vinyl seat cushion was lumpy from years of use, but she found a position that provided a bit of comfort and placed her hands on the Formica tabletop.

"How have you been, little sister?" Anion asked. "I trust your project is proceeding well."

"I'm fine," Stella replied. "And you know that I can't discuss my work. It's highly classified. In fact, I'm surprised that you found me. The location of my black project is off the radar. In fact, my black project doesn't exist."

"The NWO knows almost everything, sister. Its members can be found working in every black project operated by every government around the globe. We know the names and personal information of every employee at every governmental operation and black project in the world. Our knowledge of the clandestine operations of the United States is, of course, the most important because the United States offers the greatest possibility of resistance to the NWO's ultimate agenda. You were easy to locate."

"So, what brings you to Dulce?"

"Officially, I'm spending a few weeks in the subterranean facility beneath the Jicarilla Indian Reservation. Your mother's first husband spent some time there, I believe interfering with the NWO agenda. Unofficially, however, I'm here to see you. In fact, you're my primary agenda item."

"I'm not used to being labeled as an agenda item. It sounds so impersonal."

"No offense intended. When we first met, I had promised to share with you my plans for the hybridization of the Earth. I thought now would be an excellent time and opportunity, especially since my headquarters are beneath your feet."

"Here? In Dulce?"

Anion nodded.

A waitress brought the glasses of water and menus. "Drinks?" she asked. "We don't serve no liquor, but we got five varieties of beer."

"Just a seltzer with a twist of lime," Stella replied.

"I'll have the same," Anion said.

The waitress gave them a look of disappointment and walked away.

"You don't drink alcohol, do you?" Anion asked.

"It dulls my senses," Stella replied.

"Excellent."

"Pardon?"

"You feel the same way as I do about alcohol. It's a mind-numbing substance which is best avoided by our kind."

"I've had wine before, but I find that my psychic abilities are greatly diminished by its presence in my container, so I avoid it."

"Yes, it has the same consequence in my container, too," Anion replied, pleased to have found a similarity that he and his half-sister shared.

The waitress returned with their drinks and took their orders. Once she was gone, Anion pressed his agenda.

"I want you to see my headquarters. It's hidden secretly within the American subterranean facility here in Dulce. It's here where my team and I have planned the surprise overturn of the draconian agenda, which we will implement once the draconians have surprised world governments with their planned reptilian takeover of NWO governance."

"I don't really understand all of this, Anion. I thought that the NWO was defunct and that the United Nations was still the best hope for international peace and cooperation."

"The United Nations has never been more than a shill organization, originally established to prepare the world's governments for eventual takeover by the NWO. Its social programs were developed to drain the financial resources of the most powerful nations and to create a culture of dependence among the third world countries. And its Agenda 21 was conceived to create space on the surface for the draconians to occupy once all humans have been relocated to designated population centers. The NWO never has been defunct, but the timeline for implementation of its agenda has suffered some setbacks:

first, by the assassination of His Excellency; second, by the destruction of the Moon's habitable space; and third, by the destruction of the Hive initiative."

"Are you working for the NWO or for the draconians?" Stella asked.

"The answer is 'Yes' to both, but only to my own ends. The NWO has been led by fools. Even His Excellency was duped by the draconians into thinking that humans and reptilians could live together in harmony on this planet. The bottom line is that humans are nothing more than a food source for the pure lizards, a delicacy for the elite among them. The ultimate draconian agenda has always been the domination of the human species. Any thought of living together harmoniously on Earth has been a work of fiction contrived to lure human leaders peacefully into their own demise."

The waitress interrupted Anion's lecture. "Here's y'all's food," she said, placing a bean burrito on the table in front of Stella and an "el diablo platter" in front of Anion. "The hot sauce is in the condiment holder with the napkins, honey," she told Stella. The waitress looked at Anion. "You ain't gonna need no hot sauce with thet there plate. Maybe some Milk of Magnesia before bed tonight." Anion smiled at her. "Can I get y'all anything else?" she asked.

"I think this will do," Anion replied, waving her away.

"It sounds to me like you're playing a dangerous game," Stella said, "especially if the draconians think you're working for them and the NWO thinks you're on board with their agenda. Eventually you're going to have to choose sides and, when you do, the other side will try to kill you."

"It's all been worked out, little sister. The draconians are assisting the NWO in its preparations to assume control of all world governments. As laid out in the NWO agenda, the human population will be reduced to approximately 500 million people, worldwide. Once the humans migrate into population centers for their own survival, the draconians will emerge from their subterranean facilities and descend from the Moon, supposedly to aid in human survival by providing medicines against rare diseases and new foods that will nourish human containers. Ultimately, the draconians will turn on the humans and raise them as cattle when they assume dominion over the planet."

"So, then you will support the draconians?"

"Absolutely not. I hate them," Anion said, stabbing his fork into a fried habanera chili. "They despise me because of my predominately human container. They believe that I'm beneath them and unworthy of leadership capability. They use me only as a spy to inform them about developments in the NWO. "

"And what about the NWO?"

"I'm rising in the ranks of the NWO and soon shall be a general. They trust me vehemently, as they have seen me kill lizards. It's this trust that enables me to move freely and do what is necessary to launch my own plan."

"And what is your plan? When we first met, you told me that you plan to push the draconians back to Draco and to eliminate all humans, thus leaving the planet to us hybrids."

"Exactly," Anion replied, smiling.

"How?" Stella asked. "The draconians have greater technology."

"The NWO has captured technology from our space brothers for more than half a century, and we have retooled it to work better in our environment. We have developed fleets of our own versions of their tureens and outfitted them with their weapons. But more than that, we have the means to make our Earth uninhabitable by draconians, and that's my plan."

"Are you behind the chemtrails that are filling our skies with strange compounds?"

"No, that's the draconians. They're trying to raise the temperature of the Earth to make it more habitable for their kind. You must remember that lizards like heat. The core temperature of their own planet Draco is ten degrees warmer than that of the Earth. My plan is the opposite. I will drive the mean temperature of the Earth downward and will eliminate the desert areas that they hope to inhabit because of their similarity to the landmasses on Draco. When the lizards find the Earth intolerable, they will leave."

Stella's mind swirled with thoughts of how Anion might accomplish his plan. Could he somehow unleash a series of volcanoes that would spew ash into the atmosphere, effectively shutting out the sun's warming rays? Could he reset the Earth's orbit such that it is further from the sun?

"Little sister," Anion said, interrupting her thoughts, "you've barely eaten your dinner. Hurry and gobble it down because I want to show you my headquarters, and to do that, we must venture underground."

When Stella had finished her burrito, Anion paid for the meal and escorted her to his vehicle, an H1 Hummer painted in desert camo. As Stella and Anion approached the Hummer, two soldiers stepped out and saluted. Anion returned their salute and introduced Stella to them as "my sister, Miss Arrow." Stella noted that the driver's side door bore the emblem of a bird gripping the Earth in its talons. In its beak furled a ribbon embossed with the words "New World Order."

One soldier opened the back door and gestured for Stella to enter. Then, he walked to the other side, opened the door for Anion, and snapped to attention while Anion climbed in beside Stella.

After the two soldiers were seated in the front, the driver asked, "Where to, Colonel?"

"Let's go home." Anion replied.

The driver steered the Hummer onto Narrow Gauge Street and followed it west until they were clearly out of town, then he unexpectedly turned right and onto the desert sand, driving into the darkness following an old stream bed. After ten minutes of kidney bouncing, Stella could see a corrugated steel building in the Hummer's headlights. Its dull exterior was rusty, and a single light bulb flickered above the door in the front of the building. Instead of stopping in front of the building, the driver passed it and then spun the Hummer so that it faced the side of the building. Reaching above his head, the driver touched a button and the side of the steel building opened the way a common garage door would open. As the Hummer entered the building, Stella could see that its purpose was to disguise a ramp that dived at a 30-degree angle into the ground. The driver hit the gas gently and the Hummer began its descent.

"This is the back door into the facility that is most famous for the Dulce Firefight. Ever heard of it?" Anion asked.

Stella shook her head.

"It happened long before we were born. But it's not that important anymore." He pulled his cell phone out of his pocket and checked the time. "This facility has been used by the US government for almost a century. They conduct experiments here using captured alien technology and abducted humans as guinea pigs. The NWO has a small presence here at Level Six, and I am the commander of that presence. I oversee almost 300 soldiers, both men, and women. I also oversee a small detachment of 47 draconians who are working with us, and a smaller detachment of 25 reticulan Greys who are assisting us with retro-engineering a variety of technologies. The lizards and Greys are quartered at Level Five."

As they passed through a large vault-like door, they were greeted by three armed sentries, who saluted when they saw Anion sitting in the rear seat. Anion returned the salute and continued, "Below our facility, Level Seven houses a magnetic levitation train station that connects this facility to a dozen more facilities that are located across the west."

"Why would the US government lease space to the NWO?" Stella asked.

"Because all U.S. presidents since WWII know what's coming. Your president wants the US to be the key player in establishing the new global government. She and her predecessors think that democracy is the best way for a global government to rule the world. They are all naïve, of course. After a global pandemic, anarchy will rule the day. There will be no time for consideration of individual rights and consensus-driven decision-making via democratic principles. It will take an iron hand and swift justice to maintain control of the planet when so many are suffering from hunger and disease. You and I will take charge of that."

"You're asking a lot of me, Anion. I've been raised to love my neighbors. I don't know if I can stand to see them suffer."

"Decision-making is all a matter of resources, Sister. If you have a pound of meat, do you give it to a worker or to an invalid? If you have a quart of water, do you give it to a nursing mother or to an aged grandmother? The answer is that you allocate your resources to wherever they will do the most good for the most people. If you give a little to everyone, there will never be enough to go around and all will slowly starve. It's better to help the starving and sick out of their misery quickly so that the healthy can better survive."

"You're talking about sacrificing a few in order to save humanity, aren't you? I didn't hear that in what you've told me before now."

Anion gave her a puzzled look.

Stella rephrased her comment. "I never heard you say that your plan will permit humans to survive. That is what you intend, isn't it?"

"Yes and no, Sister. If you have adequate resources, then in the short run the answer is 'yes.' However, if you have limited resources, perhaps only a single pound of meat, do you give it to a human or to a hybrid? Which one is of greater value to the future of the Earth? When you tell me the answer to that question, I will know that you understand my perspective. For me, the choice carries with it no dilemmas."

Stella nodded. It was clear to her now that Anion, indeed, planned to sacrifice humanity for the sake of hybrids whenever a decision forced a choice between the two species. Eventually, she reasoned, humanity would die out in favor of the alien-human hybrids, known by many as the Star Children or the Indigo Children, and Anion claimed that 850,000 already were living on the planet.

The Hummer came to a stop after passing through the vault door at Level Seven. The driver and other aide opened the doors, and Stella and Anion slid out and onto the concrete floor.

"This is home," Anion told her.

A young soldier approached from a corridor to the right. "Welcome back, colonel," he said. "Was your visit worthwhile?"

"Buxton, I'd like you to meet my sister, Stella," Anion replied, motioning with his hand.

"Miss Nargas, it's a pleasure to meet you."

"It's Arrow, not Nargas," Stella replied forcefully.

Buxton blinked twice in surprise, and then his nictitating membranes blinked from the side, exposing the fact that he was a hybrid.

"But you can call me Stella," she continued, softening her tone in recognition of Buxton's species. "It's nice to meet a fellow hybrid."

"Buxton is my adjutant, Stella," Anion told her. "He is highest in command among the 50 hybrids who also quarter here. We're the vanguard, the ones who are planning to surprise the reptilians."

"Any news from Command?" Anion asked.

"There is specific concern from Astana that a spy may have leaked information to the American FBI about the existence of the nuclear weapons storage facility in Waco. It may need to be relocated, and it appears that one from our unit has betrayed us; thus, it will be our task to move the weapons cache."

"A spy in our command?" Anion snapped.

"Sir, yes, sir. The leak has been traced to a laptop issued to Sgt. Corey in Munitions. He has been detained and our IT crew is searching his laptop for evidence of his disloyalty."

"Good. Let me know what they find."

Anion turned to Stella. "Heavy is the crown, sometimes. For a human, Corey has always seemed upstanding. I'd hate to discover that he's been practicing subterfuge." He pointed at the corridor. "Come, let me show you around."

Anion shuttled Stella through the facility using a quad runner, showing her all 550,000 square feet of tunnels and rooms, each outfitted with a specific function in mind. Of particular interest to Stella was the Indigo Conference Room, a special center accessible only by hybrids whose DNA had afforded them enhanced psychic abilities. That meant all hybrids on earth had the potential of accessing the room, except for a very small handful, none of whom were quartered at the Dulce facility.

"What goes on in here?" Stella asked as her eyes explored the room. Its walls and carpet were a dark shade of lavender. A large rectangle of natural oak tables followed the four walls, with luxury leather high-back computer chairs at every seat. Stella estimated that as many as 100 people could easily be accommodated, with room for more if additional chairs were brought into the room. Hanging from the ceiling was a four-sided audio-visual unit that included a projection system that permitted life-sized 3-dimensional figures to appear on a circular pad of wood that was situated on the floor directly below the AV unit.

"This is where my team calculates each move that we need to make in order to achieve our agenda," Anion replied.

"Have you arrived at a timeline yet?" Stella asked.

"It's still fluid, but others and I have been urging the NWO to launch the viral pandemic within four months. If they do, then we'll surprise the draconians in approximately one year. You'll want to have relocated here before the virus is released. If you haven't, it may be impossible to find your way here because once the severity of the virus is understood, all mass transportation systems will be shut down by the government as a virus containment strategy." Anion smiled and added, "But it won't work."

"I have been immune to all human diseases thus far. Why should I fear this virus?"

"It's called AUAG4, a highly mutated strain of the Australian Antigen, and it's designed to kill an infected person in less than two hours. It's unclear if we hybrids are susceptible to it, and nobody has volunteered to be the guinea pig to find out. If we are susceptible, you can bend over backward and kiss your ass goodbye the moment that you inhale a single virion."

"So, are you asking me to quit my job and join you here today?"

"No, stay at your job until I notify you that the virus is about to be released. You'll have approximately two days to find your way to Dulce. Maybe less. If you never go back to work, they'll assume you were a victim of the pandemic. Nobody will look for your body because there will be hundreds of millions of virus-contaminated bodies around the globe. The principal problem faced by the survivors will be how to avoid contamination while disposing of the carcasses of the deceased. Nobody will miss you for more than a few minutes."

"And what about my mom and my brother?"

"As a hybrid, your brother is always welcomed to join us. If you must bring your mother, you may do so. But as I just told you, recognize that choices may have to be made and, for me, choices between hybrids and humans carry no dilemma."

They drove back to Anion's office, where Buxton was anxiously waiting.

"More news from Astana?" Anion asked, helping Stella from the quad runner.

"IT found more than ten messages from Sgt. Corey leaking information to the US Intelligence Services. They're currently analyzing the extent of damage to our agenda."

"Where is he?"

"In your office with Security."

"Excuse me for a moment, Sister." Anion said to Stella. He marched aggressively through a doorway and out of Stella's range of vision. Stella could hear Anion's angry voice but could only make out the words "traitor" and "honor." Then she flinched at the piercing sound of a single gunshot.

Chapter 19

ay I help you?" Mona asked the young woman who had rung her doorbell.

"Yes, I'm told that this is the home of Mr. Dan Arrow," she said with a British accent. "Is he available to speak with me?"

Mona's face fell. "I'm sorry, but Mr. Arrow is deceased. I was his wife. Is there some way that I can help you?"

"Agent Casola?" the young girl asked.

"Yes, but the last name is now Molandowski."

The young woman looked surprised. "I'm familiar with that name," she said.

Mona motioned with her hand, "Would you like to come in?"

The young woman stepped inside. Mona surmised that she was in her early twenties. Her calves and thighs appeared hard like a runner's but her face bore lines of stress and her eyes seemed older than her body. Mona asked her to sit on the sofa, while she sat in an easy chair, with the coffee table between them, just in case.

"You may not remember me, Agent Casola, but my mother once asked your husband, Mr. Arrow, for assistance in locating the person who killed her son, Max Gates."

Mona searched her memory and then said, "Yes, I remember. He was found dead in a hotel room. His body had been covered with a substance that turned it black."

"That would be poisonwood sap, Agent Casola."

"Yes, that's what the coroner told Danny….And my name is now Molandowski," Mona reminded her visitor.

"Did you know that they found Max Gates alive?" her visitor asked without skipping a beat.

"No. Danny never told me what happened in that case."

"Max showed up at a UFO conference in South America. He'd been dropped off by space aliens in the middle of the jungle where they thought that he would perish, but he managed to survive the ordeal. Somehow he found the strength to walk many miles and through many dangers before finding a small village where a peasant farmer and his wife took him in and gave him food and shelter."

"Remarkable story, Miss…" Mona told her, searching for a name.

"Gates," the woman replied.

"Oh," Mona said. "His daughter?"

"No, Mrs. Molandowski…I am Maxwell Gates."

Mona's eyes opened wide with surprise.

"When I was abducted by the space aliens, they stripped me of most of the memory of the abduction and somehow moved me from my body into the body of a five-year-old girl. Then they dumped me deep in the jungle in a country whose inhabitants spoke a language that I didn't understand or speak. My survival was purely due to good fortune."

"I'm sorry that Danny isn't here to meet you. I remember that he began his work trying to investigate your death, but then he was ordered into another assignment, one where he met an untimely death of his own."

Max Gates nodded in understanding. "I'm sorry that I wasn't aware of your loss."

"So, you've come here to ask Danny for assistance with something. Is there some way that I can help you?"

"Two ways, Mrs. Molandowski. First, Mr. Arrow was given an advance of $5000 by my mum to begin his investigation. Does any of the money remain? If so, I'm hoping to recover it so that I can apply it toward the acquisition of a new male container."

"I don't have a clue where Danny might have put the money, Mr. Gates. But perhaps I can help you to acquire a new container. If you'll give me a few days, I'll see what I can do."

"Too bad about the money, but I'll take you up on your offer of help, Mrs. Molandowski."

Mona nodded.

"And second, and more importantly, you should know what I have learned as I have continued my own investigations into alien interference in human affairs. I have learned that a young hybrid has plans to re-ignite the New World Order's goal of reducing the Earth's population to no more than 500 million humans. Humans who will be ruled by Reptilian/human hybrids."

"Really?" Mona asked, now more interested in what Max Gates had to say. "I thought that the NWO was essentially defunct."

"Yes, it went underground, and your ex-husband went to great lengths to see that happen. However, it's a new age and young radicals have plans to take over the NWO. Their leader is someone you might know."

"Who would that be?"

"Anion Nargas, son of the deceased Commissar."

A shot of anger rushed through Mona's body at the mention of Commissar Nargas. He was the reptilian who had held her captive and who had impregnated her against her wishes. He was the one who had tried to kill her and Danny several times and who had successfully killed Waam's son Doroo. Until Danny cracked the Moon, Nargas was the bastard who had been running the lunar-based facility where reptilian and NWO troops were waiting for the command to invade the Earth.

Seeing that Mona recognized the name "Nargas," Max Gates continued, "Anion Nargas is also your daughter's half-brother."

"Half-brother?" Mona asked.

"Yes, he is the son of a woman much like yourself who was impregnated by Commissar Nargas, but unlike yourself, she killed herself when she saw the baby after giving birth to it."

"He must have looked too much like his father," Mona replied with a scowl.

"Mrs. Molandowski, I had hoped to speak with Mr. Arrow about another rumor that I have heard, one involving your daughter."

"Stella?"

"Yes."

"What about Stella?"

"My source tells me that Anion Nargas has promised her a high position in the New World Order in return for her assistance and support in implementing his plan to become its leader."

"My Stella?" Mona repeated in disbelief.

"My source tells me that your current husband is NWO and it is he who introduced your daughter to Anion Nargas."

"Sarge is NWO? Are you certain that he introduced Stella to Nargas' son?"

"Yes, that's what my source has told me. He's close to Sgt. Molandowski…one of several confidantes."

"And you have the utmost confidence in your source's information?"

"He has never failed me." Max Gates uncrossed her legs and leaned forward, handing Mona a business card. "Mrs. Molandowski, you must stop your daughter from helping Anion Nargas to implement his deadly plan. If he's successful, mankind is doomed."

☙❧

Sarge arrived home from work at 5:00 pm. As he pulled into the driveway, he noticed that the front yard was littered with clothes. They were his.

Mona greeted him at the door. He could tell from the protruding veins on her forehead and her folded arms that she was angry, maybe beyond angry.

"What's wrong, baby?" he asked, extending his arms, palms up.

"You're a fucking liar," Mona gnashed at him.

"What lie did I tell you?" he asked.

"You told me that you'd always protect Stella. That you'd make sure that no harm ever came her way."

"Is Stella okay? What's happened to her?"

"You've happened to her, you fucking son of a bitch."

"Let's go inside and talk this over, honey. You're making a scene."

"This is my house. You're not coming inside, you bastard."

"Come on, Mona, you're not making any sense," Sarge pleaded.

"Did you or did you not introduce Stella to her half-brother?"

"Oh, she told you? That's good."

"No, she hasn't told me squat. I had to find out from someone else. Who do you think you are, letting anyone with the last name of Nargas into my home?"

"Stella has grown up, Mona. She has to know where she came from so she has some concept of why she is the way she is. Anion Nargas shares a similar background. I thought it would be okay with you if she learned a little about her blood line, especially since she's grown up."

"Get your clothes and get off of my property," Mona screamed at him. "If you knew anything about me, you'd know that you don't make decisions about Stella without talking with me first. It's always been that way."

"I'm sorry, Mona. I guess I wasn't thinking. I meant to talk with you. I really did."

"Well, you just bought yourself a ticket to divorce court. Now get off my property."

"Mona…"

Mona slammed the front door and rammed the dead bolt shut.

Sarge slowly picked his clothes up from the grass and threw them into the back seat of his sedan. He knew that there would be no talking with Mona until after she cooled down, and that could take as long as a week. It had happened once before, when Stella was five and he had let her walk downtown into the Villagio unaccompanied. As punishment that time, he slept on a cot at the Provost Marshal's Office for three nights and then on the sofa in his home for a week before Mona let him back into the bedroom. She had that kind of temper. And she seemed even angrier this time, especially since she had thrown his clothes out of the house that they shared, a house that she just had called "my property." Before starting his sedan's motor, Sarge looked up at the picture window, hoping to see Mona watching him. The blinds were shut. He touched a button on the dash, and his motor sprang back to life. Then he slowly backed out of the driveway and drove his sedan to the PMO.

෧෧෧

The phone rang at 7:00 pm. It was her mom on FaceTime. "I could sense your anger, Ma," Stella told her before Mona could utter 'Hello' into the receiver. "What's wrong?"

"You already know what's wrong, sweetheart," Mona replied.

"You're angry at Sarge, but I can feel that it also involves me."

Mona didn't reply.

"So, tell me about it, Ma. Why are you upset with me?"

Mona didn't know where to start. The roots of her anger began with first being abducted by Commissar Nargas, who impregnated her with genetically modified DNA. Then, when she had finally come to grips with having been impregnated against her will, he had abducted her again, this time removing the fetus from her body against her will. Add to her anger the weeks that she had spent being led around on a leash by draconian Greys, all at the Commissar's command, followed by the weeks she had been held in the hollow Moon as the Commissar's captive while she nurtured the hybrid offspring, her little Stella. Add to it, too, being re-leashed on Mars and being held captive while knowing that her lover, Danny Arrow, was being tortured or killed by the Commissar. Compound that with the disregard and dishonesty now shown by her second husband, who had knowingly and intentionally gone behind her back to connect her precious daughter to an unknown half-brother, a man who may actually be working to hasten mankind's extinction. It was all too much to think about.

But Stella read her emotions and saw the tangle of anger, hostility, and feelings of deceit that Mona was experiencing. "Talk to me, Ma," she said again.

"Tell me about Anion Nargas," Mona began.

"Who?" Stella asked, pretending that she didn't recognize the name.

"Come clean with me, Stella. Sarge has already confessed that he introduced you to Anion."

Stella had hoped to relieve her mother of the pain of revisiting the past, but it was too late for that. She admitted to the first meeting. "Okay, yeah, Ma, he introduced me to Anion when I was home the last time. I told him that he shouldn't have brought Anion to our home without first discussing it with you."

"Why didn't you tell me? You know how I feel about the reptilians, especially Commissar Nargas."

"Sarge said that he would tell you. He was confident that you'd be supportive."

"That just goes to show how little he knows about me. It also shows how little you know about Sarge. Don't ever trust him, Stella. Never trust any man."

"Come on, Ma, it's not that big a deal. The meeting lasted about ten minutes. The guy was only interested in meeting me because we share similar DNA traits, but you know all about that history. He thinks that we're related, but we don't even look alike."

"He's part of the New World Order, Stella, and they're up to no good. Your Daddy fought against them until he disappeared."

"You mean until he died."

"Maybe he died, but I'm not so sure about that anymore. I've had two official inquiries about him recently. I think he actually may be alive somewhere."

"Have you tried to Remote View him, Ma?"

"I'm too upset to Remote View. The things I see are too confusing. I'll try again when I've cooled off."

"What about Sarge, Ma? He's your husband."

"I've kicked him out. I'm done with him, Stella. I think I married him because we shared an interest in Remote Viewing and because I needed help with raising you. Neither of those reasons is good enough to move into a live-in relationship with someone. Besides, he was never straight with me. He didn't tell me that he was a hybrid until after we were married.

"But you told him about you, didn't you? Before you two were married, he knew that you suspect that you're a first-generation hybrid, didn't he?"

"No."

"Jesus, Ma. How could you expect your marriage to Sarge to last without complete openness and honesty?"

"There's always been something not right about him, Stella. There's something dishonest deep within him. Promise me that you'll never trust him."

Stella knew that her mother was right about Sarge's dishonesty. She had felt it as a child, especially the sense that he was too interested in her. Maybe it was because he knew about Anion, even back then. She nodded her head so her mom could see.

"Put your pointer finger on the phone's camera, Ma. I want to see who came to ask you questions about Daddy."

When Mona's finger was all that Stella could see on her phone's tiny screen, she placed her own finger on her phone's screen and closed her eyes.

Inside Stella's mind, images of two interviewers formed, one a pregnant woman in a flight suit, and the other a man whose face she had never seen before, but whose electrical essence clearly was her dad's. Her mouth dropped open in surprise. The young soldier was her dad in an unfamiliar container.

"Who was he?" Mona asked when she saw Stella's expression on her cell phone's screen.

"The woman who interviewed you was pregnant, Ma. She's carrying a hybrid male."

"Not her," Mona replied. "Who was the man? I think I've seen him somewhere before, but I can't recall where."

"I don't know, Ma," Stella lied. "His vibrations seem familiar, but I can't identify him. Maybe we can try again when I see you in person and can hold your hands."

"That's odd," Mona said. "You must be losing your touch."

Chapter 20

S ir, we didn't know that would happen," pleaded a young NWO noncom, who was standing at attention in Anion Nargas' office. Beside him, another soldier, a young private, fought to keep his trembling from becoming visible. Sweat poured down from his forehead.

"Bullshit, corporal," Anion growled. "You've been through the training. In damp conditions, the shafts of small internal combustion engines need to be turned so the thin oil coating on the cylinder walls prevents rust. When the walls get rusty, the cylinder heads fuse to the walls and render the motor useless."

"Sir, we thought second shift was overseeing that responsibility," the corporal declared.

"Are you pushing the blame onto your peers? Are you trying to throw them under the bus in order to save your own skin?"

"Sir, no sir."

"We needed that motor to run a refrigerant compressor on the battlefield. Now it's as useless as the two of you. I've buried men for less than this."

Before the corporal could respond, Anion's personal cell phone began playing the lead guitar riff to *Little Sister*, a ring that he had assigned to only one caller, Stella Arrow. Anion took a deep breath, exhaled his anger at the men who were still standing at attention, and answered the call.

"Little sister, what a surprise to hear from you. Have you sensed that the date for the pandemic has been accelerated?"

"Hi, Anion. Did I catch you at a bad time? I can sense that others are with you."

"Not for long, Little Sister. But, don't worry about these losers." He exhaled heavily into the receiver and continued, "Anyway, I'm glad that you called. You should plan to join me in Dulce no later than six weeks from now. It is time."

"That's why I called, Anion. I don't think I'm going to be able to join you. It's not a good time right now. My mom has thrown Sarge out of the house and has filed for a divorce."

"I was unaware of this turn of events. When did it happen?"

"A few days ago."

"That might explain why I haven't heard from Sarge. Do you know where he is?"

"No. He stayed at the Provost Marshal's Office here at the Villaggio for a few days, but he's gone from there now."

"So, you're in Virginia and not in Dulce?"

"Yeah. My mom is a mess right now. I've taken an extended leave of absence to help her. I can't leave Ma in this state, not even to serve the NWO."

"Bring her with you," Anion replied. "She'll be welcomed here and treated with respect by my men, even by the Reptilians who serve under me."

"She hates the lizards, Anion. Years ago, she was collared by one and paraded around like a pet dog. She'd never tolerate them being near her."

"Mine aren't the same as the draconians that she knew, Stella. Mine have been hand-selected. I only accept those who were born through parthenogenesis. With no testosterone, they don't quarrel over women and don't possess the drive to overthrow their leaders. I'm never challenged. Besides, they've all been rebooted."

"Rebooted?" Stella asked.

"Yes, it's a brain function that only two species share, lizards and parrots. Regardless of their loyalties, if you keep them in total darkness and silence for four days, their brains re-set and they bond to the first creature that feeds them. I ensure that all my reptilians are subjected to sensory deprivation and are bonded to me."

"I still can't come, Anion. I just can't."

"Do you have more excuses to offer me, Stella? You're disappointing me. I thought we were simpatico."

"In my heart, brother, I can't be a part of what you plan to do to humanity. After all, I'm mostly human, almost 75%."

Anion could feel his disappointment turning into anger. He squeezed the tiny cell phone and shook it in his hand, and then he yelled into it, "You're not a human, Sister. You're a hybrid like me. Humans aren't worth what you leave in the toilet. Don't do this to me. I need your assistance if I am to lead the NWO after the pandemic."

"I just can't do it, Anion."

"You're making a mistake that you'll regret in a few weeks, especially after your mother is dead and gone from the AuAg virus."

"I have to go, Anion."

"Wait, Stella…"

"Goodbye, Anion."

"Wait, Sister…" The line went dead.

Anion howled and threw his cell phone against the concrete wall behind his desk. It shattered into several pieces. Then Anion turned to the two soldiers who were still standing at attention in his office.

"What is your name, soldier?" Anion growled at the corporal.

"Sir, I'm Corporal Anders Sparskraag."

"No, it isn't, soldier. Your name is Stella Arrow."

"Sir?"

"What did I tell you your name is, soldier?!" Anion screamed.

"Sir, you called me 'Stella Arrow'."

"Tell me your name, soldier."

"It's Corporal Anders…"

Anion pulled his 40 caliber SIG from its holster and put a round through the soldier's head before he had finished giving his full name.

Anion turned his attention to the private who was still standing at attention, now whimpering. The front of his pants was wet with urine. "Aw crap," Anion snapped, raising his pistol a second time. "I don't have time to fuck with you," he said almost apologetically, and then he painted the wall with the soldier's brain.

Two military policemen burst through the door to Anion's office. "Sir, we heard shots. Are you okay?" one asked.

"Clean up this mess," Anion ordered, pointing at the two bodies on the floor. "And where's my adjutant?"

"Major Buxton is on his way down to your office, Colonel," a young lieutenant said as he entered the office door.

"Good. I need a cell phone. Mine is out of commission."

The lieutenant left the office and returned in less than a minute with a cell phone that he handed to Anion. "This one belonged to Corporal Sparskraag. It hasn't been cleared for top-secret communications, Sir. But we'll have a new one ready for you within the hour."

"Thank you, lieutenant," Anion replied.

He opened a small notebook that was lying on his desk and then tapped a number into the cell phone. "Lieutenant Ujo?" he said into the phone. "This is Colonel Nargas. How soon can your tureen be ready for flight? Good. I'll see you in twenty minutes." He dropped the cell phone onto his desk and then cleaned his hands with antibacterial gel.

"Colonel, are you alright?" It was Major Buxton, Anion's adjutant, who had just arrived at the office door.

"Yes, Buxton. Things just got a little messy here."

"Yes, sir, it appears that way," Buxton replied, looking at the two bodies that were still oozing blood onto the concrete floor.

Anion excused the military policemen. Once they were gone, he said, "Buxton, I want you to find four of the strongest men in our command and bring them with you to the Salvage Hangar. Be there in fifteen minutes, ready for combat. The Ummites are going to fly us to someplace special."

"Sir?"

"Just find me four strong men, Buxton. No lizards. Be sure they're packing military-issued pistols and meet me in the salvage hangar in fifteen minutes. Can I be any clearer?"

"Perfectly clear, Sir. I'm on it, Sir."

Buxton hurried out the door.

❧❧❧

The salvage hangar was located at the end of a seldom-used corridor on the sixth level of the subterranean facility.

Although it was a large cavern with a glassy ceiling one hundred feet above its concrete floor, the hangar was mostly full of old and broken equipment that was waiting its turn to be transported out of the facility on the five-ton stake truck that made bi-weekly dump runs to a recycling center located in Lumberton, a few miles outside of Dulce.

Anion Nargas hurried from his headquarters to the salvage hangar in a quad-runner, one with a flatbed capable of carrying at least ten suitcases or suitcase-sized boxes, if properly tied down. He brought his quad-runner to a full stop at the barn-sized garage door that sealed the hangar from unwanted visitors, and then he opened the door with a small electronic device that he had carried in his shirt pocket. Once the door provided enough clearance, he drove through it and then shut it behind him.

Inside, he drove along a narrow pathway toward the back of the hangar, where the piles of used equipment suddenly ended and a 200-foot square space sat empty, except for an Ummite military tureen that hovered quietly in its center.

"Lieutenant Ujo?" he called out as he skidded to a stop thirty feet from the tureen.

A nine-foot-tall man in an orange flight suit descended from the tureen's ramp. "Yes, Sir?" the Ummite replied, saluting his commanding officer.

"Five men will be joining us shortly. Are we almost ready to launch?"

"Darvo is checking the light-speed drive and calibrating the destination coordinates. We should be ready in another few minutes."

"Excellent," Anion replied. "Our goal is to retrieve weaponry that was stored at the target site before its location was recently compromised by a traitor."

"No problem, Sir. We Ummites have traveled through time for several decades now, and we have experienced no difficulties, not a paradox of any kind."

Noise from the front end of the hangar caused both men to look in that direction. "Buxton has arrived with our four mules," Anion said.

Once Major Buxton and the four men whom he had chosen entered the open area, they began making comments about the Ummite tureen. None had been so close to one before.

"Are we taking a ride in that baby, Major?" one asked Buxton.

Buxton stopped a few feet from Anion, saluted, and snapped to attention. The four NWO soldiers followed his lead.

Anion returned their salute and ordered them, "At ease, men." When all had relaxed, he said, "Gentlemen, this is Lieutenant Ujo, formerly of the Ummite Space Command, who recently has joined our forces. He is going to explain our mission."

Ujo stepped forward. "Thank you, Sir. We will be traveling in this Ummite military tureen to a secret weapons facility. Once we're there, we'll utilize invisibility cloaking to hover unnoticed above the facility. When we're in place and believe that we haven't been detected, Tech Specialist Darvo will teleport your team into the facility, where you will retrieve the weapons that the Colonel wishes to secure. You'll have five minutes to complete your mission, and then you'll re-cluster at the drop point to be teleported back into the tureen with your packages."

"This sounds like Star Trek," one soldier remarked.

"It *is* Star Trek, soldier," Anion replied. "Our mission is to travel more than fifteen years into the past, retrieve the weapons, and return them here safely. With any luck, we will return here a few moments after we've left."

"How are we leaving the hangar, Colonel?" Buxton asked.

"Beyond invisibility and time travel, the Ummites have other technologies unfamiliar to us. One such technology permits them to maneuver this tureen and, all of its passengers through solid rock. That's how they were able to conceal their tureen in this facility. We'll simply rise up through the ceiling above us until we enter into the atmosphere. I did it many times as a child. I can't replicate the technology, but thanks to Lieutenant Ujo, we have access to the technology which was pre-installed in this tureen before he joined us."

Two quick beeps accompanied by flashes of the tureen's blue running lights interrupted the conversation. "The tureen is ready. All aboard who are coming aboard," Ujo told them.

Anion led the procession into the tureen, where the men met Tech Specialist Darvo and then settled into webbed seats for the trip into the past. Like Ujo, Darvo was very tall by human standards, almost ten feet from toe to head. Both had steel blue eyes and blond hair, and both were intimidating due to height alone.

Darvo and Ujo positioned themselves in the pilot seats, touched a few indentations on the control panel, and the tureen rose into the air, through the ceiling, and into the bright midday sunlight above the ground. They hovered silently for a few moments and then Lieutenant Ujo said, "We have set the coordinates and have ensured that nothing imperils our journey, so we will now launch into hyperspace where we'll reconnect with the past. It should take no more than thirteen minutes, Earth time." Within thirty seconds, the tureen had lifted beyond the Earth's atmosphere and was accelerating toward light speed.

Anion had dreamed of experiencing time travel but had thought he would never get the opportunity until Lt. Ujo appeared and asked to join the NWO. It was more than Anion could have hoped for, and now it was giving him the opportunity to vent some anger, launch his own plans, and seize control of the NWO—all without Stella's assistance. Once his plans were implemented, there would be no need for the pandemic, and as he assumed leadership of the NWO, Ujo and Darvo would be his personal pilots and bodyguards. And now, with the availability of time travel, he could foil any unfortunate events after they happened by simply returning to the past and undoing them before they occurred.

Ten minutes into the flight, Darvo told Ujo, "We've reached our destination, Lieutenant,"

"Colonel?" Ujo said, interrupting Anion's thoughts.

"Yes, I heard. Tell us when and where to stand for teleportation.

"Let's ensure that we've not been detected, and then we'll proceed with the mission."

After a long minute, Ujo nodded to Darvo, who rose and told the men, "Gentlemen, please move to the grey rectangular area on the floor, opposite of the exit ramp."

Anion, Buxton, and the four soldiers rose and followed Darvo's directions.

"Men, please check your weapons. Lock and load," Anion ordered. "We're not sure who will greet us below."

Darvo reported, "Colonel, our scanners show only two individuals near your arrival area. They appear to be unarmed. You should encounter little or no resistance."

"Excellent," Anion replied. He turned to the others. "Remain alert, men. Our presence may set off alarms and bring us unanticipated difficulties."

"Yes, Sir," one of the NWO mules replied.

"Prepare to deport," Darvo said. "Deporting in three, two, one…"

Anion saw the interior of the tureen begin to blur before his eyes, then everything turned white for a second until the blurriness returned and he slowly found himself standing on a concrete floor in a darkened room with a single window near the ceiling on an exterior wall.

"Holy shit, that was cool," one of the mules remarked.

"Fuck, yeah," said another.

"Follow me, men," Anion ordered, first listening to a door that led into a neighboring room, and then barging in.

Two men in white lab coats were working on devices at tables that were illuminated by fluorescent workbench lights.

"Who the fuck are you?" one man asked, startled by the presence of six men in the workroom. "You have no permission to be in here."

Anion pointed his Kazi pistol at the man's face and said, "You have five seconds to live unless you direct us to the suitcase hydrogen nukes."

"What?" The man replied.

"Three…two…"

"Wait! Wait!" the man pleaded.

"Where are they?" Anion demanded.

"Who are you, anyway?"

"I'm Colonel Nargas of the NWO. I need a dozen suitcase nukes, preferably hydrogen. I want them here in less than a minute, and I want instructions on how to arm them."

The second man stepped forward and replied, "We're here only to clean the weapons and to replace parts that have aged out. We're not here to give away weapons without orders from Astana."

Anion grabbed the man's right ear, pulled his head downward, and shoved the barrel of his Kazi into the man's mouth, breaking his front teeth in the process. Blood ran out of the man's mouth and across his cheek. "I have no time to waste with your bullshit. I want a dozen hydrogen suitcase nukes, and I want them now, capisce?"

"Don't hurt him anymore, mister," the first man said. "I'll show you where they are."

Anion told Buxton, "Take the men with this guy and bring me the nukes. We have only a few minutes left before teleportation."

Buxton pushed the man, and said, "Lead the way." The man pointed toward a steel door with a built-in combination lock. The door was propped open by a cinder block on the floor. Buxton and the mules followed him into the room.

About a minute elapsed before Buxton and the men returned to the cleaning room, each carrying two nukes, one in each hand.

"How do we arm them and set the timers?" Anion demanded of the man with the broken teeth who was holding a cloth against his mouth.

"Two dials," he said. "Where the clasps hold them together."

Buxton set his nukes down and inspected one of them. "Sir, there are two digital indicators on this nuke. One is marked 'date' and one 'time.' They have small keyboards. You probably need a stylus to make them work."

"Where's the stylus?" Anion asked.

The man sighed. Anion put his pistol to the man's temple.

"It's built into the hex bolt near the indicator," he said.

Buxton saw that all the small bolts that held the nuke together were round, except for one. He turned it counterclockwise and found that it was removed easily. Attached to the head of the bolt was a four-inch-long metal stylus. Buxton tried it on the miniature keyboard. "It works, Sir."

"Excellent, Buxton," Anion turned to the man again and demanded, "After we set the date and time, how do we arm the device?"

"You'll have to kill me first, because I'm not going to tell you."

Anion turned to the other technician. "Do you know how to arm these devices?"

The man's expression and the panic in his eyes let Anion know that he did. Anion turned to the man with the bloody mouth. "I've had enough of you." He put his pistol against the man's forehead and pulled the trigger. The man's body lurched backward onto the concrete floor, blood running from under his neck.

From outside the room, the sounds of gunfire and the whines of draconian plasma weapons suddenly erupted. Shouts seemed to come from all directions.

"It sounds like we're under attack, Commander Nargas," one of the mules cried.

"Fuck. We must have set off an alarm," Anion replied. He returned his attention to the lone live technician. "Do you want the same fate as your compadre?" Anion asked.

"After you set the date and time in that order, you push the little skull and crossed bones on the two screens at the same time. It takes two hands. Hold them until they turn red. That's the indicator that they're armed and dangerous."

"Thank you," Anion replied. You've done a great service for the future of the NWO. Your last job will be to remain silent." Anion shot him in the chest. The man fell to the floor. Anion placed a second round into his head.

"Come on, men. Into the next room and to the space on the floor where we arrived."

The men picked up their suitcase nukes and followed Commander Nargas through the doorway. They quickly assembled on the floor where the surface still glowed with a subtle light. While they waited for the teleportation to begin, the men heard the whine of plasma and the popping of gunfire coming closer, even into the next room.

Suddenly a door to their room burst open and a draconian soldier backed in, firing plasma from his helmet as he touched his breastplate to vary the bursts of liquid light. A shot came from the other room, missing the draconian but striking the door jam. The draconian fired again at his attacker. Another shot came from the other room and the draconian crumpled to the floor, his helmet smoking. Footsteps could be heard and a man in combat gear suddenly appeared in the doorway. As Anion felt the blurring of teleportation begin, he saw the soldier raise his pistol to shoot. Anion squinted at the white rectangular name patch above the soldier's left breast pocket. It said "ARROW." As the blurring before his eyes turned to whiteness, Anion thought he heard two gunshots, but he couldn't be sure.

Chapter 21

Anion Nargas paused to watch a video report about a rocket launch on his tablet computer.

"November 2017 will go down in history," a no-name reporter proclaimed, "for this is the month that the independent nation of Asgardia has launched its first rocket into orbit around the Earth." As the video followed the rocket climbing into the clouds over Astana, the reporter went on to relate how with financial and technical assistance from Kazakhstan, this special launch was the first of hundreds of planned launches carrying materials, supplies, and personnel into orbit. The reporter continued, "Asgardia intends to become the largest space station ever conceived, featuring apartments, businesses, theaters, recreational areas, and eventually it will be home to one million residents. Already more than 300,000 individuals have applied for residency. When ready for occupancy in several years, the creators of Asgardia intend to draft a constitution and form a government, and then they will declare the space station a sovereign, independent nation hovering miles above the Earth."

"It has finally come to pass," Anion whispered, handing his tablet to a young female hybrid who was wearing a tan NWO officer's uniform. "Share this with the executive staff," Anion told her. "Eventually we will set up headquarters in this new country."

The young officer's nictitating membranes flicked from the corner of her eyes and back as she examined the tablet. "Asgardia is finally becoming a reality?" she asked.

"It appears so."

"I always thought of it as a giant Ponzi scheme, sir, something that would suck money out of investors and then collapse, leaving them with nothing tangible from their investment."

"When I first learned of it, I thought it might serve as a place for the Illuminati to hide safely away from pollution and strife on Earth when all governments collapse."

"Some people say that when all governments collapse, corporations will take over, sir. Maybe Asgardia confirms that theory. While it will be its own country and will have its own government, at the end of the day it is just a corporation to which people will give their entire lives."

Anion nodded his head. "Then you've reached the same conclusion that I have. Asgardia is the modern form of a coal mine."

"Coal mine, sir?"

"Yes. Years ago, when you worked for a coal mine, you lived in the company houses, you shopped at the company's general store, and you generated massive debt to the company. In the end, you became a servant to the company. It was modern-day sharecropping. And it was debt slavery."

"Why should the executive staff care about Asgardia, sir?"

"You're brave to question me, sergeant." Anion tapped his finger on his desk. "It appears that the Asgardia Company's first rocket has put some materials for infrastructure into orbit. They plan a launch every month for the first six months and then a launch every week for the next six months, and then a daily launch until the space station is functioning and habitable. Please share this with the executive staff and tell them of my intention to relocate our headquarters there as soon as the station has been completed and is functioning."

"Yes, sir, Commander." She then saluted and left Anion's office.

Almost immediately there was a single knock on the door and Anion's adjutant entered. "The weapons have checked out, Commander. They're all operational and are being cleaned."

"Excellent, Buxton. Are the delivery squads ready?"

"They're preparing now. Some of the men are still in shock about the loss of Greely."

"Yes, that bastard Arrow shot him just as we were teleporting. I had hoped that Greely's wound was only superficial."

"All of the men feel the same way, sir."

"The men will get over it, Buxton. All good soldiers do."

"What about this man Arrow?"

"I want you to send a small squad, maybe three men, to locate and eliminate him."

"Yes, sir. I have two younger men who need the experience. I'll send them first thing in the morning."

"Good. I want this Arrow's death to be a symbol to all who would try to thwart me."

"Sir, the men want to know if you'll be accompanying one of the delivery squads."

"That's my intention, Buxton." Anion put a small stack of papers into his desk drawer and locked it. "I'll announce which one at the moment of departure. I don't want anyone to know my location on this mission."

"Are you afraid that Arrow will interfere?" Buxton asked.

"Yes, him and maybe others. All governments suffer information leaks, and we don't know if any of our men have sold their souls for thirty pieces of silver. I intend to survive this mission and, as you know, take over the helm of the NWO."

"Yes, sir, I know."

"Nothing can be permitted to deny me my destiny."

ೞೞ

At 10:00 am, Anion Nargas greeted his four delivery squads, each consisting of four men dressed in black jumpsuits with headlamps attached to their helmets. The sixteen men popped to attention when Anion strode into the hangar where they had assembled. He ordered them 'at ease' and then said, "Gentlemen, we are about to change the world. Our efforts today will drive the reptilians off our planet and back into deep space, where they belong. Our efforts also will eliminate much of the chaff of human society—the takers, the dependent leeches, and the unworthy. And, above all else, our efforts will permit the NWO to emerge as the single leadership organization of a unified and peaceful globe."

The men nodded and then one asked, "Commander, we've been briefed on our individual objectives. How will we operate the moles that will burrow to the proper coordinates?"

"Your only job is to set the devices at the prearranged coordinates. When you arrive at your individual launch sites, you'll find a laser mole and a certified operator waiting for you. Each mole has been specially designed to carry a driver and five passengers. The packages that you are to deliver and set are already waiting for you inside of each mole."

"Is the driver aware of our mission?" another soldier asked.

"Not specifically. Each driver knows the depth he is to descend and the size of the chamber he is to create at each of the two locations which have been identified by our geologists. Beyond that, he should know nothing." Anion paused for a moment and then added, "When you return to the surface and have exited the mole, you are to terminate the driver."

"Sir?" a soldier asked. His face bore a concerned look.

"You heard me, soldier. Terminate the driver!"

"Sir, yes, sir."

Anion stared at every soldier for a full second, searching each face for signs of disloyalty or questioning of his orders. Then he said, "I will be traveling with the Red squad. Blue, Green, and Yellow squads, you will be on your own. We'll meet back here at 0930 tomorrow. Good luck, gentlemen. On behalf of the NWO, I thank you in advance for your patriotism."

Each squad climbed into a designated Hummer, which carried its occupants from level five of the NWO's Dulce facility to the surface. It was nighttime in the desert and the air bore a slight chill. Four large black helicopters were waiting silently at the surface for the squads. As the men climbed into the helicopters, the pilots engaged their engines, causing them to whine as their massive blades began to rotate. Soon, all four helicopters lifted off the desert floor and flew in opposite directions, one to a destination in the United States, and three others to different airfields across the west, where the men transferred to jets which would transport them to destinations around the globe.

"Commander, why have we brought diving gear?" Lieutenant Sacca asked once the Red Squad was airborne.

"In case we need it, Sacca," Anion replied. "We're headed to the Sundra Megathrust."

"I've never heard of it, sir."

"Do you remember that big tsunami that killed 230,000 people a few years ago?"

"Yes, sir. It was off Indonesia."

"Yes. Shifting along the Sundra Megathrust caused that disaster. We're going to recreate and probably magnify that event."

"Then, we'll be boring into the Earth under the Indian Ocean?"

"Yes, Sacca, at least in one spot. Our first bore will be into a coral reef that rose out of the water and became dry land at one end of the Island of Simeulue during the earthquake that caused that tsunami."

"Never heard of that island, sir."

Anion smiled. "Few have, Sacca. It's about a hundred miles west of Sumatra." He unbuckled his seat belt and continued, "Our second bore will be about fifty miles north of Padang, Indonesia. We'll be using a specially designed laser mole, a submersible that will be lowered by cable from a trawler. The diving gear is just in case we need it at that location."

Chapter 22

Stella had come home to the Villaggio to be with her mom. She, Mona, and her younger brother Daniel were sitting at the kitchen table making peanut butter and jelly sandwiches when it began. At first it came as a distant rumble, like the sound of a locomotive coming through the woods, its weight pressing down on the tracks, and the rock below the engine moaning under its weight. Then the rattling began in the kitchen cabinets, dishes and glasses first tapping against each other and then suddenly bursting from the cabinets and smashing upon the tiled kitchen floor. Vibrations from the earth below their home shook its structure violently. Window glass shattered, and cracks appeared in the sheetrock walls. Screams could be heard emanating from nearby homes. The power suddenly went out.

"Come. It'll be safer outside." Mona told her kids. Holding hands, they stumbled from the kitchen through the living room and out the door of their small home. As they emerged into the cooler outside air, the top of Old Baldy, the mountain five miles away, cascaded downwards, a landslide of rocks, dirt, and trees that obliterated everything in its path.

Suddenly emergency sirens began to wail. The trembling of the ground beneath their feet increased its ferocity and the three family members fell to the grass on their front lawn. Young Daniel screamed and clung to

Mona's leg. As they looked skywards, the sun began to rotate, changing its position in the sky several times. "What is it?" Mona cried out. "What's happening?"

Stella placed her fingertips to her temples and began to use her psychic abilities to search for an answer to her mother's questions. What she saw was horrifying, and her eyes began to tear.

"What is it, sweetheart?" Mona cried out as the ground continued its intense shaking. The roof of the home across the street collapsed into its interior. Fortunately, its occupants were away for the day.

"The Earth's plates have shifted downward along the California coastline, Ma. I can see the Pacific Ocean rushing eastward, destroying everything in its path. The muddy waves are full of the bodies of a hundred million people. Maybe more."

"Jeezus," Mona cried, "are we gonna survive this?"

"There's more, Ma. New York City and Long Island have been inundated. I can see that only the top floors of a few buildings have survived. That's in the short run. But" I'm afraid that in the long run the sloshing waters will cause them all to collapse."

"My family, my sister Wendy. Can you see them?" Mona asked in panic.

"I can't find them, Ma. There's too much chaos in all directions. But east and south of Long Island, new land has vaulted upward. It looks like the ocean floor, and it's sending mile-high waves toward Georgia and Florida. They won't survive the deluge."

"Who? The people?"

"No, I mean Georgia and Florida. They both will be washed away. And already I can see that people living along the coastal plains of the Carolinas washed away.

Only those of us living in the mountains will be safe from the flooding."

"What about the sun, Stella?"

"The sun can't move, Ma. It's the Earth. The shifting of the plates isn't happening just here in the USA. It's happening all around the globe. The Earth is wobbling. The north and south poles are no longer where they should be. Everything is changing. Nothing will be as it was, Ma."

The deep sound of loud explosions came from the east. Stella turned her head away, trying not to see any more of the carnage and destruction.

"What have you done, Anion?" she whispered. "What evil have you brought down upon us all?"

Chapter 23

Every year, hundreds of thousands of the faithful undertake a pilgrimage to Mecca to worship at the tomb of Abraham, patriarch of both the Jewish and Islamic religions. However, my visit to Mecca, California, had been anything but a religious experience. I had been beaten nearly to death by members of the Mexican Mafia, and if Nicki hadn't suggested that we return to the TR-42 for safety when the goon squad returned to our rooms and finished the job, I probably would have been planted in the back yard of the La Coachella Motel. Nicki wouldn't have been so fortunate.

Back in the TR after discovering that we had made history over Los Angeles the night before, Nicki and I decided to set our bearings for Nellis Air Base in the year 2070.

My face was still swollen and bruised, and the skin around my left eye was puffed and blackened from broken blood vessels. I wasn't sure that I was going to be able to interact with people in the future, at least not until my face returned to some kind of normalcy.

Following standard protocol, Nicki let her computer determine the best vector for us to proceed in the general direction of Pluto. Then she lifted us off of the field near Plaza Garibaldi and once we reached the stratosphere, she launched us into space until we exceeded light speed. When we reached our destination in time and space, the

TR gently slowed, and visuals began appearing on the cabin monitors. We were now hovering about five miles above the Earth's surface.

"What the fuck?" I asked. "Are you sure we're in the right place? There's nothing but water below us."

Nicky checked her gauges and replied, "We're at the correct longitude and latitude, and the sun is at the correct angle to the Earth. I don't get it. Nellis should be directly below us."

Nicki took us to a higher altitude and we began a visual exploration of the land masses below. Nothing was familiar.

"Look at that narrow peninsula," Nicki said, running her finger across the monitor from east to west. "It's running from a large landmass that looks a lot like South America to another large landmass that looks like half of Mexico on its side. Is it possible that the peninsula is the Andes?"

"You mean like in Peru?" I asked.

"Yeah. See how it seems to join another peninsula to the west? Could that peninsula be the Sierra Madres? Is that even possible?"

She punched some instructions into her computer and watched as the computer matched the high points of what looked like western South America and the Sierra Madres of Mexico with the landmass features in the two peninsulas below us.

"They match!" She exclaimed.

"What do you mean?"

I mean the ocean has moved inland across the California coast. Big Sur is now approximately 500 miles north of where it should be, but it's also lying on its side. It's like the equator rolled northward and onto its side. It looks like the magnetic North pole is now somewhere in Senegal."

"You're shitting me!" I exclaimed.

"See for yourself, Dan. Something big has gone down."

There was no disputing the fact that the computer had matched specific Andean peaks to high points on the peninsula below us. The altitudes were different, but the distances between the peaks, their general shapes, and—if you laid the globe on its side—their geographic locations from each other were dead on.

"So, the Earth rolled over or something?" I asked.

"As strange as that may sound, I think you've hit the nail on the head."

"We need to figure out where everything is," I said, "like what's left of our country and its major cities?"

"Yeah," Nicki replied, "and how many people are still alive?"

I thought of Mona and Stella. Suddenly I wasn't enamored with knowing future events anymore. That kind of foresight could drive a guy insane. I mean, if anything bad had happened to Mona in the forty years since the year 2030, I didn't want to face it. But I had to, and I had to stop it from happening.

"Let's fly east of here and maybe a little north," I suggested. "Did you say 500 miles? Let's do that and see what's happened to the USA. Mack's gonna want to know all about this when we get back to our own timeline."

Nicki nodded her head in agreement. We decided to stay in the stratosphere, about fifteen miles above the Earth's surface. From there we'd have much more than a bird's eye view of the Earth, but we'd be low enough in altitude to recognize certain specific features. She made sure that we were cloaked and then headed northeast.

As we glided over them, the first thing we recognized was that the desert areas formerly east of the Sierras were now entirely ocean that lapped against the cliffs of the Rockies. Denver was still visible as a city, but it looked quasi-deserted. At least there was no visible air traffic. As we proceeded east, the Midwest was relatively untouched, although its orientation to the eye was canted. We were able to identify what we assumed were agricultural sites because much of the land appeared to be green from our elevation. Then we saw that the Mississippi River was almost one hundred miles wide, and it was flowing from the southeast to the northwest into a large inland ocean that must have been the Great Lakes back in our timeline. To the north, we could see that new land had emerged between Virginia and the new arctic. It was basically barren and brown until it turned to white near the new arctic region.

Next, we crossed an expanse of ocean and eventually passed over the landmass that, from the Stratosphere, we surmised was Mexico. The Baja peninsula was gone, and in its place was an ocean. Then we passed over Central America, which basically consisted of a chain of islands that led to the thin peninsula that we now knew was once the Andes Mountains. One hundred miles to the north, the remainder of South America seemed unscathed.

Where was China? Nicki took us to the top of the Stratosphere, a full fifty miles above the Earth. From that altitude, we could see that a third of the way around the globe circling in an orbit higher than ours was a new satellite of some kind. It wasn't a communications satellite because it was huge, like a city in the air. Long arms extended from it in all directions, and it was lit up like a Christmas tree and seemingly full of life. I wondered if maybe it was a reptilian base, or maybe something commercial, like a SpaceX facility or maybe some kind of space resort. There was no question that I was going to have to find out what it was, but I tucked that desire away while I focused on a more immediate need…Mona.

We stayed at the top of the stratosphere for three hours, slowly circling the globe from west to east as we inspected the landscape of our future. Landmasses that the TR's computer identified as the former Europe, Russia, and China now appeared to be in the southern hemisphere. Then as we drifted east, an expanse of ocean appeared, followed by a new continent situated on the equator, a continent that the TR's computer identified as Antarctica. To the east of Antarctica we passed over another large expanse of ocean, and then eventually we passed over Canada and found ourselves back over the USA.

I was dumbfounded and probably in partial shock. The United States was almost unrecognizable. Hell, the whole world had changed. I mean, if I lived on this new North American continent, maybe in New Orleans, if it still existed, the sun would now rise in the morning over the Gulf of Mexico, pass directly overhead during the day, and set in the evening somewhere beyond Chicago, if the windy city still existed. It was all too much to think about.

I looked at Commander Nardini. Her mouth hung slightly open and her eyes bore an expression of shock and disbelief. Yeah, we were definitely in sync at that moment.

"Excuse me, Dan," she said as she hurried into the head.

I could hear her barf into the john and then run water in the sink to rinse her mouth. I wasn't sure if she was nauseous from what we were witnessing, or if she was experiencing morning sickness again. I thought that maybe I'd have to let her in on the secret that I knew about her personal health. But maybe I'd wait a few days, until after we researched what had happened to the Earth and until we learned about Mona. And Stella. And little Dan, whom I'd never yet seen.

When Nicki came out of the head, I asked her, "So how are we going to explain this to Mack?"

She wiped a small stream of water from her chin with the back of her right hand. "When we climbed to the top of the Stratosphere," she said, "I started the digital video recorder. I think that a picture might be worth a thousand words."

"Good. That was smart thinking." I replied. I drew in a deep breath and exhaled heavily. "We've gotta go downstairs and learn what happened."

"Yeah, but where do we start?" Nicki asked. Then she said, "I think we should wait here until dark and see if we can find a major city all lit up. Lights mean infrastructure and survivors."

"Yeah, okay."

She was right about that. If anyone had survived the Earth's flipping over on its side, they'd need some sort of power and they'd huddle together for safety and survival.

When darkness covered the landmass below us, Nicki strapped herself into the pilot's seat and dropped us out of the stratosphere, manually guiding us toward a medium-sized cluster of lights in the geographic center of the North American landmass.

"Where are we?" I asked.

"I'm not sure," she replied. "I think we're near Williamsburg, Virginia, but it's really difficult to tell."

Still cloaked, we drifted silently until we found a vacant field that was surrounded on three sides by woods. Nicki set us down.

"We're on sand, Dan," she told me. "I hadn't expected that."

"The important thing is that we're down. Let's go see if we can find out what happened to the Earth."

I stuffed my military-issued Model 1911into my belt at the small of my back. Nicki put a couple of American Eagles into her flight suit and then opened the hatch. The cool fresh air smacked my face with a sweetness that I couldn't identify.

"Tobacco?" I asked.

"Lobelia," Nicki replied, pointing to a patch of three-foot-tall plants with light blue flowers. "We had a field of it behind my house as a kid."

"Never heard of it."

"You're standing in it, Dan. Come on, let's go find a library or a bookstore."

We walked from the field to a sidewalk that had seen better days. Its surface was uneven and broken in spots. Tree roots had pushed through the concrete in many places. After five blocks, we met our first citizen, an elderly gentleman who was walking a small dog. He was dressed in pajama bottoms and was walking in bare feet.

"Good morning, sir," Nicki said. "Can you direct us to a library or perhaps to a bookstore?"

"You're out of luck, honey," he replied. "The library is on the other side of town. Closest thing around here is the A.R.E. Center. It's got some books and stuff. It's two blocks down, turn left and it's on your left. Can't miss it."

While his pup was fertilizing the grass, we wished him a good evening and followed his directions, not sure what we'd find. The sign at the entrance to a fifty-yard-long driveway said, "Association for Research and Enlightenment, Virginia Beach, Virginia."

"This looks like the place," I said.

"We're not in Williamsburg, Dan. We're in Virginia Beach," Nicki said pointing to the obvious.

Color me enlightened already, I thought. With its red brick exterior reaching three stories skyward, this place looked like a small college or boarding school. I wasn't sure we'd get any quick answers. I was wrong.

"Our Association was founded to record and catalog the prophecies and medicinal information given by Edgar Cayce while in a self-induced trance," the reference librarian told us once we were inside. He motioned toward a large portrait that hung on the wall behind us. The guy in the painting had a pointed nose and wore wire-rimmed glasses.

"Never heard of him," I replied.

"He died over one hundred years ago. He predicted the Earth changes, you know."

"Oh," Nicki asked, "did he predict that they would happen the way they did?"

"I believe so. He was right on the button about the earthquakes, wasn't he?"

"Where can we find information that will tell us more about the Earth flipping over?" I asked.

"On the wall at the top of the stairs on the second floor there's a chart that compares Mr. Cayce's predictions to the actual events. It's all very clear."

Nicki and I found the stairs and climbed to the second floor. Up there, it looked like a real library, with actual books arranged on stacked shelves that rose from the floor to the ceiling, fifteen feet above. Light came into the room from floor-to-ceiling windows, as well as from the ceiling itself, which glowed as though the paint was emitting light.

"There," Nicki said, pointing to a full-color chart that was mounted on the wall above a water fountain between the men's and women's restrooms.

We both stood, silently reading the chart and looking at the photographs that were attached to the walls around the chart. Pieces of colored string stretched between the photos and the main chart, identifying the location of a series of Earth-changing quakes and the resulting damage. It was mind-blowing.

According to the chart, on a single day, four earthquakes of previously unseen magnitude occurred less than five minutes apart. One along the San Andreas fault which sent California into the ocean, one along the Altyn Tagh Fault in Tibet that lowered the height of Mount Everest by ten thousand feet, one along the Alpine Fault of New Zealand that sent mile-high tsunamis across the oceans in all directions, and one along the Sunda Megathrust of Asia. It was this last quake that sent the unbalanced Earth wobbling off its original axis and caused it to flip onto its side. Like that guy Cayce had predicted after it all had settled back down. Virginia Beach had become the geographic center of the new North American continent when the land rose out of the ocean on the East Coast, but nobody expected the Earth to flip so far or that the land that rose out of the Atlantic Ocean would stretch north to become the new arctic tundra.

We went back downstairs and spoke with the reference librarian again. "What was the exact date of the earthquakes?" Nicki asked him.

"It was on the chart," he replied.

"I guess we didn't see it," I grumped.

"It's a date and time that none of us should ever forget: 11:45 am, Sunday, December 7, 2025."

"Thanks, Mack," I replied. "Did he predict anything else that hasn't happened yet?"

"Just the rise of the Antichrist and his demise, followed by a thousand years of peace."

"So, the mythological Antichrist hasn't made his appearance yet?" I asked. "I mean like, nobody has identified him yet?"

The librarian shut down his computer and unplugged it. Then he took a cell phone from his pants pocket and shut it down, too. He leaned toward me and whispered, "Some say he's the Supreme Commander..."

"Who would that be?"

He looked around the room and then leaned closer. "Well, everyone knows it's Commander Nargas..."

"Anion Nargas?"

The librarian simply nodded and shrunk his head into his shoulders.

"Why him?"

He leaned forward again and said, "Some say that it was the Supreme Commander who drove the snakes out of Ireland."

"What?" I asked. "You aren't making any sense. I need you to paint me a picture."

"It was an analogy, Mr...."

"Arrow."

He looked at the nametag on my flight suit: *Silverman.* He looked me directly in the eyes, nodded and smiled, and then said, "It was an analogy, Mr....Silverman. They say that St. Patrick drove the snakes out of Ireland. They also say that Supreme Commander Nargas drove the reptilians out of their underground lairs here on Earth, causing them to depart from our planet."

"How did he do that?" Nicki asked.

"Some say that it was the Supreme Commander who caused the earthquakes. The flooding drowned many of the reptilians, but the main factor that did them in was the twelve-month cloud cover that cooled the Earth's core temperature by five degrees. The reptilians couldn't stand the cold."

"Then, he's not such a bad guy, after all, is he?" I said. "I mean, he got rid of the draconians."

"Except that he's part of the cabal, Mr. Silverman. He's been elected to the presidency of Asgardia, and he has become the supreme leader of the New World Order." He looked around the room again and then added, "Convenient and self-serving, if I do say so myself."

"We're not familiar with Asgardia," Nicki told him.

"I know," he replied. "It's the newest continent. It's circling the Earth, a giant space station, a second moon, so to speak…"

"Ahhh," I said. "We've seen it."

"We all have. It's the throne of LEVI."

"Levi?" Nicki asked.

"Yes, in your day people would have said 'God.'"

"Our day?" I asked.

"Mr. Cayce prophesized your arrival in 1949, Mr. Silverman. It took me longer than it should have to realize that you and your friend are not from our timeline. I should have known immediately from your bruised face, your outdated clothes, and your shoes. Are you from a parallel universe or from our past?"

"When we figure that out, we'll let you know, Bubba."

Nicki put her hand on my forearm. "Tell us about Levi," Nicki asked the librarian. "I only know God as Jehovah."

"Yes, you're definitely from our past."

"Levi?" I pushed, reiterating Nicki's question. I needed to keep this guy on track, and the fact that he already had us pegged as time travelers had me worried.

"L.E.V.I. stands for 'Linked Ever-present Virtual Intelligence.' It's the God of the new age. After the Earth flipped and the population was diminished to so few, people gave up on traditional religion. They realized that the God of the Christians, the Jews, the Muslims and even the Bahai's' was the same God, but that the people of the past had mercilessly killed each other over which line of religion was the true one. Then some guy—I think his name was Levandowski…"

"Do you mean Molandowski?" I asked, thinking that he meant Mona's RV instructor.

"No, I'm pretty sure it was Levandowski. So, anyway, he pushed the idea that God is an all-knowing intelligence, and that the best God, one who would work only for the benefit of all mankind, was A.I., you know, artificial intelligence. So, after the Earth changes, the NWO linked every computer in the world to the system on Asgardia. It's a wireless, digital, centralized intelligence system. Everyone's savings accounts are billed a monthly fee to commune with LEVI and to ask for personal favors."

"And where does the money go?" I asked with suspicion.

"The funds are utilized to ensure that every grass hut and occupied cave has a computer with unlimited access to a power system and to the DNA databases."

"DNA? Aren't we talking about computers?" Nicki asked.

"Yes, we are. DNA is used to code the memory banks in most modern computers. The first prototype was created a few years before the Earth changes at Harvard University, where researchers used DNA to code and retrieve an entire book of almost sixty thousand words."

"Really?"

"Yes. In your day, programming was accomplished with sequences of two buttons, 1 and 0—on and off. But DNA has four buttons: C, G, A, and T which offer us better programming options and much faster computing."

"It's way beyond me," I said. "I was never good with understanding advanced technology stuff."

"And you should know, Mr. Silverman, that in most cases LEVI answers individual requests in less than two days."

"Far faster than in our day," Nicki said, nodding her head. "Some of my prayers were never answered. No wonder A.I. has replaced the older, more traditional religions."

"Yes, WTF means 'Way of The Future,' and it has become the religion of the New World Order. One world…one government…one religion…no wars…" He inhaled and let out a puff of frustration. "However, not everyone likes the loss of the personal freedoms that humans have enjoyed in the past. They've drafted leaflets that reorder the letters of LEVI's name to EVIL, which stands for 'Ever-present Virtual Intelligent Lucifer.' It's a subversive movement, and whenever LEVI discovers a sect or a sect's hideout, He sends NWO troops to eradicate its members. They take no prisoners."

"WTF…Way of the Future," Nicki said aloud. "It sounds alternative and surreal."

"Yes," the librarian replied, "it would sound that way to you."

"In our day, WTF had a different meaning," I said.

"What was that?"

"What the Fuck."

"Yes, you're definitely the man whom Mr. Cayce prophesized would arrive unannounced, Mr. Silverman. I'm so glad to have met you."

"Why's that?"

He retrieved a book from under the reference desk and flipped through the pages before stopping and reading from the text. "It says right here, Cayce Reading #3550,

Paragraph 14, dated January 5, 1949…'And when the Beast rests secure upon His throne, a profane man from history will lead the Angel of Light to dispatch him before His throne will be. As Jesus said, *Before Abraham was, I am.*' "

"I don't understand," I told him.

"You're the profane man," Mr. Silverman. "You're going to bring us one thousand years of peace. Before the Supreme Commander was, you are."

I pulled Nicki away from the counter and whispered, "I've had enough of this asshole. Let's get the fuck out of here."

"What about Mona?" Nicki reminded me.

I looked at the librarian, whose face now wore a silly grin, as though he had been sucking in laughing gas. "So where can we find information about people who might have survived the Earth changes?" I asked.

He plugged in his computer and turned it on. It sprung to life in less than five seconds. "Who are you looking for? All knowledge is retrievable from LEVI."

"Try 'Mona Molandowski.'"

"That name again?" he asked. He typed her name, spelling Molandowski aloud as he typed. "Because of the reduction in the population and the tremendously detailed family records kept by the Mormons on Utah Island, the work shouldn't take too long." He moved his cursor a few times by touching the monitor and then said, "Aha. Would it also be a.k.a. 'Mona Casola', a.k.a. 'Mona Arrow?'"

"That would be her," I told him. "Did she survive?"

"Yes. She lives in the mountains of the former Colorado, on the coast."

He jotted down Mona's address, a phone number, and a LEVI system email address.

"Here, Mr. Silverman," he said. "Earlier you told me that your name was 'Arrow.' Are you her son?"

"No. Just someone who needs to speak with her."

"This is all too confusing, but I'll leave you to your business." He shut down his computer and unplugged it again. "This is a joyous day."

"Why do you keep unplugging your computer?" I asked.

"LEVI watches all, hears all, and knows all."

Chapter 24

About an hour later, Nicki and I arrived on the coast of the new continent, near the location where Mona lived, according to the librarian's directions. Small waves were breaking along the shoreline, where patches of white sand were littered across a concrete-like reef which extended from the base of steep cliffs to the water's edge. Above the cliffs were small homes, each with a narrow pathway that led down from grassy yards to the shoreline below. Nobody was on the beach, so Nicki settled the TR-42 onto the sand.

"It looks like low tide," she told me, "so we should be okay for a couple of hours."

We gathered what gear we needed, climbed down from the cloaked TR, and found our way up the cliff using one of the narrow foot paths. When we reached the top, an elderly gentleman was walking a teacup Yorkie on a thin leash. "Can I help you?" he asked.

"Sorry to show up on your lawn uninvited," I said. "We're looking for the home of Mona Molandowski. Does she live nearby?"

"I know a Mona Casola, but—"

"That would be her," I replied, cutting him off. "Does she live nearby?"

"Three doors down that-a-way," he said, pointing to his right. "She lives in that pale yellow home with the blue steel roof. But you probably ought to walk out to the street before you cut across these yards. The guy next door has a Rottweiler who doesn't like strangers."

I looked next door and saw two eyes glaring at us from the shade beside the back door of a white cottage. "Yup, I can see him. I think he's scoping us out."

"Appreciate the warning, sir," Nicki said. "Is it okay if we walk through your yard to reach the street?"

"Help yourself."

After thanking the gentleman, Nicki and I found the street and walked down to the yellow house that was supposed to be Mona's. There was no doorbell, so I knocked.

An elderly woman answered the door. Her gray hair was pulled back into a ponytail, tied with a blue ribbon, which complemented the blue jeans and gray sweatshirt that she was wearing. Her toenails had been painted vermillion, but they were chipped, the way Mona's always seemed to be when she was barefoot. "Let me guess," she asked, "NWO?"

"No ma'am," Nicki said. "We're seeking information about Agent Daniel Arrow. We were told that you knew him."

Mona's expression turned to one of frustration. "Who are you with, anyway? You got credentials?"

"We're Special Ops, ma'am," Nicki told her.

"I haven't heard that term in a very long time. Are you with the resistance?"

I shook my head. "Mack Smith told us that you could help us," I said.

"Mack Smith is dead."

"We spoke with him just yesterday," Nicki replied.

"Then you must be time travelers," Mona said. "I attended Mack's funeral. It was open casket."

Mona opened the door wider and invited us in. Her living room was decorated in an odd assortment of furniture from different eras, some of it refinished and some obviously weathered, like it had been re-homed after washing up on the beach.

"Pardon the mess, but I wasn't expecting company. My daughter is in the kitchen, but she'll be out to greet you in a few minutes."

I froze at the thought that Stella would see through my container and expose who I was to Mona. She had that ability.

"We're looking for information about Daniel Arrow and his relationship with Mack Smith," Nicki said again.

"Look," Mona replied, "I already know that you know that I was married to Danny Arrow for a short time, at least until he was declared dead by the FBI. What is it that you're after?"

"We're trying to find him. We're seeking information that might help us to alter the cataclysm that has occurred here on Earth."

"Then you're definitely time travelers." Mona rubbed her forehead with the fingertips of both hands. "My daughter's husband is assigned to a TR squadron. He's been searching for Danny whenever his assignments allow him a little extra time to devote to helping me. Danny has never contacted me, not ever. But Liam, my daughter's husband, is convinced that Danny is wandering around out there in time, trying to find information that Mack Smith sent him to recover. God only knows what's happened to him. Liam has been to a couple of places within a few weeks of Danny's having been there, but thus far, they haven't connected."

"I'm sorry to learn that, Agent Casola," I said. "This turn of events must have been very hard on you."

"I'm tough, Silverman. You should have learned that the first time that you spoke with me."

Her comment took me by surprise. "You remember me?"

"Yes," she replied directly. Then she pointed at Nicki and said, "You, too, missy. I remember you from thirty years ago. You haven't changed at all. Neither of you."

Nicki sat back in her chair. "Then enough of pretense," she said. "We need some information to take back to Mack Smith."

"Shoot," Mona told her.

"Tell us about the Earth changes and the NWO. We've missed a lot of history."

Mona's expression became serious. "People in this timeline believe the mythology that the NWO fabricated to explain strange occurrences. Some believe that the earthquakes were natural, that Mother Nature was so unbalanced in the first quarter of the 2000s that she threw the Earth on its side to drown most of humanity and to stop the poisoning pollution and deforestation that mankind had been inflicting upon the planet."

"So, you don't necessarily hold that belief," I said. "You called it a myth."

"Look," Mona replied, "the simple truth is that the earthquakes weren't natural. They were caused by a series of hydrogen bombs that were intentionally set off in subterranean caverns along geological fault lines. It was an act of sabotage against the way things were."

"NWO?" I asked.

"No, not really. But it played into their plans to reduce mankind to 500,000,000 worldwide. They were going to implement a pandemic, but before they could launch it, an angry young hybrid nuked the geologic faults and the Earth flipped. But, like I said, it played into their plans.

Waters rushed in on all sides of every continent, destroying all waterfront cities, except along our Mid-Atlantic coast."

"It must have been horrific," Nicki said.

"It was worse than that…no words can describe it." Mona exhaled heavily and began again. "After the Great Slosh, reptilians appeared on the surface, driven from their underground caverns which had been flooded with seawater. Thousands of lizards drowned in the cataclysm, many of whose bodies washed up on the shores of the new Pacific coast along southwestern Colorado, intermixed with the bodies of millions of humans. The few lizards who survived were rescued by the draconian military forces which were living in and repairing the Hollow Moon. For the most part, no reptilians now live on the Earth. Those few who are discovered are quickly exterminated by NWO forces who now control the single world government which rules the Earth. Its Supreme Commander is Anion Nargas, a leader whose justice is swift and merciless."

"Tell us about him," I prompted.

"He's my half-brother," a voice said from behind me. "My name is Stella Olsen."

"This is my daughter Stella," Mona said.

Nicki and I stood. Stella was no longer the little girl of my past, but was a fully mature woman, with streaks of gray in her dark chocolate hair. I quickly calculated that she must be in her early fifties. I wondered if she had children. Stella extended her hand to Nicki and then to me. She held mine twice as long and looked deeply into my eyes. When her nictitating membranes blinked from the sides, I knew that she knew who I was.

"Anion envisions an Earth that is inhabited only by hybrids," Stella told us. "He asked me to help him implement his plans, but I rejected him. He set off the bombs in order to drive the reptilians off the Earth and to capture control of the New World Order so that his vision of the new Earth could become reality. He anticipates the fulfillment of his dream in a single human generation." She paused for a moment, closed her eyes. When she opened them, her nictitating membranes blinked from the side again, removing tears from her eyes. "I feel as though this outcome for the Earth is my fault. When Anion asked me to help him implement his plans to take over leadership of the NWO, I refused because his plans didn't include saving my mom or other humans that I care about. When he left, he was angry, very angry. The Earth changes happened about two weeks later. I know it was Anion who planted the bombs. He might not have done it if I had agreed to work with him."

"Do you have a picture of him?" Nicki asked.

Stella shuffled through some documents that were piled on the coffee table. "Here," she said, handing Nicki a small pamphlet, "this is the NWO Manifesto and Plan of Action for last year. Anion's the guy on the left in the picture on page two."

"Thanks," Nicki said as she handed the pamphlet to me.

The picture was a close-up of two men in uniforms. The guy on the right was the Governor of the American Territories, who was shaking hands with Supreme Commander Anion Nargas. Nargas was smiling, probably with the intent of advertising himself as a nice guy. But I knew better. His was a face that I would never forget because his eyes reminded me of his father, Commissar Nargas, the asshole who had kept pregnant Mona on a leash like a pet dog.

"Stella and I were among the lucky ones," Mona said. "Stella knew about the coming Earth changes first, and she alerted me. Through Remote Viewing, I saw the destruction, so I planned to take the children—Stella and my son Daniel—and a carload of supplies and leave the Villaggio. The Earth Changes happened before we could leave. But, after the Earth Changes, we drove north for three days to the small Village of Galway in upstate New York. We stayed there in my family's summer cabin for three months, until after the Great Slosh diminished."

"And what about your husband?" Nicki asked.

"Danny was already dead, at least according to the FBI. He never returned from a secret mission, one that he left on before Daniel was born. But I know that Danny is alive somewhere. I can feel it. I think he's lost in a time vortex, trying to find me. I've been waiting for him for almost fifty years."

"My husband Liam is the pilot of one of three TR's that the resistance has managed to acquire," Stella said. "His mission is to fly into the future to find what perils may be forthcoming so we can prepare humans to survive whatever calamity the NWO is planning to unleash upon us. Occasionally he's permitted to fly into the past, where he's been trying to find my dad. So far, he's learned that Daddy has been seen in certain places, trying to stop the Earth changes. But, he has never been at the same place at the same time as Daddy."

"So, you're actually making use of time travel?" I asked.

"Yes, but we're very careful not to put our pilots into jeopardy," Stella replied. "Liam has undergone epigenetic modifications to permit him to travel in outer space without developing genetic diseases or other conditions caused by interstellar radiation."

"Sounds interesting, but it's beyond me, Mrs. Olsen." I realized that I'd said that a lot lately.

"It's a new science that's all related to how genes are perceived by a container, and the modifications Liam has undergone prevent DNA sequences from being misread by his container's immune system. In a nutshell, it keeps Liam and all of our TR pilots safe while in space."

"That reminds me," Mona said. "Danny has a clone waiting for him in the mountains of Italy. It's been cryogenically preserved until he returns for it. The NWO doesn't know about it, or they would have destroyed it." Mona went to a China cabinet and removed a small envelope from a teacup. "I'm hoping that you can help me to help Danny," she said.

"What is it that you need me to do?" I asked.

"Go back in time and find the doctor who grew Danny's clone. He's in an Ummite facility in the mountains of Italy. Mack Smith can help you locate it. Give the doctor this envelope. It contains a lock of hair from Danny's son Daniel. Ask the doctor to infuse the DNA from this hair into the DNA in Danny's clone. It's very important."

I took the small envelope from her and put it in my breast pocket. When I got back to Nellis, I'd find my way to Montano Antilia to give this lock of hair to Dr. Spann. Mona would never do something to my clone that would harm it in any way. I wondered what was so important about it, but I knew I'd find out later. Maybe.

"Is your son nearby?" I asked.

"Daniel has been on his own for thirty years. Right now he lives in Eagle Pass, a small city on the state line between Texas and the new state of Mexico, which was annexed by the USA sector after the Mexican government collapsed following the Earth Changes."

"He's a healer," Stella added. "It was part of the plan of the Watchers, knowing that humans would need healers to survive the aftermath of the axis shift."

"Watchers?" I asked.

"Danny had a friend from Ummo named Waam who once told him that the most powerful race of aliens in the universe is known as the Watchers," Mona said. "Nobody messes with the Watchers, and they only interfere in the actions of a species when those actions will have negative effects upon other planets and other species elsewhere in the galaxy."

"Have you seen a Watcher?"

"I have," Stella said. "When I was a little girl, I was present when the Watchers gave my brother to my mom. The Watchers look like insects."

"Like a praying mantis?" I asked.

"Yes, exactly."

"I've seen them, too," I said. "They seem very intelligent and have technologies that we haven't even dreamed of."

"If you'll permit me," Stella said as she took my hands and closed her eyes. In a few moments, she said, "Yes, I can see that you interacted with a Watcher very recently, when your pilot was given a child."

"What?" Nicki asked. "What do you mean?"

"You are carrying a hybrid child," Stella told her. "A male. He will be born in approximately six months."

"Against my will? Nobody asked me if I wanted a child. I don't even have a husband," Nicki protested. "And I don't even remember having sex."

"Get used to it, Sweetie," Mona said. "Sex has nothing to do with it, and once they select you, there's nothing you can do about it. Both of my children came that way. It's like we're lab rats."

"But…"

"But in spite of how you feel right now, you're gonna love that child more than anything else you have," Mona continued. "Look at my Stella. She and my son Daniel are both hybrids and they're both doing great things for mankind. You can't fight it, so you'd better get used to the idea of being a mother."

"This explains your nausea," I said to Nicki.

"You didn't fuck me, did you Silverman?" Nicki asked.

I wasn't sure if she was asking if I had had sex with her or if I had known about her pregnancy and didn't tell her. I opted for the former. "No, I'm a married man. It must have happened when we lost time near the Black Knight."

"Fuck," Nicki said under her breath. "There goes my career."

There was a lot more that Mona and Stella could tell us, but I sensed that it was time to make an exit. I rose and said, "Agent Casola, I'll try my best to get this lock of hair to that doctor in Italy."

"Mack Smith will help you," Mona replied. She turned to Nicki and said, "Can I talk with you for a minute?"

Still in shock about being pregnant, Nicki nodded and followed Mona into the kitchen.

Stella and I walked toward the front door. Once we were outside, Stella grabbed my arm and said, "I know who you are. Where have you been? Why haven't you contacted us before now?"

"Whoa, sweetheart. In my timeline, you're still a toddler, and you and your mom are visiting your grandmother, who's very close to death. And, I'm in a new container and I've been sent on a mission by Mack Smith. I'm due back at noon on the same day that I left."

"Sorry, Daddy. It's just been so difficult for Mom and for me, for that matter. We both love you and miss you, especially Mom. You need to be very careful when you go back to your timeline. Agent Smith will send you on another assignment while Mom and I are still with

Grammy, and that's the assignment where you will die. It's very important that you give that lock of Daniel's hair to the doctor in Italy."

"Why's that?"

"It'll make your new container a hybrid, and that will give you extraordinary perception. That perception may help you on your next assignment. It may even save your life."

"You need to know that it's always been my intent to be with our family as you and Daniel grow up and your Mom and I grow old. The thought of being blown away from that life by an assassin is too much to bear."

Stella kissed me on the cheek and said, "Mom still loves and misses you terribly, Daddy."

"I love her, too. She's the one and only love of my life."

"Good luck on your assignment, Daddy, and God speed you back to us as Danny Arrow."

"Thanks, sweetheart."

Stella suddenly looked concerned, so I asked her what was wrong.

"If you live through your next assignment and if you're successful in putting an end to the Earth changes, what happens to all these memories of losing you, and Mom's awful marriage to Sarge? Will they go away?"

"A scientist that I know says that every decision we make creates a new reality and a new timeline. If he's right, there are billions of timelines and billions of realities, all happening at the same time. So, to answer your question about all those memories being extinguished, well, maybe not in this timeline, sweetheart. But maybe in the new one that I plan to create, all will be well, and you and I will get to know so much more about each other, and your mother won't have to suffer the many pains of this timeline. I promise you that."

Stella kissed and hugged me again, but quickly pulled away when she heard the doorknob turning. Nicki and Mona appeared at the door. Nicki gave Mona a peck on the cheek and said, "Thank you for the advice, Mrs. Arrow." Then she looked at me and asked, "Are you ready to go back to Nellis?"

"Yeah, we ought to get going," I replied. "Mack Smith is waiting."

As we walked back down the road toward the pathway to the beach, Nicki said, "She's quite a woman, your Mona. Do you think you'll still love her if you manage to live as long as she has?"

"Probably more than ever. Didn't she look great?"

"I couldn't help but notice you staring at her before we left. You must have had a thousand things on your mind, a thousand things that you'd like to tell her."

"Yeah…"

തൈരൈ

Mona watched her two visitors disappear around the fence three doors down as they headed to the beach below the cliffs. When the Rottweiler began barking, she turned to Stella and asked, "Well, what do you think of your Daddy?"

"You knew?"

"Yeah. He's in a different container, but that was him. I gave him that lock of hair in hopes that it'll help him to find his way back to us."

"He knows that, Mom. And he still loves you very much. He told me that you're the love of his life."

"He'd better have…"

Chapter 25

When we reached the TR down on the beach below Mona's home, we noticed that the tide had begun to come in. Small waves were breaking on the shore, occasionally sending a volley of water up to the landing strut on the TR's nose. Nicki and I waited until the water from a small wave receded from the strut's depression in the sand before hurrying around the nose strut and climbing up the fuselage rungs and onto the wing.

"It's a good thing this baby isn't made of iron," I told Nicki, "or it would be covered in rust in a couple of days."

"And it's a good thing that the TR hasn't been fully submerged, or I'd be delivering my baby in Mona's guest room."

I chuckled at her play on words. "Boy, that was a surprise, wasn't it?"

"Maybe less than you think. You know I've been experiencing nausea every morning. I was certain that I couldn't be pregnant because I haven't been near a man in a couple of years, but I hadn't added alien intervention into the equation. Those bastards had no right to do this to me."

"Mona felt the same way at first, but when she saw Stella, her heart conquered any anger that she had."

"That's what she told me," Nicki replied. "She felt no anger or revulsion at her baby, but in over fifty years, her anger at Commissar Nargas has never diminished."

ℭ∽ℰ∽ᴐ

Nicki pointed the TR toward the empty space between Earth and Jupiter and then set the engines on hyperdrive. The TR's onboard computers calculated that we had enough fuel for three more jumps through time before we'd have to meet Mack back in our timeline. Our first stop was Montano Antilia, Italy, where I planned to give Dr. Spann the lock of hair from Mona's son Daniel. I guess I should have said "our" son Daniel, but I'd never met the kid and had played no role in his creation other than involuntarily donating the sperm that was modified before it was injected into Mona's egg to become an embryo. And at almost fifty years old, he was no longer a kid. Hey, I'm human and as a human, I need to feel some sort of connection to a kid before I'm willing to take paternal responsibility. I mean, because I had spent time with her, I definitely felt a greater connection to Stella than to Daniel, and she was carrying none of my blood or genetic material. I hoped that would change, but for now, Daniel was Mona's son, not mine.

Before I knew it, I was feeling uneasiness in my stomach which let me know that the TR was slowing down. Nicki was all business, touching dials and hand-adjusting our altitude and angle of approach. "We're here," she said. "I've programmed the TR to hover a few feet off the ground on the ledge at the coordinates that you gave me."

I looked outside. Yup, we were surrounded by mountains and the ledge looked very familiar. "We're definitely here," I said. "You coming?"

"No," she replied. "I'm feeling a little nausea and this thing you're doing really has nothing to do with me."

She was right about that. "Okay, I'll be back as soon as I see Dr. Spann."

I opened the hatch and climbed down to the ground using the fuselage rungs. As I turned to walk toward the rock face that served as the elevator to the below-ground facility, I saw that it was already blurring, which meant that someone was coming to greet me. I hoped it was Dr. Spann.

Three Ummite soldiers stood in the alcove that had appeared in the solid stone." Hands up," the patrol leader ordered. I did as directed. All three were pointing plasma weapons at me, but I knew that because they were Ummites, they'd never shoot. Waam had taught me that all Ummites had taken the pledge to never harm a human being. I hung my hopes on the possibility that they hadn't changed their minds.

"I'm here to see Dr. Spann," I told them with hands reaching for the Moon.

"He's not expecting you," the squad leader replied. "He's available by appointment only."

"Call down and ask him if he'll see an emissary from Agent Mack Smith."

The squad leader spoke quietly into his collar microphone and then nodded. "Alright, you are to come with us. Are there any others in your vehicle?"

"Just the pilot and she's not feeling well. She'd rather stay topside."

The squad leader instructed one of his men to stand outside the TR and to arrest anyone who came out of it. Then he and the other soldier and I took the elevator to the migration facility deep within the mountain.

When the elevator door opened, I turned to the right and led the way to Dr. Spann's clone growth room within the facility. "Dr. Spann will see you in his office," the squad leader told me.

"First, I'd like to see Agent Arrow's clone," I replied.

I stopped when I heard a voice to my left. "Agent Arrow's clone has yet to leave the Petrie dish." It was Dr. Spann.

"It's good to see you again," I said offering my hand.

"Who are you?" Spann asked without shaking my hand.

"Dan Arrow, but I'm in a different container, Dr. Spann."

"Agent Arrow? When I saw you last, you left here as a Grey."

"Yes, and Mack Smith will be calling you in a few days to ask you if I can be migrated from that Grey into Nevada Ritter's clone container."

"Mr. Ritter is finishing a film. He is expecting to be migrated into that container as soon as the picture has gone to editing."

"Yeah, well…maybe." I figured out pretty quickly that Nevada Ritter's horse hadn't rolled over on him yet. *Should I call the poor bastard and tell him to take a few days off?* "Listen, Dr. Spann, Mack Smith sent me here with a lock of hair. Apparently, it's from a hybrid that I fathered. He'd like you to extract the alien DNA from the hair and infuse it into the clone of me that you're developing. You know, the one that you've begun to grow from my DNA that you extracted from the blood and tissue sample that Agent Casola gave you on that handkerchief."

"It *is* you, isn't it?" Dr. Spann exclaimed, grabbing my hand and shaking it. "You're a man of many surprises, Agent Arrow."

"Can you do it, Dr. Spann? Can you extract the alien DNA from a lock of hair and integrate it into the DNA that you're growing in that Petrie dish?"

"Yes, but there is always the risk that when it's mature, your clone won't look as same as you anticipate, Agent Arrow. You may take on some physical characteristics of the new DNA donor."

"Come on, Doc, I know better than that. You guys can manipulate all sorts of things. Just give me the intellectual capabilities of the donor and leave the rest as the original Dan Arrow."

"Such manipulation will cost an additional fifty thousand dollars. You know, it requires special equipment and many hours of additional staff time."

"Cost is not a problem, Dr. Spann," I lied. "Just send the bill to Mack Smith. He'll cover all the incidentals."

"Excellent. Do you have the lock of hair on you?"

I removed the lock of hair from my flight suit's breast pocket and handed it to Spann. He held it up to the ceiling light, inspecting the quality of the hair. "It appears to be clean," he said aloud to himself. Then he turned his attention to me again. "There is little time to waste. I'll need to extract the DNA soon since your clone has already grown to more than a thousand cells in size. Before long, you'll be able to see it with the naked eye."

"Don't let me keep you, Doc. If these gentlemen will escort me back to the surface, I'll be on my way."

Dr. Spann nodded to the squad leader. I thanked the doctor and told him that I'd see him again in a few days. He gave me a quizzical look. I told him, "When I see you next time, if I don't say anything to you about this lock of hair, it's not out of lack of interest. Mack and I want to keep this kind of secret if you know what I mean." Dr. Spann nodded. Then I turned to the squad leader and said, "Can you show me the way to the elevator? I think you left one of your own topside."

"Yes, I did," the squad leader replied. "It's this way…"

⁂

When I entered the TR, Nicki was standing with her back to the pilot's seat. She nodded to her left. "You have a visitor."

I looked in the direction of her nod. A young man in an NWO uniform was standing against the interior gravity control panel, pointing a small pistol in Nicki's direction. He was a PFC. His face was blotchy with acne, and the sweat stains in his armpits let me know that he was stressed. "Who sent you?" I asked. "Was it Anion Nargas?" The PFC didn't respond to my question. "How did you get past the Ummite guard outside?"

"He just appeared inside our TR, Dan," Nicki said. "I think he teleported here."

"Shut up," the young soldier ordered. He pointed his pistol at me. I could see that it was a pistol that I used to carry, a German-made Walther PPK, and I could see that its safety was still on. *This kid isn't too bright*, I thought.

"Listen, kid," I said, "you don't want to go pulling that trigger inside this TR unless you want its hydrogen condenser to reduce this whole mountain into a pile of pebbles." His irises grew in size, so I figured that I had him thinking. I kept lying about his situation. "You got me fair and square, but this lady is an innocent bystander, and I don't think Nargas would want you taking her out as collateral damage. How about we go outside this TR and talk this over?"

"There's nothing to talk over if your name is Arrow."

"My name is Dan. You heard the lady call me that a few moments ago." I pointed to the name tag on my flight suit. "Dan Silverman. See?" I turned both palms toward the ceiling. "Who is this Arrow guy, anyway? Do you mean Arrow Aronowitz? Are you looking for him?"

"I want the guy named Arrow who saw Commander Nargas and shot Corporal Greeley when they were taking the nukes from the storage facility. That's you, isn't it?"

"No, it's not me. I think you want Arrow Aronowitz. They teleported you to the wrong TR. Now let's step outside and see what we can do to rectify this situation." He raised his pistol and pointed it directly at my face. "Don't pull that damned trigger, kid. Not in here, anyway. The flame from the gunpowder will set off the hydrogen vapors, and we'll all be in Hell before you can count to one."

He lowered his pistol to waist level, but it was still pointed at me. I raised my arms and backed slowly out of the hatch and onto the wing section of the TR. He followed, keeping himself at a safe distance from me, but never letting me out of his line of sight.

Once he was outside on the wing of the TR, I saw Nicki quietly close the hatch. As she did, its lock clicked. The moment that he turned to see what had caused the sound, I leaped from the wing to the ground and rolled under the wing. Springing to my feet, I ran beneath the fuselage and under the other wing, where I squatted to the ground to see if he would follow me. Suddenly I saw movement on the far side of the TR. The PFC's head appeared, dangling from the far side of the TR. He was lying on the wing, aiming his PPK under the TR to shoot at me. I could see him try to squeeze the trigger, but the pistol didn't fire. That bought me a couple of seconds, as he had to bring his arm up and roll onto his back to fumble with the safety. Before he could roll back onto his stomach, I took off running toward the granite door of the Ummite elevator. I smacked on the rock with my open palm, but it was of no use. Everybody was downstairs, and I could see that I was on my own.

Two shots suddenly shattered the air: Bang! Bang! The bullets ricocheted off the granite several feet above my head. The PFC was too far away, and a PPK isn't necessarily accurate at distances over fifty feet. Especially if you're shooting it upside down.

His head disappeared again, which meant that he had rolled onto his back again, probably to climb down from the fuselage and hunt for me on the ground. However, before he could reach the ground, Nicki started the TR and lifted it a hundred feet into the air and over the canyon that abutted the ledge where I was huddled. Then, she rolled the TR upside down. The kid screamed as he fell toward the canyon floor, at least a quarter of a mile below.

I was safe for the time being. But just knowing that anybody could be teleported into the TR at any time of day or night left me feeling like a dead man walking. How would I ever be able to sleep? Obviously Nargas had figured out a way to locate me in time and space. It had to be some kind of alien technology, and I had no idea how it worked or how to shut it off.

∽∾∽

After I was back aboard, Nicki once again pointed the TR toward the empty space between the Earth and Jupiter. Before launching into space, she had to maneuver into the stratosphere to avoid a possible collision with our Moon. It was a piece of cake for the TR's onboard computer. This time our destination was a quick return to our recent location, Montano Antilia, Italy, but eighteen months in the future. To play it safe, Nicki set the time and place for a full twenty-four months. It was a prudent idea,

When we returned from outer space to Montano Atilia, several smaller tureens were situated where we had hovered twenty-four months before, so Nicki had to descend half the distance to the valley floor before she found a small horizontal outcropping where she could set down. Rather than trying to climb the mountain on foot, we decided to wait until the tureens left the ledge above, and then we would return to our intended parking spot. Nicki kept the TR cloaked.

While we waited, Nicki and I climbed down from the wing to stretch our legs. The morning air bore a slight chill, but it felt clean and invigorating as it entered my lungs. In the valley below, we could see smoke rising from several chimneys, and dozens of brown cows dotting the landscape of pastures. As we walked along the edge of the plateau, Nicki turned to me, her breath white in the crisp air. "How am I going to explain this pregnancy to my parents?"

"I'd wait before I did anything like that," I replied.

"They're going to need time to process this."

"If you tell them too soon, you may have a more difficult time explaining to them what happened to your baby, especially if those bastards come to pluck it out of you to put it in a growth tube."

"Is that really what happened to Mona?"

"Yeah, and she was as pissed as you are about being artificially inseminated against her will. But she was even more pissed about having the baby removed from her without her permission. She felt that the reptilians were treating her like nothing more than a lab rat."

"I know how she felt." Nicki stopped walking and kicked at a round stone that was buried in the mud. "It's a rabbit's skull," she said, as it rolled to the surface.

"Come on," I replied, "Let's go back to the TR before we accidentally find the skeleton of that kid that you slid off the wing this morning."

⌘

Nicki hadn't planned to come with me to see Dr. Spann but I talked her into it. The two tureens that had been parked on the narrow ledge a thousand feet above us had taken off for parts unknown, and Nicki had quickly lifted our TR to be sure that we were next in the queue. After she shut down the engines, I asked, "Wouldn't you like to see a growth tube in action? Your baby might be swimming in something similar in a month or two."

"Maybe if I'm lucky," she replied.

I texted Dr. Spann to let him know that we were topside and needed an escort into the facility.

Dan Arrow is deceased, he texted in reply.

Migrated, I replied. **Not dead. Not yet. I need my clone if you still have it.**

What about Nevada Ritter's container? he asked.

Mack Smith has it.

I want it.

You saw my current container when I brought you a hair sample about two years ago. It belongs to a black ops guy named Silverman. You can hold onto it for exchange...or ransom. Mack has lots of money.

It is you, isn't it, Agent Arrow. Nobody thinks the way you do. I'll be right up.

Two minutes later the granite wall at the base of the cliff beside our TR began to shimmer. Soon Dr. Spann and an Ummite guard walked from an alcove that had appeared where solid rock had been only moments before.

"Agent Arrow," Dr. Spann exclaimed when he saw me. "I believed the reports of your recent demise." We shook hands. "And who is your friend?"

"Commander Nicki Nardini," Nicki told him, extending her hand to shake his.

"Pleased to meet you, commander."

I decided to get right down to business. "How's my clone?" I asked.

"Very well, indeed, Agent Arrow. Let's go meet him."

Nicki and I followed Dr. Spann into the Ummite solid matter elevator. The Ummite guard backed into the elevator, keeping his plasma weapon pointed toward the ledge.

"Sorry for the extra caution, Agent Arrow," Dr. Spann said. "We recently had unsavory visitors from the NWO."

"The two tureens that were here about an hour ago?" I asked.

"So, you saw them?"

"Yes. What did they want?"

"You or your clone."

"Oh."

"But they didn't get either. I told them that you were last here two years ago and that your clone was destroyed after your untimely death."

"And they believed you?"

"Well, not at first, but after they searched the premises, they left convinced that I was telling them the truth."

"But you said that my clone is well."

"Yes, it is. We dressed it in women's clothes and they never gave it a second look."

"That's amazing in itself."

"Well, we haven't cut its hair yet, so all we had to do was to shave and dress it. The clone's hair is halfway down its back. A few strokes with a curling iron and we had a beautiful woman."

"Can I see it?"

"Certainly."

"And Commander Nardini would like to see the growth facility."

"It's on the way."

I knew enough about the growth facility to give my own guided tour, but I thought I'd let the doctor continue playing the role of welcoming host and tour guide.

When the elevator door opened, we turned right and Dr. Spann led us to the growth facility. It was a large, dimly lit room furnished with six aisles of growth tubes, each filled with translucent green fluid. Only three of the forty-eight tubes were empty. The remainder contained clones of every race and gender, all naked, and all resting in a form of suspended animation.

"Do you have any babies?" Nicki asked.

"Yes, over here," Dr. Spann replied, turning to his right and leading us to the row of tubes that was closest to a polished granite wall.

"How young are they when you put them in the tubes?" Nicki asked.

"We begin their growth in Petrie dishes like we did with Agent Arrow's, and then we move them to smaller devices that mimic the environment of a woman's womb. Once they reach three pounds, we move them to the growth tubes. If they're smaller than that, they tend to perish in vitro."

"Don't you mean in tubio?" I asked.

Dr. Spann didn't grace my comment with any kind of reaction. But Nicki rolled her eyes and gave me a look of disdain. At that moment she reminded me of Mona.

"So, I have a question for you, doctor." Nicki began. "If a woman were to discover herself pregnant, could you remove the fetus from her and finish the growth process in one of these tubes?"

"That would be highly unethical, commander." The doctor cleared his throat. "If the woman participated in its conception, shouldn't she continue participating in the fetus' development through the birth process?"

"If the woman was a rape victim, would that make a difference?"

"A human fetus requires almost two years to fully develop into adulthood in our tubes. To develop a baby to the birth stage, however, takes less than two months. It requires a major commitment on our part, and if something went wrong, we wouldn't want the negative publicity or the probable lawsuit. If the woman didn't want the fully developed baby, we would not want to be responsible for seeing to its adoption."

"What if the baby was a hybrid?"

The doctor raised his eyebrows. "Do you mean part human and part alien?"

"Yes. Would you consider it then?"

"How long have you been with child, commander?"

∽∾∽

Nicki's discussion with Dr. Spann had ended abruptly. He had guessed her secret and she had walked out of the room and into the hallway, partially out of embarrassment and partially out of frustration.

Dr. Spann changed his focus to my needs. "Come, Agent Arrow. Your clone has been waiting for you for a long time."

I followed him into the hallway, where Nicki was leaning against the wall, arms crossed and eyes looking at the floor. "Commander Nardini," Dr. Spann said, "I think I can help you if you really want to rid yourself of the demon that grows inside you."

"It's not a demon, doctor. It's a baby, and I'm just having difficulty accepting the fact that it's there at all. Maybe we can talk about options later when I've sorted out a few things."

"Will you join us to inspect Agent Arrow's clone? Perhaps you'd like to watch the migration process."

Nicki nodded and unfolded her arms. As Dr. Spann walked down the hallway, she was soon walking beside me.

Dr. Spann opened a swinging door and we entered the migration preparation room. On a gurney to our left was a man with bright orange hair. He was naked, except for baby blue boxer briefs. Wires which were attached at one end to his chest and arms led to several monitors which displayed numbers and graphs related to his vital signs. "A rodeo clown," Dr. Spann told us.

To the right, another gurney supported a woman with dark brown hair. She was wearing a navy-blue dress with white polka dots, reminiscent of one of Jackie Kennedy's famous dresses. "Is that my clone?" I asked, noting the heavy make-up on its face.

"Yes, that's you," Dr. Spann acknowledged. "You make a pretty woman, Agent Arrow, although your clone's heavy eyebrows gave us concern that it would be discovered. We redirected the observers' eyes to its fake breasts, size 38 D."

"Speaking as a woman, it was a nice touch," Nicki said. "Most of us have contemplated breast augmentation at one time or another because it's just about the only thing you men ever think about."

"Guilty as charged," I smiled.

"Are you hoping to be migrated into your clone today, Agent Arrow?" Dr. Spann asked.

"That was my intent, doc."

"We'll need an hour to prep the clone. You know, a haircut, manicure, and a full medical exam. I don't anticipate any problems, but we should perform our due diligence."

"Sure. Nicki and I will get something to eat and then we'll meet you in the waiting room."

"You should eat nothing, Agent Arrow. You know that's the protocol."

"I was hoping things had changed in the past two years," I replied.

๏ยด

So, I sat in the cafeteria with Nicki while she stuffed herself with a hot dog, french fries, and a chocolate milk shake. I was hungry and watching her eat wasn't easy for me. Everything she shoved in her mouth was a favorite of mine, except I'd pass on the chocolate shake in favor of a cold beer. Especially with a hot dog.

When she finished, we walked into the family waiting area, where spouses and sometimes children eagerly wait for their loved ones to emerge from the migration room in a new container. Today, we were the only people there. Nicki passed the time leafing through a couple of Hollywood gossip magazines. After ten minutes, she threw three magazines onto the coffee table in front of her. "These are such shit," she said.

"Yeah, I don't know why people read them, except they

like to see a little dirt thrown at the movie stars.”

“Most of the people they write about aren’t even stars, Dan. Hell, I’ve never heard of half of them. They’re mostly wannabes who believe that any kind of publicity is good.”

I was going to say something about most of them being minor actors in low-budget movies and unpopular television shows, but a nurse interrupted our conversation. “Agent Arrow?”

“Yes, that would be me.”

“Your container is all prepped and the doctor is ready for you.”

“It’s okay if my pilot comes to observe, isn’t it?”

“The policy is that spouses and other family members must remain here, but if you two aren’t related or in a pre-marital relationship, then I guess Dr. Spann won’t mind.”

“Come on, sweetheart,” I said to Nicki. The nurse gave me an odd look.

“He’s kidding,” Nicki told her.

“Okay, yeah,” the nurse replied. She offered to help me to my feet, but I declined. I’m not that old yet, and she wasn’t dressed in a Boy Scout uniform.

I turned to Nicki as we walked toward the door to the migration facility. “Did you know that they now let girls into the Boy Scouts?”

“What?” she asked.

“Never mind,” I said. “It isn’t important, anyway.”

When we entered the migration facility, Dr. Spann greeted us. He was dressed in a surgical gown, but the flowered collar of a Hawaiian shirt protruded from above the gown around his neck. “Agent Arrow, before we do this, I think you should know that I followed your advice.”

“My advice?”

“Yes. I contacted Agent Smith to tell him that I was in possession of the Silverman clone. He asked me where I got it. I lied because you're supposed to be dead. He wanted it back—something about Silverman needing it and that it was the property of the United States government. I told him that I would exchange it evenly for the Nevada Ritter clone if he still had it. He said that it was in no condition to travel, but he'd trade it for another of equal value. I opted for one of Carrie Underwood's clones. He said that we had a deal, but then I told him that I also wanted an additional three hundred thousand dollars to cover the maintenance costs of the Dan Arrow clone that I've been storing. He wasn't happy."

"Did you expect him to be?"

"No, I suppose not, but he finally agreed to it. The exchange will take place tomorrow, here in Italy. He's bringing Silverman with him, but he told me to destroy the Arrow clone."

"Nice, Mack," I replied, holding my middle finger up in the air in a futile gesture. I huffed and then said, "I guess we'd better get me out of this container and into my own, so you can ready this one for Silverman. Besides, I don't want Mack to see me here."

"Nonnie has been preparing your clone. We should have you out of the old and into the new in very short order." I remembered that Nonnie was Dr. Spann's Ummite assistant. He had operated the equipment when I was migrated into Nevada Ritter' s clone not so long ago, at least in my timeline. By now, equipment operation must have seemed like old hat to him. That was comforting.

"Please undress. Agent Arrow," Dr. Spann told me.

"Should I excuse myself?" Nicki asked.

"No, commander," Dr. Spann said. "He'll keep his skivvies on, won't you, Agent Arrow?"

"You can count on it," I replied, looking at Nicki. "You can inspect the goods when I'm no longer in them."

Nicki gave me another one of those looks that she must have borrowed from Mona. I don't know why the women in my life can't just roll with the humor.

When I was undressed, Nonnie helped me align my container on the padded oak migration table. He attached a series of those sticky electrodes that the technicians use when they give you an EKG, and then he clipped colored wires onto each electrode. While Dr. Spann adjusted buttons on the main control panel, Nonnie placed a metal ring around my head. I imagined that I looked a little like a king, with the exception that my crown was full of wires instead of jewels. Then he rolled the paddles over to the table and told Dr. Spann, "Ready here, doctor."

"Begin their rotation, Nonnie."

Nonnie gave the paddles a gentle spin and they seemed to accelerate on their own, spinning in a counterclockwise direction around my head. I closed my eyes and felt the breeze of the paddles as they spun, but I heard nothing.

Soon, I felt a wave of vertigo and then the sensation of climbing to the top of the first drop of a rollercoaster. Then, suddenly the race was on. I felt the rush of free-falling combined with several twists and turns. Then, long before I expected it, I was slammed to a stop in thick pads of memory foam. This was a new sensation. The ride seemed very short and I had experienced none of the ripping and scratching that I had felt just a week ago when I was migrated into Silverman's container at Nellis. Everything was dark, but I was fully aware of my surroundings. I felt my new container arch one time and then a light began to appear in the distance.

Soon, my vision became clear again. Nicki was standing near Silverman's body, looking down at it. "It just went limp, doctor," she said.

"Yes, commander. He's no longer occupying that

container. Go look at his clone."

Nicki's attention turned to me. As she walked toward me, she said, "Oh, the clone is breathing. Its eyes are open."

"No shit," I said groggily. "Dan Arrow is back in familiar surroundings."

"Welcome back, Agent Arrow," Dr. Spann said. "You should rest for a few minutes before beginning normal activity."

The door to the migration facility opened and in walked two greys. Dr. Spann conferred with them and then told me, "Tryl and Baaz have informed me that Mack Smith is departing Andrews Air Base and should be here in approximately three hours."

"Good, we'll be out of here by the time he arrives," I replied.

"How do you feel, Dan?" Nicki asked me. "It's going to be weird having a new person aboard the TR."

"I'm the same old me. It's just a new container."

"Still, you look entirely different, and your voice is definitely someone else's."

"You'll get used to it," I replied, "and when we're back in the TR, I'll tell you all about the ride I just experienced. This was my fourth trip through the migration wires, and each one was unique."

Nonnie helped me rise to a sitting position so he could remove the electrodes from my skin. "Time to get dressed, Agent Arrow. Get yourself something to eat and drink before you leave the facility."

"Good idea. You got any beer?"

Chapter 26

We were low on fuel, but Nicki estimated that we had enough to find our way back to Nellis and Mack on our timeline. However, she told me that we'd be limping in. I was okay with that, as long as we actually found our way back. Mona and Stella would be coming home from Mona's mom's in a few days, and I intended to be there to greet them. Alive.

In addition to that, I had some disturbing news to convey to Mack about this guy named Anion Nargas and the Earth changes that he would be inflicting on humanity in a few years. He had to be stopped, but I wasn't sure where to find him or how to dispatch him without its being outright murder. Maybe Mack could send a couple of black ops assassins to do the deed. I mean, that's their job and it doesn't seem to bother a black op's conscience, as long as the target is considered a threat to our national security.

Nicki set the proper coordinates and we lifted into space at "warp speed," as they used to say in Star Trek. We traveled for almost fifteen minutes. Then, when I felt my stomach pushing outward, I knew that we were slowing down. Soon Nicki announced, "We're here, Dan. We're a brief trip east of Nellis on our timeline, and I can glide us down if necessary."

"Glide?"

"Yeah, our mercury supply is basically expended. I'm going to glide us toward Nellis and use the few remaining drops to set us down on the runway."

I hadn't realized how desperate our situation was. But I was glad to be back in our timeline and approaching our goal. Nicki radioed Nellis and told them that we'd be dropping in. It sounded like a friendly visit, but I think she really meant that we might be dropping out of the sky like a piece of space junk. The guy in the conning tower told her that he'd be scrambling the emergency vehicles. Then he asked, "Commander, you guys just left ninety minutes ago. How could you already be out of fuel?"

Obviously, he didn't know that our mission involved time travel, and Nicki couldn't tell him that we'd been gone for more than a week, so she replied, "Don't know. Maybe a leak in the fuel tanks." Then Nicki turned to me, "Mack's gonna be worried about us."

"Why's that?"

"He was expecting us back a few minutes after we launched. You heard the guy in the conning tower. We're over an hour late."

As we descended toward the runway at Nellis, I could see the flashing red lights of the emergency vehicles following our trajectory toward the TR hangar. Something inside my head told me that the emergency vehicles wouldn't be necessary—that Nicki would bring us in safely. Call it a reassuring premonition. When we were a hundred feet from the hangar doorway, Nicki brought the TR to the tarmac. I felt the struts open and then suddenly the engine died, and we fell the last three feet, dropping with a "Clunk."

"Damn close, wasn't it, Dan?" Nicki exclaimed.

Even though I had known that we weren't in peril, I told her, "Another second and we'd both have had our spleens in our throats."

Within a few moments, we were surrounded by the emergency vehicles, their sirens blaring and lights sweeping in circles. Nicki opened the hatch, walked onto the wing, and signaled that we were okay. One by one the sirens stopped their infernal blaring, but the emergency lights continued to illuminate the area. I joined Nicki on the wing. Coming toward us at breakneck speed was a black Hummer with its emergency flashers working overtime. It had to be Mack.

As the Hummer screeched to a halt beside our TR, its front passenger door opened and Mack hopped out. "You made it back," he shouted up to us. Nicki waved, and I followed her down the fuselage ladder and onto the tarmac.

"You made it back," Mack repeated as he grabbed our hands and shook them.

"It looks like we did," I replied. "We had our doubts for a few seconds, but our TR was piloted by the best in the world. I think she had our fuel measured down to the last drop."

Mack stared at me briefly and tilted his head as if he wanted to ask me a question. But instead of asking, he turned and escorted us to his Hummer, where Nicki and I slid into the back seats and he climbed into the front passenger's seat. The moment his door clicked shut, the driver put the hammer down and we were whisked back to the debriefing center, a steel Quonset hut situated by itself on a couple of acres of land and surrounded by antennas and television disks.

"What's with all the technology?" I asked as we pulled to a quick stop.

"Most of that stuff is here to scramble signals and eliminate any eavesdropping," Mack replied matter-of-factly. "Let's talk inside."

I got the message and kept my yap shut while we entered the building. The Quonset hut was divided into several small meeting rooms surrounding a center room that was outfitted with a coffee maker and a frost-free refrigerator. Mack led us to a small room that opened into the center room from the rear. Inside was a standard military-issue gray table with four chairs. Lighting came from two fluorescent units which were hanging above us. "Lovely décor," I said as I sat down across from Mack. Nicki sat adjacent to him, on his left.

Mack got right down to business. "So, what did you learn?"

"Where do you want us to start?" I asked.

"Let's begin with the fact that you're in your own clone. Where's Silverman's clone?"

"It's in Italy. Dr. Spann is holding it for ransom. He wants Nevada Ritter's clone and some additional money. He'll be contacting you about it in about eighteen months."

"Silverman will need it before then."

"I left it eighteen months in the future, Mack. Maybe somebody can go get it for you."

"I'll have to put Ritter's clone on ice and see if we can do anything to salvage it. Our doctors don't have the technology that the Ummites have. I'm not sure we can save it."

"Spann's got a thing for Carrie Underwood. Maybe he'll cut a deal with you for one of hers."

Mack shook his head and blew out a puff of frustration. I hoped he wasn't mad at me. "So, what about the Black Knight? What's its purpose?"

"We don't really know, but we don't think it's hostile," Nicki told him. "When we approached it, it took out our instrumentation. The next thing we knew, we woke up over southern California in the 1940s. Neither of us was harmed. I think it's observing all of us, you know, like what we humans are doing to the Earth. Maybe how our technology is affecting the climate and stuff like that."

I nodded. I didn't want Mack to know that we were the cause of the famous Battle of Los Angeles.

"What about the pandemic? Will Anion Nargas successfully implement it?"

"Not exactly," I replied. "He does far worse." Mack tilted his head, waiting for me to tell him, so I did. "You know that beach house that you own in Maine?"

Mack nodded.

"Sell it. Nargas is going to set off a series of nuclear devices and the Earth is going to flip on its side. The oceans will flood all of the coastal cities of any importance, killing several billion people around the globe. When it's all over, you won't recognize the continents that you know today. Everything's going to be different."

"That's unbelievable."

"We've got a ninety-minute video for you to watch," Nicki added. "We shot it from the stratosphere. The entire Earth is flipped on its side and in many places, the only things left of familiar coastlines are the mountain ranges that are inland from them. You should post it on YouTube to warn the world."

"There's a good side to it, Mack," I added.

"What's that?"

"Most of the reptilians who are living underground will drown."

"Good. Those bastards need to die."

"It gets better. The Earth's core temperature will drop a few degrees, cooling everything down. The surviving reptilians won't be able to tolerate the cold, and they'll evacuate for warmer planets, like Draco and Mercury."

"What about the NWO?"

"Anion Nargas will become its leader. They will make him president of the NWO. He'll move their headquarters to Asgardia, where he'll set up the global government and a computer system that will become God."

"You're shitting me. Asgardia is a bunch of hooey."

"I wish we were, but Dan's telling you the truth," Nicki replied. "That's what we learned."

"When does all this happen?"

"We didn't get an exact date" Nicki replied, "but Nargas will do the deed somewhere between fifteen and twenty-five years from now."

"We've got to take him out," Mack said.

I nodded in agreement, but Nicki changed the subject. "Where's the head?"

"To the right of the coffee station," Mack told her, pointing to a white door.

"Excuse me, gentlemen."

Nicki left the room to do her thing, either to pee or to puke. It didn't make a difference to me. When the door closed, I leaned forward. "Mack, you need to know something. I was awake when we were abducted by the Black Knight."

"Do you mean when it shut down your controls?"

"No." I was tongue-tied trying to explain. "I mean, 'yes,' it shut down our controls, but we were removed—you know, abducted—from our TR, and were taken into the Black Knight. I was fully conscious. They wanted me to see what they were doing, to be a witness when the Praying Mantis operated on Nicki."

"Praying Mantis? Operated? Why?"

"They called him 'Master Enki.' Does that mean anything to you?"

"Never heard of him. Who called him that?"

"His helpers. The Praying Mantis seemed to be the head guy on the Black Knight. He oversaw everything that went on. His helpers removed a small cancer from Nicki's left breast, and then they impregnated her. She's carrying a hybrid child."

"She didn't say anything about it."

"I don't think she wants to talk about it. It's not like she ever planned to be a mother. And she doesn't know everything that I know about what they did."

"So, then she knows she's pregnant?"

"She was nauseous for days. Then she finally figured it out."

"How'd she do that? One of those over-the-counter pregnancy tests?"

"No. Stella told her."

"Stella? Was Stella there?"

"We saw Stella fifty years in the future. She and Mona were living in a coastal town in Colorado. Stella held Nicki's hands and told her that she had been impregnated just like Mona had been."

"Coastal town? In Colorado?"

"Everything's gonna change, Mack."

"What about me?"

"You're gonna make it to retirement if that's what you mean. You'll be living up near Lake Placid when we contact you."

"How's my health?"

"We didn't ask, but you'll still be driving a car in fifteen years."

"I guess that's some comfort."

ᏅᎦᏅ

After our debriefing and after I enjoyed a shower and a meal, Mack sent an NCO to my room to ask me to meet him in the C.O.'s office. The NCO conveyed a tone of urgency about it, so I hurried over. I had no idea where Nicki was.

"What's up Mack? Did Dr. Spann contact you already?"

"Nothing so minor, Dan. We need to attend to something more immediate. Our guys have identified an NWO weapons cache, a fully loaded combat arsenal. Worst of all, it includes a bunch of nukes."

"Don't you mean 'best of all?' Isn't it better we take them out than they use them on us?"

"That's exactly what we're gonna do. We'll be leaving in forty minutes, a complement of four squads, full combat gear."

"Do I have time to call Mona?"

"Make it a quickie."

I stepped outside the building and punched Mona's number into my cell phone. "How's your mom?" I asked when she answered. God, it was good to hear her youthful voice.

"She seems to be getting better, Danny. I think Wendy's and my being here has brightened her perspective a little. She told us an interesting story that I want to share with you, but not over the phone."

"What's it about?"

"Wendy and me, but don't ask me any more questions. I don't want to discuss it over the phone. But I'll give you a clue…it's about gnomes."

"Okay, I can wait, especially if it's about some stupid garden statue malarkey. Listen, babe, the reason I called is to let you know that Mack is sending me on a small assignment. It shouldn't take too long, maybe a day or two. I should be back in the Villaggio in a couple of days."

"Danny Arrow, you never tell a girl that you're calling her for any reason other than needing to hear her voice. Somebody has to give you lessons on keeping your girl wrapped around your little finger." Mona paused for a second and then changed the tone of her voice when I didn't reply. "So, what strange place is Mack sending you this time?"

"He was very hush-hush about the location, but it's somewhere in the USA. We're gonna recover some weapons and secure a facility. That's all I know. I'm going with a couple of squads of Green Berets."

"Well, watch your backside. There's always more to it than Mack ever lets on. But I guess you already know that."

It was interesting that Mona told me to watch my back. When I spoke to her fifteen years in the future, hadn't Mona told me that I was shot three times in the back of the head and that my funeral had been closed casket? Had Mona seen something in her remote viewing? I needed to think about this, but for the moment I refocused on family. "How's Stella?"

"She's doing wonderfully, Danny. She and Wendy get along like long-lost friends, and she's taken to Ma, too. She keeps saying that Ma isn't sick anymore. She's just so cute."

"Well, maybe your mom *will* get better, sweetheart. Maybe this was just a temporary setback and the doctors are wrong about everything."

"I pray you're right, Danny, but the doctors have given up, and you know what that usually means."

"Yeah, I know." I didn't know what else to say. I've never been too good at these kinds of conversations. Besides, I knew that her mom was going to pull through. "Listen, I gotta go. Mack needs to brief me about the target, and I still need to get outfitted for the mission. Kiss Stella for me and ask her to give you a big kiss from me."

"I will. Bye, honey. And you tell Mack that I expect him to send you home safe and sound and all in one piece—or I'll kick his ass."

"Yeah, I will. He'll appreciate the sentiment."

Just like that Mona hung up. God, I missed her. I hoped I would get to see her again, not as an old woman like she was fifty years from now, but as the vivacious woman she was in today's timeline.

Chapter 27

There was a knock at Mona's door. Normally, Stella would have answered it, but she was with her husband Liam, who had just returned from a two-week flight into the future. She had kissed him goodbye this morning, and he had unexpectedly returned at noon, unshaven and tired from his trip.

When Mona opened the door, she saw a familiar face, although she couldn't remember where she had seen the woman before. "Mrs. Molandowski?" the woman asked.

"Arrow," Mona replied. "My last name is Arrow."

"I don't know if you remember me, Mrs. Arrow. I'm the guy who was abducted by reptilians and returned to Earth a few days later in the body of a little girl. I visited you about thirty years ago to warn you about Anion Nargas and his evil plans."

"Yes, I remember you now," Mona replied. "Weren't you supposed to get a new container from the Richmond Migration Center? I remember arranging that for you."

"Yes, thank you. I was given a male container that lasted almost ten years before it contracted an incurable form of bone cancer. I was fortunate that the Center had retained this female container, and I was able to reoccupy it. I don't have the funds to obtain a new male container, but at this point, I don't think I'd even want it."

"And you were right about Nargas, weren't you," Mona offered.

"Yes, I wish that your husband had been alive and had been able to stop Nargas. I tried several other individuals, but none were able to get the job done. You can see what a mess Nargas has made of the Earth."

"So, what is the nature of your business today, Miss…"

"Gates, Mrs. Arrow. Maxwell Gates, although I now go by Maxine for obvious reasons. But people still call me Max or Maxie."

"Okay, Maxie, so what's your business today?"

"I have a reptilian with me that I'd like you to meet. He's out in my van."

Mona looked over Gates's shoulder. In her driveway was a nondescript white van that could have been rented at any airport.

"Is he dangerous?"

"No, not now. I found him hiding in a cave beneath the Beaver Run Super Chair at Breckenridge. He was weak from malnourishment, but I was able to nurse him back from near death."

"You're breaking the law. You were supposed to turn him over to the NWO. They've been exterminating the last few remaining lizards."

"I'm aware of that, but I just couldn't do it. In the process of nursing him back to health, I discovered something that I don't think anyone else knows, Mrs. Arrow. And it's important."

"What's that?"

"The lizards are like parrots."

"How so?"

"They can be rebooted."

"What do you mean?"

"Parrots are loyal creatures, Mrs. Arrow. Think of Long John Silver in the Treasure Island story, the pirate with the parrot on his shoulder. The parrot warned him if anyone was sneaking up from behind, and the parrot also savagely bit anyone who got too close. Parrots are one-man birds. But, if their owner dies, who are parrots loyal to, Mrs. Arrow?"

Mona shook her head. She had no idea.

"Parrots can live for more than fifty years, Mrs. Arrow. They often outlive their owners. What you have to do in that situation is to reboot the parrot, like you would a computer. You do that by putting a hood over the parrot's head for four days. You don't feed it and you prohibit it from hearing noise of any kind. After four days, its little brain is totally rebooted. Then, when you remove its hood, it bonds to the first person it sees who feeds it and speaks gently to it."

"So, you're saying you can do that with a lizard?" Mona asked.

"Yes. Wally is a prime example of a rebooted reptilian. You have to come see."

"You're really asking me to trust that your lizard won't try to kill me?"

"He's perfectly harmless, Mrs. Arrow. He's been my companion for more than four months now and I trust him with my life." Maxie took Mona's elbow and tugged slightly. "Please, come out to my van and meet him."

After years of FBI training, Mona wasn't about to get into a van with a virtual stranger, especially one who claimed to have a pet reptilian waiting inside. She excused herself for a minute, went to her bedroom, and slid her Glock .45 into the belt in the small of her back. When she returned, Maxie escorted her to a road-weary Tesla commercial van. Through the van's oxidized white paint, she could see the famous golden tiara and the word "Meritage," which indicated it once had been part of the defunct Winery distribution fleet owned by a past president. "This truck has to qualify for antique license plates," she said to Gates.

"I found it under a tarp in an abandoned garage," Gates replied. "Its owner perished in the deluge. It has only a hundred and twenty-five thousand miles on it, which for a Tesla means that it has at least a hundred thousand miles of life left in it."

"How do you charge it?"

"The solar panels on top charge it during the day, but I have a small charging unit that I can use at night or on particularly dreary days."

Mona nodded. "So, where's your lizard?"

Gates opened the rear doors of the van. Mona stepped back at the sight of the reptilian who was seated on an old convertible sofa with missing legs. "Mrs. Arrow, let me introduce you to my friend, Chuckwalla. I call him 'Wally' for short."

Mona looked into the reptilian's eyes. His irises were black and round, unlike the Commissar's, which had black slits from top to bottom. She sensed no hostility or evil in his gaze.

"Nice to meet you, Ma'am," Mona heard Wally tell her telepathically. Mona nodded. She thought Wally's greeting was almost comical.

"Wally's greatest value is his ability to serve as an interpreter," Gates said. "You never know what a lizard is saying when he's speaking reptilian. Wally is ready to help us in any way that he can. He's grateful for having been saved from starvation."

"I have no use for an interpreter at the moment, Maxie. But can I call you if the need arises?"

"Mrs. Arrow, surely you have need of a reptilian who can help you and your friends to eliminate Anion Nargas. He'd be perfect for the job."

Mona gave Gates a look of suspicion. "Maxie, I have no intention of assassinating Anion Nargas, and anyone who told you something like that was lying."

"No offense intended, Mrs. Arrow. It's common knowledge that Nargas had your first husband assassinated, what with how he destroyed the hollow moon and killed Nargas' father. I just thought that you might find Wally useful if you wanted to equal the score."

"If I were a younger woman, I might think that way, but a lot of water has passed under the bridge since my husband's untimely death. I'm in my eighties and I plan to spend my last few days enjoying my children and grandchildren." Mona turned to walk back into her home.

Gates held out a small piece of paper onto which he had written something. "Mrs. Arrow, here's my cell phone number. If you change your mind, just give me a call."

Mona took the piece of paper. "You'd better keep your lizard out of sight. If the NWO learns that you have him, you'll both be terminated." Gates nodded, shut the doors to his van, and drove away.

☙❧

After dinner that evening, Mona walked down the narrow path that wound from her back yard to the beach below, her eighty-year-old frame carefully negotiating the dusty, loose-packed surface of clay and pebbles. As she descended, she heard the calls of a dozen seagulls that were fighting over dining priority on a large chunk of something that had washed ashore. *Probably a dead sea lion,* she thought. *Maybe partially eaten by an orca.*

But when she approached the corpse, she realized that it was human. Its head had been twisted entirely around, perhaps more than three hundred and sixty degrees. She picked up a stick and swung it at the gulls, who scolded her loudly as they departed to wait until she had finished with their meal. Then she used the stick to twist the cadaver's head so she could see its face. "Maxie Gates," she exclaimed aloud as the head flopped toward her. Its eye sockets had already been plucked clean by the birds. "You poor fuck," she said shaking her head, "I told you never to trust a lizard."

Mona hurried back up the pathway to her house in order to notify the authorities. She was breathless as she reached the top. She continued across the dark green grass as quickly as she could to the back door which opened into her kitchen. Once inside, she sensed that something wasn't right. She quietly opened a small drawer beside her refrigerator and removed a black Walther PPK .25ACP, the pistol that her Danny had carried on this ankle when he first descended into the deep underground military base at Dulce, New Mexico.

As she turned to enter her dining room, Mona heard drawers being opened and closed in her living room. Small objects were hitting the carpeted floor. Mona peered left as she stepped quietly into the dining room. A reptilian was ransacking her home. It was Maxie's Wally.

"What the fuck did you do to Maxie?"

Wally turned toward her, throwing a handful of pencils and ballpoint pens at her face. Mona stepped aside as they flew by her. She raised her pistol. "Did you kill Maxie?"

The reptilian's eyes met hers. *"You stupid bitch. Did you really think that Gates had trained me? She was expendable, especially once I found you."*

Mona pulled the trigger on her PPK. Nothing happened. She realized that she had forgotten to pull back the slide to chamber a round. It was a rookie mistake, one that she would never have made back when she and Danny were younger and fully engaged in hunting reptilians. As she grabbed the slide to pull it back, she felt a hammer hit her neck. *No, it wasn't a hammer*, she realized as her knees buckled, and her face found the floor. *I forgot to clear the dining room. I didn't look to the right.* Mona realized that she had been wounded by something sharp that had entered her neck in a downwards motion, severing arteries and piercing her lung. She struggled to remain conscious, but it was a battle she could not win.

As darkness consumed her, Mona felt a boot kick her ribs twice, rocking her body like a piece of jellied meat. Then she heard a man's voice say, "Mission accomplished, corporal. Let's go."

Chapter 28

At eleven in the morning, Mack and I walked into the briefing theater, where two officers were speaking to a group of soldiers. "Four fireteams will assault the building from its sides, two fireteams per side. Fireteams Able, Charlie, and Delta will enter South, East, and West, in that order. We expect the weakest resistance will occur on the north side, where there are two entrances. Fireteam Bravo will enter the door on the right. The FBI has asked to be included in this mission. Their team will enter the door on the left." The officer looked at Mack. "Agent Smith, how many men will comprise the FBI's team?"

"Just one," Mack replied, pointing at me. "Agent Arrow is well experienced with reptilian resistance and firepower."

"That's highly irregular, Agent Smith. Your man will need at least one backup."

"I'll volunteer for that assignment," said a soldier near the front of the group.

"Okay, Molandowski. If your squad leader agrees, then it's a go."

"Let him help the FBI," the squad leader replied. "Molandowski is just standing in for Eggleston anyway."

"Okay, Molandowski, you're now entering with the FBI."

Molandowski turned and saluted me with his pointer finger.

So that's the sonofabitch who plans to snuff me out and move in with Mona, I thought. My mind sent me a picture of him making love to her. When Molandowski turned back toward the officer who was addressing us, I glared at him. I wanted to slam a red-hot iron through his eyeball or peel him alive and nail his skin to a barn door.

Mack elbowed me twice. "Dan," he whispered.

"Yeah?" I asked.

"The colonel just asked you a question."

I looked away from Molandowski and toward the front of the room. "Excuse me, Colonel?"

"I asked if you have any words of advice for the men?"

"Just that if we run into any lizards when they touch their breastplates, they're shooting at whatever they're looking at. Their weapons shoot plasma that exits from their helmets. It's white-hot, like the sun, and it'll cut you down in less than a tenth of a second. The noise will be incredibly different from our weapons. It's a loud whine, like something you'd hear in a video game."

"Are you shitting us?" asked one soldier. "If I see a lizard wearing a helmet, I'm going to stomp on the sonofabitch and kick it out the door." The others laughed.

"You'll be lucky if he's only seven feet tall and four hundred pounds," I replied. "They grow larger." The men grew silent. "And, 'no,' I'm not shitting you. If you've never seen one before, they're as strong as ten men and they smell like snakes." I looked at the colonel. "Haven't your men been in combat with NWO forces before?"

"Listen to Agent Arrow, men. He's had experiences that none of us have enjoyed. I've never seen a reptilian soldier either. If he says there are seven-foot-tall lizards that shoot plasma from their helmets, as crazy as it sounds, you ought to believe him." He turned to me. "Is there anything else we ought to know?"

"Yeah. The lizards are working with the NWO and plan to take over the Earth. No lizard is a good lizard, and no lizard gives a shit about a human, except as a side dish at the dinner table. If you see a lizard, put a bullet in him before he slices you like a pizza."

"Thank you, Agent Arrow."

After the colonel finished the last details of his briefing, we all followed him to four choppers that were waiting outside to fly us from Nellis to our target, ninety minutes away. We were going to drop in unannounced and assume control of the facility in less than five minutes, if everything went according to plan.

By habit, I ducked as I walked under the chopper's spinning rotors and climbed in behind the members of Fireteam Bravo. Molandowski climbed in after me. Before the chopper lifted off the ground, he offered me his hand. "It's great to meet you, Arrow. I've heard a lot about you," he shouted above the rotors' noise.

"Yeah, from who?"

"Your wife, Mona. I've been her remote viewing coach for the past year. She's really good at it."

"If you're stationed at the Villaggio, what are you doing here at Nellis?"

"Special opportunity to see some combat. My CO offered it to me and I jumped at it. Besides, I'm a desk jockey and I need a few campaign ribbons to dress up my uniform."

As I smiled and gave him the thumb-up sign, the chopper's rotors began their deafening beat. Within a few seconds we were airborne, heading southeast, toward Phoenix.

Our choppers pushed on for a full ninety minutes. I couldn't talk with Molandowski because of the noise of the rotors, which was probably a good thing because all I wanted to tell him was to keep his slimy hands off my wife. Soon, however, the squad leader for Fireteam Bravo pointed out the window at our target. It was a warehouse, supposedly an abandoned Toys- R-Us facility, with several military-like vehicles parked outside its main entrance.

Our chopper veered to the left, circling the warehouse. On command, our chopper descended to the ground at the same moment as the other choppers. Fireteam Bravo exited first. Molandowski and I followed, going to the door on the left as instructed during the briefing.

When we reached the door, we hugged the cinderblock exterior with our backs. I pulled my SIG P220 from my holster. "You going in first?" I shouted at Molandowski.

"Age before beauty," he shouted back.

So that's how he plans to position himself to put a bullet in my head.

I reached for the nickel-plated doorknob. It was unlocked. That surprised me. I pushed on the door with my shoulder. It opened into a short corridor with another door to open, about ten feet away. As I approached the second door, something inside my head told me to look up. In the reflection in its glass window, I saw Molandowski raise his pistol toward my head. Instantly, I dropped onto my back, pointed my forty-five at Molandowski, and fired. The bullet completely missed his torso, but as luck would have it, it struck his pistol, sending it spinning backward onto the floor. Molandowski grabbed his right hand with his left and squealed in pain. I pulled the trigger again, but nothing happened. *My goddam gun is jammed,* I realized.

I'm not waiting around for him to pull another weapon, I thought. I jumped to my feet, opened the inner door, and slammed it behind me. There was no way to lock the door, so I weaved through the piles of clothing and stacks of equipment that littered the floor inside. As I neared another doorway on the far side of the room, I heard the door behind me open. A shot rang out, and its bullet hit the concrete wall a few feet behind me. I could hear shooting and the whine of plasma weapons in the next room, but with Molandowski in hot pursuit, I had no choice except to take my chances on the other side. I opened the steel door and closed it behind me. Then I dropped to the floor so I could survey the fighting.

Two lizards and an NWO guardsman were battling it out with the four soldiers of Fireteam Bravo. One reptilian saw me come through the door and sent a volley of plasma in my direction. It hit the wall above my head and splattered hot shit all over the place. I rolled onto my back and pulled on the slide to try to unjam my pistol. I had to release the clip before the spent casing fell free. I rammed the clip home, chambered a round, rose to my knees, and fired. One lizard grabbed his right arm and squealed. Then, someone from the Bravo fireteam took him out with a round to the forehead. Next to go was the NWO guardsman, knocked backward into Hell by a hand-held anti-personnel rocket. *One lizard left.*

Suddenly I was knocked onto my side by a blow to my ribs from something hard. It was Molandowski, swinging a pipe in his left hand. He pulled back, swinging again, missing me. Another swing smashed into my left arm at the shoulder and bounced against my cheek. Suddenly, I was seeing stars and hearing chimes. I pointed my pistol at Molandowski's large frame and squeezed the trigger. It was jammed again. *Goddamn shitty ammo!* Molandowski pulled the pipe back to strike me again, but before he began his downswing his ear exploded, a mist of blood filling the air beside him. His body leaned to the left and hung in the air for a moment before collapsing to the floor.

A soldier in an unfamiliar khaki uniform came through the door, a futuristic weapon still smoking in his hand. "Are you okay?" he asked.

"Yeah, thanks," I managed to say as my ears continued ringing.

He took my hand and lifted me to my feet. "This room is all secure now," he told me. "Let's see if we can collect those nukes."

I checked the room. Fireteam Bravo was nowhere to be seen, but the bodies of the two reptilians and the NWO guardsman lay heaped on the floor. "Who are you?"

"The name's Liam Olsen. I believe you know my wife."

"Me?"

He pointed at Molandowski's body. "Yeah, you were married to her mother until that sonofabitch killed you today."

It all came back to me. "You're Stella's husband, aren't you? Mona told me you've been looking for me for a while."

"Yeah, like fifteen years. This is the second time that I've tried here and now. I arrived ten seconds too late the last time, but I dispatched this bastard Molandowski that time, too."

"Jesus, you're making a mess out of a few futures, aren't you?"

"Listen, Dad, we're wasting time. We've gotta see if we can eliminate Nargas before he gets away with those nukes."

It was strange hearing a fully grown stranger calling me "Dad," even if he meant it as father-in-law. We were going to have to sort out the details later. Liam was right about getting our asses in gear. "Since you've been here before," I replied, "how about leading the way."

"Let's go," he said.

We exited the room and hurried down a hallway to a door identified by a sign that read RADIOACTIVE MATERIALS. DO NOT ENTER. *Great,* I thought. *All I really need to make my day is a dose of a hundred roentgens.*

Liam entered first, his military green synthetic weapon held at the ready. The room was empty, but we could hear noise in the adjoining room. Liam pointed at the door to that room. Standing to the right side of the door, he slowly turned the knob. *What the fuck,* I thought, *surprise is the best assault.* So, I kicked the door in.

Two lizards looked up in surprise. One lizard wasn't wearing his helmet. I fired two rounds at him and he went down like a rubber chicken. The other touched his chest plate and fired a burst of plasma that passed between me and Liam and struck something in the other room. Liam fired several shots at the lizard, hitting him in the arm and possibly in the leg. The lizard roared and backed through a steel door into another room. He fired another blast of plasma at us, but it struck the ceiling. Sparks fell like the afterburn of a roman candle. I fired two quick rounds at him, striking him in the throat. He fell backward into the room. I quickly followed him into the room. Eight men were standing close together, each man holding two objects that looked like nuclear devices. Suddenly their bodies began shimmering. *They're fucking teleporting,* I realized. I raised my pistol and fired two rounds. I know I hit one guy because he doubled over and fell before he disappeared.

Liam entered the room. "Did the bastards escape again?"

"It looked like they were teleporting," I told him.

"Well, crap. We were so close this time."

"Where did they go?"

"To a DUMB, a deep underground military base. It's someplace in New Mexico, but we've never been able to locate it."

"I guess it's my fault. If I had kept my guard up, Molandowski wouldn't have surprised me with that pipe."

"It's not your fault, Dad. He killed you back there the last time and then married Mom a couple of years later."

"But I'm not dead."

"Not this time. This changes everything." He pointed at the door we had come through. "Let's go before anyone else knows that you're alive. Molandowski might not be the only one who's planning to do you in."

I stepped over the dead reptilian and peered out the door. "All clear."

Chapter 29

Liam's TR was cloaked and waiting for us on the asphalt not far from where the chopper had set down earlier. I could hear the choppers from Nellis circling above, waiting for the signal to return for the fireteams.

"My co-pilot is ready to take off as soon as we're on board," Liam told me.

He helped me find the footholds which were built into the invisible fuselage and I climbed onto the wing and into the cabin.

"Greetings, Dan. Long time no see."

I looked at her familiar face. She was leaner, though not frail, and much older, with a few lines arcing from the sides of her lips, like the sun's rays at dawn. "Is that you, Nicki?"

"What other aging female would they let fly one of these crates?"

I gave her a hug and we touched cheeks. "So, you joined the TR command."

"Yeah, our friend Mack helped me get assigned to the squadron about three years after my baby was born. I'm set to retire when I turn eighty next month."

"What did you have?"

"You mean the baby? It was a little boy. He works as a healer with your son Daniel. They're doing great things for humanity. You know, what's left of it."

"How did he meet Daniel?"

"Through Mona. The last thing she told me when we visited her and Stella was to look her up when you and I got back to our timeline. She's a great lady, Dan. She's still waiting for you, you know."

I saw Liam give her a stern look. "Look, Dad, there's something you've got to know."

The tone of his voice let me know that something serious was coming my way. "Mom's dead."

I felt my heart fall into my stomach. I grabbed the edge of the TR's control panel and sat down in the co-pilot's seat. "How?" I asked.

"You'd think they'd have left her alone, the bastards. Goddamn, she wasn't a threat to the NWO anymore. She was eighty-three and retired."

"Who?"

"Nargas," Liam snarled. "Stella felt Mom's death psychically. She hurried home and found Mom dead on the dining room floor. Nargas had stabbed her through the jugular with a sickle. She bled to death, Dad."

My hands shook uncontrollably as I realized that my world had just ended. The love of my life was dead, killed by the very sonofabitch that I was trying to stop from flipping the Earth over and killing off most of the world's population. My emotions careened like a car tumbling down a cliff, first the horror of Mona's ugly death, then the rush of anger and the lust for revenge, then the sense of penultimate loss. Suddenly I was alone, and yet on my timeline, Mona was still at her dying mother's side with her sister Wendy and our baby Stella. It was all too damn confusing.

"Where to, Dad?" Liam asked. "Back to Nellis?"

"No. Back to your time, but the day that Mona was killed."

"They already know that she died. She can't suddenly come back to life."

"She was eighty-three years old. I have a different strategy." I turned to Nicki. "Take me back there."

Nicki looked at Liam. He nodded his head. Nicki lifted the TR into the air, let the computer determine the best trajectory toward Jupiter, and set the controls to auto-pilot. Soon we were leaving the Earth's atmosphere and rapidly accelerating beyond light speed.

When I felt that queasiness in my stomach, I knew that we were slowing down. Soon, the Earth appeared, still laying on its side. Nicki ensured that we were cloaked and then guided us back to the western coast of Colorado.

"I'm not sure that this is a good idea, Dad," Liam told me.

"Listen, Liam, I was married to your mother-in-law for a very brief period of time. In reality, although she has two children, we weren't together long enough to have two kids. And I wasn't around long enough even to see my son Daniel. When that bastard Molandowski killed me, Mona was only four months pregnant. What I'm planning to do I'm not doing for her as much as I'm doing it for us, and maybe more for me. We were cheated out of a life together. But more than that, I was cheated out of a life with Mona.

"Nearing Mona's home. There's someone on the beach."

"Get a visual," Liam ordered.

"It's an older woman. She's moving quickly toward the pathway to Mona's home."

"Zoom in, damn it," Liam said.

"It looks like Mona," Nicki said.

"Yes, it's her," Liam replied. "Set us down in her backyard."

Nicki guided the TR to the ground, spinning it so that its hatch faced the cliffs to the ocean. As she did, Liam opened the hatch and waited until we had settled onto the sandy yard before stepping onto the wing.

When Mona's head appeared coming up the cliff on the pathway, Liam called out to her. "Mom, up here."

Mona looked up, only to see Liam standing midair. "Are you cloaked, Liam? What are you doing here? I'm in a bit of a hurry. I have to report a cadaver on the beach."

"You're coming with us," Liam replied.

"What's so important that it can't wait ten minutes?"

"Somebody wants to see you, and it can't wait. Not even a single minute."

Liam jumped off the wing and helped Mona ascend the steps that were set into the TR's fuselage. As she reached the level of the wing, I stepped out of the cabin and offered Mona assistance. At first she grabbed my hand without looking up, but when she saw me she said, "You stupid bastard. What took you so long? You never even wrote me a goddamn letter. It's been a fucking lifetime."

"I love the way you always put things into perspective, baby."

I helped Mona to her feet and gave her a hug. "No kisses, Danny, I had onions in my salad this afternoon."

I kissed her anyway. "I've never kissed a mature woman this way, baby."

"Your kisses have lost their zing, Danny. Maybe you're out of practice."

"Maybe you're out of progesterone."

"Maybe you need to brush your teeth."

She had me there. "Come on, Mona. You need to get inside the TR and out of your backyard. Anion Nargas is in your home right now, and he plans to kill you."

"Let me go home and we'll goddamn see who'll be pushing up daisies this spring."

"It's not worth the risk, baby. Besides, I have a different agenda."

"Where to, Dan?" Nicki asked as we stepped inside the hatch.

I turned to look at her and pointed my finger. "Richmond, Virginia. Make it June 2021. Find the FBI's Migration Center."

Liam closed and secured the hatch. "Everyone take a seat and buckle up."

⌀⌀⌀

The FBI's Migration Center was located a few clicks outside of Richmond in Varina, Virginia, a small town most famous for being the site of union and confederate prisoner exchanges during the Civil War. It also was the site of the first tobacco plantation in the American colonies prior to the American Revolution. I didn't know this, of course, except that it was printed on the plaque that hung in the atrium of the migration center. "That's some unique history for a Podunk town like this one," I told Mona, who was sitting on an oak bench beneath the plaque.

"Give it up, Danny," she told me. "Every small town has to find reasons to be important. It promotes civic pride, and it gives their children a reason to stay local after they graduate from high school."

Just as I was about to say something stupid, a young woman entered the room from a swinging door to our left. "Can I help you?"

"Yeah," I replied. "We're here to get my mom migrated into her clone." Mona gave me a dirty look.

"Do you have an appointment?"

"Of course not," Mona replied, waving a gnat away from her face with her hand. "He never follows protocol."

"Can I ask the name?"

"Mona Arrow," I replied.

"I believe it's listed under 'Casola,'" Mona said.

The young lady moved her finger around the screen of her digital pad. "Oh, yes, I've found the clone. We were just about to put it into nitrogen storage. It's scheduled for next week."

"What's that?" I asked.

"When a clone hasn't been called for, we freeze it through a process we call 'cryogenic preservation.' The process ensures that the clone stops aging while it's waiting for its owner to occupy it."

"Well, this one's owner is now ready," I said. "When can we get it done?"

"I'll have to make a phone call. Migration into Mrs. Casola's clone requires special permission from the FBI."

"Call Mack Smith.," I said. "He'll verify that this is legit."

"Agent Smith is my supervisor at the FBI," Mona said. "Do you need his number?"

"No, I have everything I need right here." The lady looked at Mona suspiciously. "According to my data, you should be thirty-five years old. Are you sure you're Mona Casola?"

"I've had a rough couple of weeks. How about a blood sample? Would that do?"

"I can do a DNA analysis in less than thirty minutes, if you'll let me take a sample. If you are who you say you are, we can slide you in for migration at three this afternoon."

Mona agreed to a DNA sample. The lady disappeared into the swinging door and returned in less than a minute with a lab technician who swabbed Mona's mouth, plopped the swab into a test tube, and disappeared back into the inner works.

"While you're waiting, please feel free to get some light refreshments in our cafeteria, except for you, Mrs. Casola. If we migrate you later, it should be on an empty stomach."

Mona nodded. "Go tell Liam and Nicki what we're doing, Danny."

"I'll be right back," I replied. I exited the building and found the TR-42 on the grass at the end of the small parking lot, where Nicki had set it down in between two pecan trees. After letting them know that we'd be a couple of hours, I went back to sit with Mona.

When I entered the cafeteria, I didn't see Mona. Instantly I realized that I should never have left her alone because doing so had put her safety into jeopardy. *You're an asshole, Arrow*, I told myself. If anything bad had happened to her, I knew I'd never forgive myself for making such a stupid error.

I was startled by a voice from behind me. "Back so soon?"

It was Mona. "Oh God, I thought…"

"You thought I had been kidnapped by a Nargas again?"

"Yeah, that or something more bizarre."

"Come sit with me, Danny."

I held Mona's arm as we walked to an unoccupied square table. Her skin felt loose and crinkly under my fingers, as though the muscle had disappeared, leaving only the bone beneath.

The cafeteria was only half full, probably a few people waiting to be migrated and probably more waiting to greet relatives who were undergoing migration. I helped Mona into her seat and then sat beside her. Her eyes had a tired cast to them.

"I'm not sure I want this clone, Danny. Although I've missed you terribly, I've led a good life, and I've been enjoying retirement in Colorado. It's the life I've known."

"It's for me, Mona," I replied. "The migration is for me. You've been alive more than twice as long as I have. You've had an opportunity to know Stella and Liam. I've had none of that. I guess maybe you'll think I'm selfish, but that's not true. I'm jealous, jealous of the opportunities you've had with them. You know, the stuff that parenting is about—the birthdays, the swimming lessons, the little league baseball, the graduations, the weddings, and all that soppy stuff. In my timeline, I've only begun to learn about it, and even now, if Liam hadn't come to my rescue in this timeline, I'd never have had the possibility of learning about it. It's something that was stolen from me by Molandowski. That bastard shot me in the back of my head so he could get to you and Stella."

Mona's face stiffened. "I didn't know that. It was Sarge who killed you? I let him touch me, Danny. I felt him inside me. I feel so dirty."

I brushed her cheek with my knuckle. "Mona, this clone means that we can be together again, no matter how long. Wouldn't you like to be young again and with me?"

"Yes, being with you again would be great. I mean it *is* great, right now. I'm just not sure if I can handle another lifetime stacked on top of this one that I'm living right now."

"Baby, you're already living another lifetime. At least, you're living in another timeline. In your timeline, you're already dead. Stella's half-brother Anion killed you with a garden sickle. If you were back in your own timeline, you'd be a bloody corpse waiting for Stella to find you."

"So, in my timeline, Stella found me dead?"

"Yes, but not just dead. She found you murdered. But in this timeline that fate hasn't fallen upon her shoulders. At least not yet. It'll be some other act of fate, or maybe it'll be nothing at all, ever."

Mona sighed. "It's so confusing, Danny. I'm too old to deal with this horse shit."

"In a new container, you'll feel a burst of energy that you haven't felt since you were thirty, baby. It'll give you the energy to do some of the things that you always wanted to do, but that you didn't get done. You know what I mean. Trust me," I coaxed.

"Are you just trying to get me into a new container so you can get into my pants?"

Mona's question surprised me. "I'll never deny that there's an element of that in me, baby. We haven't really made love since before I was in that alien grey container."

"God, that was so many years ago."

"In my timeline, it was only a few months ago. But that was way too long ago, and I miss the hell out of you, baby."

"You've gotta promise me that if I do this migration thing, you'll stop going on Mack's stupid assignments. If I blame anyone for your death, it's Mack. You had no business going on that mission. And if I had been at home instead of with my mother, I'd have told you so."

"I promise, baby." But how could I really promise that? When we got back to the Villaggio, I'd be at Mack's beck and call whenever he damn well felt like sending me on some wild ass trip to wherever.

A nurse came into the room and called out Mona's name. "Over here," she replied.

"Ma'am, everything is ready for you now."

"Do you mean my migration has been approved?"

"Yes, ma'am. The doctor is waiting for you. Do you need a wheelchair?"

Mona gave her a dirty look. "Do I really look that goddamn old and feeble?"

The nurse looked at me and shrugged her shoulders. Then as she helped Mona out of her chair, she told me, "You can wait here or in the family waiting room. Are you family?"

I nodded. "Thank you, I'll wait here."

Mona walked unassisted through the door ahead of the nurse. I would have enjoyed being a fly on the wall when they strapped her onto the gurney and started pasting electrodes onto her private parts. Twice I heard her complain, "Give me a goddamn minute," and "Wait until you're my age sweetie. Your boobs will be knocking the electrodes off of your abdomen, too." I chuckled as I pictured the goings-on. But, it was best that I stayed where I was and let her experience the thrills of the migration process without my yapping warnings about what to expect. Hell, each of my experiences with migration had been different, anyway.

Exactly thirty-five minutes after she had left the room as a woman in her eighties, Mona strode through the door as the young woman I remembered: vibrant, feisty, confident, and brunette.

"So how do you like the old me?" she asked, spinning like a ballerina when our eyes met.

"You're beautiful, baby, maybe younger than when you went home to see your mom a few days ago."

"Danny, that was fifty years ago."

"No, baby, it was less than a week ago. Now we have the chance to recapture the life we should have enjoyed together."

"Maybe, except now on this timeline there are two of me. How are you planning to fix that? Kill the other one?"

Oh shit, I thought. *Mona is right. We have to avoid having her clone meet Mona or we'll risk setting off some kind of paradox.* "We'll manage it," I replied, but I wasn't certain how. The best strategy, I thought, was to move to a different timeline, perhaps one where a second Mona wasn't around to complicate things. Or maybe to a timeline where we'd know exactly where the second Mona would be at a specific time, and we'd simply stay away from that location. It seemed simple enough.

We said goodbye to the nurse, left the facility, and joined Liam and Nicki in the TR-42.

"Where to?" Liam asked.

"Do you still have the timeline coordinates for when we rescued Mona?"

"Of course. They're in our memory banks."

"Good. Set us for one year after our rescue of Mona and set us for Asgardia."

"Asgardia?"

"Yes. That's where Nargas is, and I have a date with him."

"Danny, are you sure about this?" Mona asked.

"When have I ever been wrong?"

Mona rolled her eyes. "Are you sure you want me to answer that question?"

"Let's go to Asgardia," I told Liam.

"Aye, aye, Dad," he replied.

Chapter 30

Commander Anion Nargas appeared agitated when Buxton entered his office. "Sir, is anything wrong?"

"Have the two men whom you sent to dispatch Agent Arrow completed their mission, Buxton?"

"Sir, I haven't heard from them. I apologize, but I have nothing tangible to report."

"That's what's bothering me, Buxton. You sent them back in time to eliminate Arrow, and yet as of the present we have no report of their success. I fear that Arrow may have eluded them."

"Sir, the first was to intercept and terminate Arrow at Villaggio Ibrido and, if the first was unsuccessful, the other was to dispatch him at the Montagno Antilia Migration Center. Years have passed since either encounter took place and there has been no sign of Arrow since then. I am convinced that he is dead."

"Without absolute proof, I disagree with you, Buxton. I suspect that Arrow is hiding somewhere in the skein of time, waiting for the proper moment to strike a blow against our cause."

"Sir, our cause has been unquestionably successful. The reptilians are no longer in the bowels of the Earth, the population of pure humans has been reduced as dictated by the Guide Stones, and the planet's affairs are overseen by a single government, our New World Order. How could this man Arrow strike a blow against our new and perfect existence? We are living in the future that you envisioned as a youth, where the declining number of remaining humans are subservient to our new race of hybrids."

"Hybrids. I hate that term, Buxton. When all the humans are finally deceased, there will be but one race remaining on this orb. We will be known as Homo Asterians, and our dominion will have advanced the intelligence and capabilities of mere Homo Sapiens by two thousand generations in less than fifty years."

"Yes, sir, it's been a leap greater than that of Cro-Magnon to Homo Sapiens."

"Greater than garden lizard to reptilian, Buxton."

The Commander's communication device signaled that an important message had arrived. He pulled it from his pocket. "Nargas."

The voice from his device sounded excited. "Commander, this is Lt. Hunter in the tower. An unauthorized triangle has entered our perimeter."

"Is it one of ours?"

"Yes, but one that has been missing for more than a decade. It didn't respond to our query for an identification sequence. Should we obliterate it?"

"Did you scan its occupants?"

"Yes, sir. Two males and two females. One male and one female are pure humans. Both are known to us as pilots and are suspected resistance fighters. The other two occupants are low-functioning first generation hybrids. The male is unknown. However, the female's DNA sequence has identified her as Mona Casola, former FBI special agent."

"Impossible," the Commander snarled. "She was terminated. I was there."

"Sir, our records also show her as deceased. So, we ran the DNA scan again and it verified her identity as Mona Casola with ninety-eight percent probability. Except..."

"Except what, Lieutenant?"

"Except that the human Mona Casola should be in her eighties and this female is approximately thirty years of age."

Commander Nargas's eyes grew wide and gleamed with excitement. "She's in a new container. Thank you, Captain. Do nothing to the triangle unless it launches an attack."

"Sir, I am a lieutenant."

"No, Hunter, you are now a captain. And if my senses are correct, you have brought me news of significant importance."

Nargas shut his communicator and turned to Buxton. "Tell the teleportation center to expect my arrival in fifteen minutes. I have another appointment with Agent Casola. And, if I'm correct, I'll personally terminate that bastard Arrow."

"Sir, yes, sir." Buxton hurried out of the Commander's office.

CXƆCXƆ

Commander Nargas entered the teleportation center briskly, the clicking tabs on his boot laces announcing his arrival a few moments before he filled the doorway. Dressed in state-of-the-art flexible Kevlar battle garb and wearing a surround vision metal matrix helmet, Nargas was carrying a short-range personal protection plasma pistol. He was clearly ready for combat and not on a diplomatic mission.

The three soldiers in the center quickly popped to attention. Nargas waved them away. "I won't be needing you on this mission."

The sergeant cleared his throat. "Sir, Major Buxton thought we should offer our assistance. He thought we might be useful."

"I'm going into tight quarters and three additional bodies would just be in the way. Tell Buxton that I appreciate his concern, but that I prefer to handle this matter alone."

"Aye, aye, Sir."

When the soldiers were gone from the room, Nargas handed the teleportation officer a small slip of paper. "This is where I want to go."

"This is almost here, sir. In fact, it's right next door. Are you sure you want to teleport instead of just catching a shuttle over to it?"

"Who are you to question me?"

"Sorry, sir. It's just that this seems to be a waste of transmission energy."

"Set the coordinates and send me on my way. I have an important appointment and I don't want to be late."

"Sir, the triangle is moving at a slow rate of speed toward our spaceport. Accurate placement within the cabin will be difficult unless we ask the pilot to come to a complete stop."

"Do your best because your life depends upon it. The triangle is to have no notice of my pending arrival."

The teleportation officer's face broadcast his concern about sending his commander into a moving vehicle. He also was familiar with his commander's temper and reputation for quick retaliation. Using his keyboard, he inputted in the triangle's current coordinates and approximate speed and heading. When his computer signaled that it was prepared, the officer told Commander Nargas to enter the transportation cylinder, and when things looked as good as they could be, he punched the key that sent Commander Nargas into the ethers. "God, I hope this works," he said as the Commander vaporized into atoms that would be teleported and reassembled within a single second's timeframe.

Chapter 31

Liam set the coordinates, told us all to buckle up and directed the TR toward Asgardia, the artificial country that was circling the Earth at the edge of its stratosphere. Only, as before, we shot into space in a trajectory toward Jupiter, but on a path that would permit us to avoid collision with space junk. When we passed light speed, we continued accelerating for another few minutes before the TR began to slow down. Soon, a mild tone let us know that we were approaching our destination, a position in time and space that was nowhere near Jupiter but which, instead, was somewhere above Earth a year into the future from our most recent location near Varina, Virginia.

The fuzziness of our observation monitors began to dissipate and Asgardia slowly came into focus. As good luck would have it, we had settled to a crawl at the perimeters of Asgardia's territorial borders, an artificial barrier which it had claimed as its safety zone in space. "It's like territorial waters that were in place back in your day, Dad," Liam explained. "You know, a place where fishermen from other countries could not net fish and where military vessels were not supposed to travel."

"Yeah, that makes sense," I replied, "but enemy submarines always violated those artificial boundaries. The safety that territorial waters provided was strictly an illusion."

"There's no need for them now," Nicki chimed in. "With no countries anymore, the NWO has eliminated their function."

"Maybe that's not such a bad thing," I replied. "No countries means an end to territorial disputes and wars."

"Don't be too fast to think that the NWO is a good thing, Danny," Mona said. "Remember that the bastard who ushered in a period of no wars did that by killing off ninety percent of humanity and by setting the Earth into a tailspin that reconfigured all of its landmasses. Can you even begin to calculate the number of your friends and acquaintances that he exterminated?"

"The entire Earth is ruled by a dictatorship," Liam added. "As a former American you need to remember that you now have no voice in your government or the laws that it creates,"

"And no say in which people that son of a bitch Nargas decides to eliminate," I said.

Our TR's communication device pinged. "We have a request from Asgardia for our authorization code," Nicki cried. "They think we're an NWO vessel. What should I tell them?"

"Don't answer them," Liam directed. "This was an NWO TR until we captured it. Besides, we just came from the past. There's no way that we'd ever have their latest protocols. Maybe we can signal that our communicator is out of order."

"Aye, aye, Commander. I'll follow the old protocol. They probably haven't changed that."

Nicki flipped the TR ninety degrees, so that its wings were perpendicular to the horizon, and then she reversed direction a full circle, and then returned us to our original position. A moment later, the communication device pinged again. "We've been ordered to hold our position until they verify that we're NWO. I think they're not sure what to do with us."

"Drift us toward Asgardia's spaceport very slowly, Nicki," Liam ordered. "We don't want to appear aggressive, but we need to get closer. Maybe if we appear to be limping in, they'll let us continue. And put our shields up in case they decide to take us out."

"Aye, aye, sir."

We drifted toward Asgardia, inching slowly closer for about twenty minutes when suddenly I sensed that something bad was coming our way. "Incoming," I shouted.

"There's no indication on our TR's warning system," Nicki responded.

"Damn it, there's something incoming," I repeated. "I can feel it."

Within a second, we heard a strange sound, like a whirlwind of sand pelting the side of a fiberglass panel, coming from inside the head.

"What was that?" Mona asked. She unbuckled her seat belt, approached the door to the head, and reached for the latch. Unexpectedly, it sprung open, pushing her against the wall behind the door. Commander Nargas stepped out in full battle gear.

Nicki turned at the commotion and screamed when she saw Nargas. A bolt of liquid light shot across the cabin, severing her right arm. Blood splattered across the forward monitors, and Nicki slumped unconscious in her pilot's seat.

Liam drew his pistol and fired, missing his target. A second bolt of light leaped from Nargas' pistol and struck Liam in the leg as he rose to shoot a second time. He spun and fell against the bulkhead, smoke rising from his thigh.

Nargas threw off his helmet, then aimed, intent to fire his plasma pistol at Liam again, but before he could squeeze the trigger, Mona savagely pushed the head's door into him, knocking him sideways and into me. I had already unbuckled my seatbelt and was preparing to jump on him when Nargas suddenly came hurtling in my direction. I grabbed him from behind, holding his arms downward and wrestling him to the floor. He smashed the rear of his head into my face three times and spun to free himself. But I managed to hold onto his right arm, the one that grasped his pistol and tried to kick him in his crotch. He was stronger than I was, and he fended off my blow with his knee. As we wrestled, Nargas used his left hand to begin prying my fingers off his arm. Somehow, my left hand found its way to his pistol's trigger mechanism, and a volley of plasma splattered against the TR's ceiling, surprising both of us.

Mona squealed as a fountain of sparks ricocheted off the wall in her direction. Then she saw Liam's pistol on the floor against the wall on the opposite side of the cabin from Nargas and me and she dived for it, sliding across the cabin floor on her belly. She grabbed it, rolled onto her back, and fired.

I felt the shot hit my shoulder with a wallop like a ball pein hammer in the hand of an ironworker. Nargas cried out and then released me, pushing his torso away from mine with his pistol still in his hand. As he stood, blood dripped from the bottom of his flak jacket. He had been hit, too, but I don't know which one of us took the first hit and which took the ricochet.

Mona dropped Liam's pistol and rushed to my side. "Danny. I'm sorry, Danny."

I felt her grab my chin and turn my head toward her. Her touch and her voice were distant, almost surreal. I felt thick warm fluid run down my arm. It had to be blood.

"Danny," she cried, "stay with me. Don't leave."

I didn't know how severe my wound was and I wanted to tell her that I didn't have much choice about staying or leaving, but I couldn't form the words.

"Danny, stay with me. I can't do another lifetime without you."

Nargas took Mona by her arm and pulled her off me. "Maybe you took out his lungs, sweetheart. He's already probably a goner."

"Don't 'sweetheart' me. You're the bastard who should be lying there. Not Danny. I had my sights right on your head. They must have been knocked out of alignment when Liam dropped the gun. I should have just hit you in the head with the gun butt, but instead, I did something stupid, and look what I did." Mona wept, "I just killed the love of my life."

Suddenly the power in the TR died and the cabin became eerily quiet. Nargas dropped his weapon, pulled his communicator from his breast pocket, and pushed the call button. "Damn thing isn't working," he complained. "Can you operate the TR's communications system?"

"If I could, I wouldn't tell you how it works," Mona replied. "But I'm just a passenger, and you've just injured the only two people who could help you."

Nargas looked at Nicki and Liam. Nicki was still unconscious, but Liam was lying on his side, gripping his thigh. Nargas grabbed Liam's collar and pulled him to the center of the cabin. "How do I use your communicator?" he asked angrily.

"Fuck you," Liam replied.

Nargas pressed two fingers into the wound on Liam's thigh. Liam cried out in pain.

"I'm not going to ask you again."

"Look around you, you stupid asshole," Mona cried out. "Nothing is working on this ship, no lights, no fans, no monitors. Even if he told you how to operate the communicator, it wouldn't work. You're stuck here like the rest of us. You're a rat in an airtight box. You'd better hope they come to rescue you before we're out of oxygen, or you'll suffocate with the rest of us."

Nargas turned back to Liam. "We can make this easy or we can make it difficult. How do I operate this triangle's communicator?"

With Nargas' back turned toward her and his plasma pistol on the floor, Mona quietly picked up Liam's pistol and ran into the head, closing the door behind her.

At the sound of her footsteps, Nargas wheeled around and saw the door to the head close. "You stupid bitch." He picked up his plasma pistol and melted the lock away in a quick volley of sparks. Mona screamed and fired two quick shots through the closed plastic door. They missed her target. She pulled the trigger again, but the pistol was empty.

Nargas could hear Mona's frustration and could sense that she was out of options. He opened the door, pulled her out by her hair, and sent her tumbling across the cabin floor to the far wall, where her head smashed into the metal and she was knocked unconscious. "Good idea, sweetheart, but you lose again."

Nargas pointed his plasma pistol at Liam's head. "This'll make one less set of lungs using up our oxygen."

"Wait," Liam said, holding up one hand.

"So, you've come to your senses?"

"Arrow and I need medical attention. From the looks of it, so do you. If I tell you how to operate the communicator, will you promise not to harm us any further?"

Nargas smiled. "Sure, whatever you want. I'm certain that you know you can trust me."

Liam knew that Nargas would kill him as soon as he got the information that he wanted, but Liam tried to buy some time. "Help me over to the console. The communicator requires my thumbprint to be activated."

"You'll have to get there by yourself, pilot. If you come close to me, I'll cut you in half."

Nargas watched as Liam struggled to pull himself across the cabin floor to his pilot's seat. Then using his hands to pull himself to a standing position on only his left leg, Liam fell into the seat and doubled over in pain.

While Nargas was engaged with Liam, I rolled onto my left side and quickly pulled myself into the head. Once inside, I found Liam's pistol that Mona had dropped to the floor. Its slide was open, exposing the fact that it was out of ammo. I stuffed it into my belt anyway. Then I reached up to the small sink with my left hand and pulled myself to my feet. I was weak, but I was determined to implement the plan that had presented itself to me while I lay on the cabin floor.

The mirror above the sink was attached by four L-shaped brackets made of thin metal, two at the bottom and two at top. I pulled the pistol from my pocket and removed its clip. Using the top end of the clip, I pried the bottom brackets open until the mirror slid into my hands. As I caught the mirror, the clip fell to the floor with a loud clatter. Then I heard Nargas snarl, "Where's that fuck Arrow?" I readied myself, holding the mirror to my side and I pointed the pistol at the door.

I heard Nargas approach the door to my hiding place. When he threw the door open, he fell backward in surprise before realizing that my pistol was the same one that Mona had emptied through the door. Regaining his balance, he smiled. "At last I'm going to be rid of your interference. Goodbye, Arrow."

Nargas raised his plasma pistol to take me out. When his trigger finger began to squeeze the trigger, I quickly raised the mirror. The whine of the white plasma was deafening as it rebounded from the mirror and struck Nargas in his chest. I was temporarily blinded by the explosion and sparks that flew everywhere.

As my eyes adjusted to the cabin's darkness, I saw Nargas lying in two pieces on the floor. Smoke from his wounds wound upwards toward the ceiling.

"Dad, are you okay?"

It was Liam, dragging his right leg behind as he limped toward the head. I stepped toward him and fell into his arms. We both collapsed to the floor, and everything went black for me.

Chapter 32

As she regained consciousness, Mona could hear motion in the form of rustling cloth. Then she saw them, six little dwarves, all wearing dark green hooded robes. Two of them lifted the unconscious Danny and carried him effortlessly through the cabin wall, as though Danny weighed less than a pound and the wall was simply an illusion. Two others did the same to Nicki.

An entity emerged silently from the wall behind Mona. It was at least seven feet tall, wearing a floor length purple robe with its hood covering his head. Silently it motioned to the two remaining dwarves. They nodded and removed Liam in the same manner as the others had removed Danny and Nicki.

Where are you taking them? What have you done to my Danny? Mona wanted to demand, but she couldn't move her lips to form the words.

The entity's response came into her head, the same way that she received thought communications from Commissar Nargas when he spoke to her while she was his captive in the hollow Moon. Its words were firm but reassuring. *I am allowing you to see so that you will know.*

"Know what?" Mona wondered.

It turned to look at her. Mona gasped. It was an insect with an iridescent green triangular head like a praying mantis. Its bulbous eyes resembled white pearls with jet black irises that reflected Mona's fearful face. Above them, two fern-like antennae protruded from its head. It nodded at Mona and pointed a claw-like hand in the direction that the dwarves had carried their captives. *Do not fear me. You will know the dispensations meted to all within this vessel. Their destinies have been determined by their actions. You alone shall know.*

The mantis touched Mona's temple with its claw and she fell into unconsciousness.

∽∾∽

When she awoke, Mona realized that she was lying on a table of some sort. It was hard and cold against her back and legs. She heard the sounds of busy hands to her left. She tried to see what was going on, but though her eyes could move, she couldn't turn her head. Mentally she called out, *Who's there? Where am I?*

Within a few moments, a square-headed creature somewhat like a grey alien appeared beside her, looking down into her eyes. It was wearing a green robe, but its hood no longer covered its pasty cube-like head. Inside her brain, Mona heard it say, *Master Enki has given you permission to watch.*

The creature gently turned Mona's head to her left, toward the noise of the busywork. As it waddled away from her, Mona could see that she was in what appeared to be an operating room. Metallic medical tools and hoses of various sorts hung from the ceiling and protruded from the pure white walls. The devices moved freely from their resting places to the hands of the green-clad surgeons as they needed them, almost as though the devices knew when they were needed at a precise moment. Then Mona recognized that Nicki lay on one table, Liam on yet another, and Danny lay on the table closest to her. *They're doing something to him, so Danny might still be alive.*

Mona watched the surgeons work for several minutes before the one who had turned her head waddled back to debrief her. *We arrived in time and your male has survived. Master Enki is pleased that your male fulfilled his mission. The master has restructured his container to be less susceptible to disease and he has enhanced its subtle cerebral capabilities. Your male will need your assistance to understand this new awareness.*

Are the others going to be okay? Mona wondered. *My son-in-law and the woman?*

The male's container has been patched, the surgeon told her. *There will be slight discoloration for a few days. He will have no pain. The female's arm has been reattached. A seed has been inserted and she will grow a new little finger in a year of your time.*

And what of Nargas, the other male, the one who was severed by liquid light in the TR?

Do you mean the inhabitant of the container which was left in the spacecraft? His electrical essence has already found its new container in the next dimension where he has a new role to play in a developing timeline. Master Enki would not restore his old container in this dimension and timeline.

The surgeon left Mona's side and waddled back to the table where Nicki was being dressed by the other workers. Mona thought that possibly her surgery was over and Nicki was being prepped for the recovery room. And Mona saw that Liam was sitting erect on the side of his operating table, being helped back into his clothing by the strange little creatures. His surgery was clearly over. She looked at Danny. He was still lying on his back, but his clothes were being gathered by one of the surgeons or an assistant.

Possibly soon, she assumed, he would be moved to a recovery room somewhere in this facility for observation and monitoring.

As she remembered the events of the day, thoughts of Anion Nargas filled Mona's head. That bastard had appeared in the TR's head out of nowhere, and clearly he was intent on killing everyone in the cabin. Was he teleported there? Could his dismembered body be teleported back to Asgardia? And she puzzled over Nargas' fate. What was the "next dimension" that the surgeon mentioned? Was it Heaven? If so, what role could Nargas possibly be playing there when he certainly should be relegated to Hell? But the surgeon said that this next dimension where Nargas had gone has a "developing timeline." Does Heaven have a timeline? It just didn't make sense to her.

Mona saw the door to the operating room open. Master Enki entered and conferred with each group of surgeons, moving his claws purposefully as he gave directions. Then he turned his attention to Mona. *Welcome to our observational satellite, what your military calls 'the Black Knight.' You are free to move*, he told her telepathically. Mona felt control return to her arms and legs. She rolled onto her side and sat on the edge of the table, her feet dangling a few inches above the floor.

Enki approached her. *Peace unto you. Have no fear of me.* Mona nodded and placed her hands in her lap. Enki continued, *I know you have many questions, and you will have many more over the next few days and weeks. Know that I mean no harm to humans whose intent is to serve the best interests of their fellow beings. Your friends and your male have been reconstructed and will live long lives unless those lives are interrupted accidentally. Soon, you will be reunited so that you may move forward in your timeline.*

"Who are you?" Mona asked aloud.

One whose assignment is to watch and to prepare the Garden Planet's inhabitants for the coming vibratory change.

"I don't understand."

The vibration of your planet is soon to increase such that all creatures will know the thoughts of all others. Plants will communicate their feelings in new ways to those who tend them. The truth behind all actions will rule the day.

"Will humans survive or only hybrids?"

It has been preordained that humanity must pass the way of the dinosaur. When this occurs, there will be one thousand years of peace.

"So, Danny and I will perish in some sort of calamity, or will this 'passing away' be peaceful?"

You and your male possess the traits of the first generation of the new inhabitants of the Garden Planet. Your children will teach you the ways of the future. Your grandchildren will honor your memory for generations.

"I don't understand."

Master Enki raised his claw to touch Mona's temple, but she pulled away. "I know you can let me see the future if you want to. Will you? I want to see."

Master Enki placed his claws on Mona's hands, and suddenly her mind was filled with images.

Chapter 33

When I woke up, I was in bed. From the sliver of light that entered the bedroom through the closed venetian blind, I could see that Mona was sleeping beside me in the young container that we had obtained for her in Virginia. *What the fuck?* The last thing I remembered was falling into Liam's arms inside the TR.

I didn't recognize the surroundings, so I threw back the covers and walked out to see where I was. But first, I found a bathroom a few feet down the hall and relieved myself. The top of the bathroom vanity was full of female stuff—powder, hairspray, cotton balls, nail polish remover, and bobby pins. There was no sign of a man's presence.

When I entered the living room, I realized that I had been here before. We were in Mona's home, not in the Villaggio but in Colorado, high above the Pacific Ocean.

The rattle of glassware alerted me that someone was in the kitchen. I quietly peered around the corner. It was a woman. From the shape of her hips and the grey streaks in her shoulder-length hair, I judged her to be at least in her late forties, if not early fifties. "Good morning, Daddy," she said without turning around.

"Stella?"

"Who else would call you 'Daddy'?"

I walked over to Stella and gave her a peck on the cheek. She was folding blueberries into batter. *Muffins or pancakes*?

"You haven't kissed me like that since I was a little girl."

"When are we?" I asked.

"You should learn to use your insight, Daddy. It warned you when Anion was teleporting into Liam's triangle."

I wanted to ask her how she knew that, but I already knew that she is tapped into everything that goes on. When she was a little girl, she knew that I was freezing to death in Antarctica. And when I came home in Nevada Ritter's clone container, she was the only person who knew who I was.

"Maybe I will," I replied, "but recently I've been all over the space-time continuum, and I really need to know when I am right now."

"Eight o'clock in the morning. It's a Saturday in June. Is the year all that important?"

"Only if Anion Nargas is still alive."

"Mom's laptop is on the counter. It's open to today's news."

I tapped on the touchpad of Mona's laptop and it sprang to life. The Denver Post was running a story about the new leader of the NWO, a woman from Kazakhstan who had promised to end the tyrannical leadership styles of her predecessors, His Excellency and Anion Nargas. It looked like she was trying to fulfill her promise by implementing a variety of advisory groups.

"She promises absolute transparency," Stella told me. "She was elected almost unanimously."

"When was she elected?"

"Next week will mark six months ago."

"And you believe her?"

"When she was younger, she was a healer, and she was one of my co-workers for almost three years. I trust her implicitly. Besides, most of us on Earth can now read what someone is thinking. There's almost no crime anymore."

"How do you read someone's thoughts, Stella? I wasn't born with that capability the way you were."

"I'll teach you, Daddy. And so will Daniel. He's retiring soon and will be moving to the Pacific Palisades to be closer to you and mom."

Mona came into the kitchen, her slippers scraping the floor with each step. She grabbed my shoulders and spun me around so we could look into each other's eyes. "Don't look, Stella," she said. When Stella turned away, Mona planted a passionate, deep tongue kiss on my lips. I felt old desires rising if you know what I mean.

"They told me that I wouldn't see you for a few weeks," Mona said, "but the least you could have done was to get me up when you found yourself at home." She winked at me. "Stella told me that you'd be here this morning."

"I just woke up, baby. I just woke up and we were in bed together. I didn't even know where I was until I came out here."

"That's how it happens, Danny Arrow. When you leave the Black Knight, you just wake up somewhere and have to figure out where you are and when it is."

Mona was right. I remembered that when Nicki and I were in the Black Knight, she was impregnated by the Praying Mantis, and then we woke up in our triangle in the 1940s. Go figure.

Mona pinched my cheek and brought me back to the present. I gazed into her deep brown eyes and felt the tickle of love run up my spine. She pulled my face toward hers and kissed me again. It was promising. More than promising.

"Okay, you two," Stella said. "There'll be plenty of time for that sort of catching up later. We have company coming this afternoon and we have to get ready."

Images of Liam and Nicki flew into my head. And a new face, a middle-aged man who looked a bit like Mona. It had to be Daniel. I was beginning to understand that knowing stuff would be a natural thing in this new container. Maybe. When it comes to this stuff, I've been known to be a bit of a hard head. Mona calls me "Capa Tosta."

∞

When she learned the date that I would be arriving, Mona had invited family and friends to come to her home to greet me. Family arrived at noon. Stella and Liam brought their daughters, Monique and Danielle. They were obviously named after Mona and me. I learned that in their early twenties both women had been "sealed" in governmentally sanctioned mating relationships, which had replaced marriages, and both had one child each. They live nearby in what had been eastern Colorado before the great slosh, but they didn't bring their mates or children to meet me because they thought it might be too much for me to handle. They were probably right about that.

Daniel arrived a little after noon. He was my size but looked more like Mona than me. He was sensitive that his hairline was receding, and Stella called him "slick" a couple of times just to rub it in. He confirmed that he would be retiring from public service in two years and would move closer to our home on the Pacific Palisades so he could get to know me better. He also figured that in retirement he'd need a younger guy to lift heavy things and to mow his lawn. He told me that he'd hire me if I needed a job. I hoped he was kidding.

Nicki arrived at 1:30 pm. She came alone and brought a couple of bottles of imported wine. When I read the label, I was surprised to learn that the vineyard actually was located on Mars. It was some sort of indoor farming cooperative that had been operated by SpaceX colonists for the last fifteen years. When I asked her about her surgery in the Black Knight, she told me that she couldn't remember anything, but that Mona was there to greet her two months earlier when she woke up in her own apartment in the former Montana. Mona had become a great friend over the years and had helped her to come to grips with both her first and second abductions.

Over wine and hors d'oeuvres, I learned that all of us had been relocated in time and place by Master Enki according to our needs. Mona was the first to return, followed a week later by Liam, and then by Nicki two months ago, and finally by me, a full six months after Mona returned. Mona reminded me we all were returned at the same moment, but Master Enki had plugged us into different times. I still can't figure that one out, except that he gave Mona the opportunity to observe and to help us all comprehend what had happened to us.

❧❦❧

The welcome home party was nice, especially meeting my son Daniel for the first time, but it delayed what I really wanted, and that was time alone with Mona. When everyone had gone, we sat together holding hands in the backyard beside a fire. In my real timeline, we had been apart for only a few days while Mona and Stella were visiting her sick mom. In Mona's real timeline, however, we hadn't been together for over fifty years, many of which she had spent essentially living alone after the kids left home. So, we came at our present circumstances from different points of view.

"I'm glad that I woke up to find that bastard gone," I said. "And it wouldn't have happened if you hadn't slammed him with that door to the head. You were always quick on your feet."

"I had to do something, and I used the only weapon that I had."

"You can improvise your way out of just about any situation, baby."

"Danny, I wanted him to kill me when I thought that you were dead. I thought it was the only way that I could be with you."

"I'm sorry. I didn't know that. If I had, I'd have dodged your bullet and kept on fighting him."

"I'm sorry that I shot you. It was an accident and I hope you won't spend the rest of my lifetime throwing it into my face whenever we have an argument."

"I never throw anything into your face, baby."

"You might want to get a second opinion on that."

That comment started me thinking. I picked up a stick and stirred the fire, sending sparks flying toward the stars above. "Do you still love me, Mona? I mean after everything that we've been through, you could be tired of my antics and bull-headed stupidity."

"Yeah, of course, I've still got a thing for you, you asshole. You're all I've thought about for the last fifty years. Remember, bucko, that it was you who broke off our relationship in the early days. You really hurt me back then."

"I know, and I regret the hell out of that. I was just a stupid prick. I think I was afraid of the feelings that I had for you. You know I was afraid to commit. But we've been through all of this before."

"And it took a trip into the bowels of the earth to wake you up. I'm afraid that the new you might still be afraid to commit to the new me. I mean, here it is fifty years later, and your container is not even thirty-five years old. You're a galactic hero and you could probably score with any woman you want."

I poured the rest of my beer onto the fire. It made a hissing sound as the cold liquid evaporated on the hot coals. Then I took Mona by the hand and pulled her to her feet. I kissed her passionately.

"There were other women before you, Mona, but there's never been anyone since you. Here in this crazy, flipped-over world, I think I love you more than ever before."

We walked arm in arm back into her home and found the bedroom. Quietly we undressed each other. The sight of Mona's naked body drove me crazy with anticipation, and I guess that my naked body pointed to my genuine interest in making love to her.

"Danny, in my mind I may be in my eighties, but in this new container, I'm a fully fertile female. We need to use protection."

I kissed Mona's neck and nibbled lightly on her ear. "I'm not worried, baby. I've always wanted to have children with you, you know, the natural way. Yours and mine, fully developed in the human oven, not in an alien growth tube."

Mona touched my private parts. "You're bigger than I remember."

"That's what you asked Doctor Spann for, baby. I was okay with the way I was."

Mona's eyes searched mine. "Be gentle, Danny. Okay?"

I gently lowered Mona onto our bed. "Always, baby."

I kissed her, and when I touched her breast, Mona moaned. She pushed my hand away and told me, "No, I mean it, Danny. You've got to be gentle with me."

I kissed her again. "What are you afraid of? It's me."

"That *is* what I'm afraid of. This container is still a virgin."

—THE END—

POSTSCRIPT

Life has given me more adventures than I ever expected. In fact, in this single timeline, I'll be living two lifetimes, the original one given to me by my parents and the new one given to me by Master Enki in the Black Knight.

Mona is not as excited about living a second lifetime in this timeline, mostly because she has already raised a family of two children and has experienced her spouse dying before her. She says that she doesn't want to go through that again. I guess that I can't blame her. As short as life can be, her perspective makes a full lifetime sound long, perhaps too long.

Unlike Mona, I'm looking forward to raising a family because I was cheated out of it on the first go around. And, I'm really pissed that the son of a bitch who killed me moved in with Mona and raised my kids until she threw him out.

I'm also a bit perplexed with my changing opinion of this New World Order. When the earth was overloaded with people and was divvied up into two hundred individual countries, the thought of a one world government bothered the shit out of me. I didn't want any group of self-elected yahoos setting the rules and changing the way things were. But now that we have fewer than five hundred million people left on this planet, and now that the earth has shifted on its axis and everything seems convoluted, a one world government doesn't seem so bad—so long as the people in power actually make laws and take actions for the benefit of the people instead of themselves. The nice thing, however, is that this new generation of mankind, and I mean all of us hybrids with human bodies and telepathic capabilities, knows if a leader is lying or cheating or seeking power for the wrong reasons. That gives me great hope for mankind and great expectation for a long, peaceful future, the kind of future that will offer Mona and me the kind of lifetime that I never could have offered her under the old way of doing things,

So that's where it sits until something comes along to try and fuck it up. So long as the reptilians and the reticulan greys stay away, old Mother Earth should be in good hands. And, so long as we have colonists on the moon and Mars who are exploring deep space every day, we should have advanced warning of any threat to our existence.

Oh, and one more thing…Mona missed her period this month. Things are looking up!

Born in Massachusetts, Ed Baker traveled widely as a child because his U.S. Marine father was transferred to new assignments across the U.S.A. on a regular basis. By the time Ed was twelve, he had crossed the United States three times. And at the ripe old age of sixteen, he drove a stick shift Ford across the nation, following his dad, who was pulling a camping trailer behind the family's station wagon.

An English major at Elon College, Ed earned a master's degree at Appalachian State University and a doctorate in Educational Leadership at the Sage College's Esteves School of Education. After thirty-five years in higher education and after retiring as Interim President of a public community college, he turned his attention to his first love, writing, while continuing to teach undergraduate and graduate courses on an adjunct basis at a private college in upstate New York.

During the warm months, Ed and his wife Edna reside in their cabin on Galway Lake, New York. During the cold months, they "hole up" in their winter quarters in Saratoga Springs, New York. When he's not writing or teaching, Ed is playing with his four grandchildren or his four-legged canine companion Sudsy.

Ed saw his first UFO as a young man while camping out at Green Lakes State Park near Syracuse, New York. He saw his second while living on the beach and surfing at Emerald Isle, North Carolina, back when it was still a wild and undeveloped stretch of dunes. And he chased a black Triangle along the Taconic State Parkway a little later in life. Ed's four-volume Dan Arrow series is based upon these experiences and upon current conspiracy theory lore, combining the UFO mystery with national and global politics and the rumored agenda of the New World Order.

Ed says that the *Dan Arrow* novels are fun to write because they permit him to delve into seemingly unrelated elements that mesh together into a fabric offering many clandestine possibilities. You can learn more about Ed and read his blog on his author web site at: www.edwardsbaker.com